The Model

Lars Saabye Christensen

The Model

Translated from the Norwegian by

Don Bartlett

Arcadia Books Ltd
15–16 Nassau Street
London W1W 7AB

www.arcadiabooks.co.uk

First published in the United Kingdom by Arcadia Books 2007
Originally published by Cappelen as *Modellen* 2005

A catalogue record for this book is available from the British Library.

ISBN 1–905147–21-X

Designed and typeset in Minion by Discript Limited, London WC2N 4BN
Printed in Finland by WS Bookwell

This translation has been published with the financial support of NORLA

Arcadia Books distributors are as follows:

in the UK and elsewhere in Europe:
Turnaround Publishers Services
Unit 3, Olympia Trading Estate
Coburg Road
London N22 6TZ

in the USA and Canada:
Independent Publishers Group
814 N. Franklin Street
Chicago, IL 60610

in Australia:
Tower Books
PO Box 213
Brookvale, NSW 2100

in New Zealand:
Addenda
Box 78224
Grey Lynn
Auckland

in South Africa:
Quartet Sales and Marketing
PO Box 1218
Northcliffe
Johannesburg 2115

Arcadia Books is the *Sunday Times* Small Publisher of the Year

Lars Saabye Christensen is Norway's leading contemporary writer. He is the author of twelve novels as well as short stories and poetry. His international best-selling novel *The Half Brother* has been published in nearly thirty countries. It won the Nordic Prize for Literature as well as the Norwegian Booksellers' Prize, was shortlisted for the 2005 International IMPAC Dublin Literary Award, was longlisted for the *Independent* Foreign Fiction Prize and was chosen as one of the twenty-five notable titles of 2004 by the American Library Association. *Herman*, published in English by Arcadia, was shortlisted for the 2006 YoungMinds Award. Lars Saabye Christensen lives in Oslo.

Don Bartlett lives with his family in a village in Norfolk. He translates from Scandinavian literature and has recently translated, or co-translated, novels by Roy Jacobsen, K. O. Dahl, Jo Nesbø and Ingvar Ambjørnsen.

Prologue

When I was finally given the chance to interview the artist Peter Wihl on the evening of his fiftieth birthday and the opening of his new exhibition, it would transpire that we would be unable to print it because of the terrible accident which occurred afterwards. We were sitting in the restaurant, directly opposite the gallery, where I could still hear people going to and fro. I almost had a bad conscience about laying claim to Peter Wihl, the evening's honoured guest, in this way, but it was at his suggestion that we went there to talk. He seemed nervous and expectant; not so unusual perhaps, considering that his exhibition had just opened, and he had enough on his mind. I noticed he kept turning towards the window while he was talking. He even ordered champagne for me. And I had the feeling that most of what he had to say consisted of quotations, things he had read or heard, borrowed phrases, well, especially what he said about the devil, that the devil had liberated the colours from objects. Yet, it was as though he wanted to tell me something else, something more, something important; perhaps that was why he was also so impatient. He had said before that he wanted to tell me everything, although I didn't know what that meant.

The tape recorder was on the table between us. I checked it was working. It was. Peter Wihl's voice was everywhere. He went on speaking. I cannot say I understood every word, but of course I would have time to listen with greater care when I got home. After a while I interrupted, perhaps emboldened by the champagne, and went straight to the point.

'Did you ever fear you wouldn't finish?' I asked.

I heard something fall to the floor – a fork perhaps; he was eating cake.

'Finish?'

I'm sure he understood what I meant. Nevertheless, I had to say:

'Finish in time for the exhibition while you still have your sight?'

His face was close to mine, his voice forced, intransigent.

'You don't finish a picture; you forsake it.'

He went quiet, turned away from me; I could hear it in his breathing and I was afraid I had ruined everything. I wanted to say something. I searched for the right words. I wanted to say something to the effect that forsaking a picture, not finishing it, was both a beautiful and terrible thought, but before I got that far he must have seen them through the window, because he stood up and said, in what was now a relieved, almost happy voice:

'Please excuse me for a moment. My wife and daughter are here.'

Then Peter Wihl went out into the street to meet them.

1

Six months earlier he had lost his eyesight.

One October afternoon Peter Wihl was working in his studio on paintings for the anniversary exhibition; twelve large canvasses. He was wearing his uniform, ready to do battle: bare feet in shabby sandals, a long, stained smock, a scarf around his neck. He had finished the groundwork, the base. Now all that remained was the art. And he was in that effortless flow, which can happen now and again. It was almost like controlled inebriation. His hand was steady and obedient, his mind clear. He knew where he wanted to go. It was just a question of finding the way. He moved with ease from motif to motif. They began to take form: anatomical sections, muscles, a shoulder blade, a sinew, a finger joint. He could scarcely remember the last time he had experienced such control: he was now the master of his tools again, the master of his craft, at the very moment when the craft was to be elevated to art, when the workmanship, the toil, was to be made to shine, and it felt like happiness. It was happiness. But, all of a sudden, he experienced a terrible pain in his eyes, as if something had shattered inside them and burst, as if his eyes had been filled with noise. Colours merged, lines dissolved, all perspective was lost, everything went black and he sank to the floor. It did not last long. It was already over. All he heard was the echo of pain, the throbbing beat of his heart. Peter Wihl was on his knees and remained there for a long time, resting his forehead on his hands. He came round. Everything fell into place with the same swiftness it had fallen apart. By degrees, he rose to his feet and, turning to the tall windows, he could see Helene and Kaia at the bottom of the garden, framed by the bars and crosses of the windows in the fading October light, and this sight filled him with a joy, or relief, which was so deep, so vast, that he was on the verge of tears, because seconds before he had been plunged into darkness. Helene was sitting on the white bench beneath the apple tree thumbing through a manuscript. He had never seen her with greater clarity – short black hair, purple fingerless gloves, an ochre-coloured coat – while Kaia was scraping together fallen leaves with a rake that was much too big for her. And it occurred to Peter Wihl that he had never painted these two people, neither his wife nor his daughter.

Perhaps that was the reason: they were too close to him and he did not dare.

He put on his windcheater and went out to join them.

Kaia continued raking; the leaves lay around her in a yellow circle.

The branch above Helene's head was black; at its tip hung a frozen, red apple.

'What are you reading?'

'What am I reading? *The Wild Duck*, of course.'

'Yes, of course. Is it going well?'

Helene put down the manuscript and looked up at him.

'What's the matter?'

'Nothing.'

She sat observing him for a while.

'What's the matter?' she repeated.

'Just a bit tired.'

A gust of wind swept all the leaves away and Kaia stood in the midst of a yellow storm. Peter went over to her and together they tried to catch the leaves; some were dried up and crumbled to dust between their fingers and disappeared while others were wet and just slipped through, landing somewhere else in the garden. It was impossible to get them all and in the end he went down on his haunches in front of his daughter.

Her eyes were green.

She had her mother's eyes.

'Let's leave the leaves till next spring,' he said.

'Should we?'

'Yes. Then they can have a rest under the snow.'

Kaia laughed and pointed at him.

'You've got paint on your face again.'

'Have I really? What colour?'

She dropped the rake and pressed her forefinger against his forehead.

'Blue.'

'Just blue?'

'Black, too.'

'No others?'

'Yes. A bit of brown.'

'Brown?'

'Yes. There. And white. On your nose.'

'What do I look like?'

Kaia thought about that as they looked into each other's eyes, and Peter Wihl was once again overwhelmed by those green eyes, his child's eyes, open, undaunted, so unsullied, as though they always saw everything for the first time.

But then a shadow flitted across her face.

'I don't know,' she murmured.

'You don't know?'

Kaia lowered her eyes and shook her head.

And she said these strange words, her voice almost sounding frightened, and it scared Peter, too:

'You don't look like you.'

He tried to laugh, to laugh it off.

'Don't I look like me?'

Kaia shook her head again.

Helena rose from the bench – the wind blew open the pages of her manuscript – and went over to them. Peter slowly rose from his haunches. She put her hand on his shoulder.

It was already dark.

'Go and have a rest before they come,' she said.

'Come? Who's coming?'

Kaia shouted first:

'Uncle Ben!'

Peter sighed.

'Uncle Ben.'

Helene leaned against him.

'Had you forgotten?'

'Now I remember. Uncle Ben's coming.'

'With company.'

'My God. With company again?'

Kaia laughed, as though relieved to be able to talk about something she was looking forward to.

'Uncle Ben with company!'

'And food,' Helene added.

Peter did as she said; he went to the studio and rested on the mezzanine floor. Soon, to the smell of turpentine, he fell asleep, not into a profound sleep, but just beneath the surface, on the margins, enough to dream even so: he is standing alone in the schoolyard by the fountain; he is perhaps eleven years old; he is cold. Then another boy comes over to him. Peter, if that is what he is called in the dream too, is frightened and steps backwards, but the boy, who is bigger, or heavier, than him, keeps coming until he is very close, almost right up to him. The boy asks: 'If you could choose, would you prefer to be blind or deaf?' At that moment Peter wakes up, the answer to the question in the dream on the tip of his tongue: This is not a choice. This is a threat.

And he remembered Kaia's strange, startling words: You don't look like you.

He got up, showered, then leaned closer to the matt mirror, which began to clear, and his face loomed up as though coming out of fog and all he could see was that he was the person he was, Peter Wihl, on the cusp of fifty, one day older than yesterday and one night younger than tomorrow.

In his eyes, though, he could still see the vestiges of that sudden horror, the panic that overcame him when he went momentarily blind.

That was the difference.

Peter Wihl thought: Will I ever be free of it?

He returned to the studio and sat there in the dark among the pictures.

Then he put kindling in the stove, crumpled up some dirty old newspapers, lit them, opened the damper, and the heat soon began to radiate from the black iron, causing the glass doors to mist up.

Ben arrived at half past seven. He had a bottle of red wine with him and one glass. He sat down on the other chair – there were two in the studio, one which was good to sit on and one which was not. Peter was sitting on the good one. Ben poured and drank. He was the only person allowed in the studio while Peter was working; not even Helena or Kaia was allowed in; that was an agreement they had, Peter's sole law, apart from alcohol, and it was absolute.

Peter drank water.

Ben drank wine and started the conversation in the way he always did:

'You should get a lamp in here.'

'You know I paint in natural light.'

'Soon be working short days, Peter.'

'Is that a problem for you?'

'I hope the pictures won't be as dark as the surroundings.'

Peter stood up and turned one of the canvasses to face the wall.

'Where's the friend?' he asked.

'The friend's entertaining Helena and Kaia.'

'And who is the current friend?'

Ben chuckled.

'Do I detect a certain scepticism, or should I say, condescension in your simple question?'

'Not at all.'

'Or a monogamous, masculine criticism of my lifestyle?'

It was Peter's turn to laugh.

'Touchy tonight, Ben?'

'His name's Patrick and he's twenty-nine years old.'

'Where did you find him?'

'At the swimming pool in the Grand on Sunday morning. Or to be more precise, in the sauna. Happy?'

Benjamin Rav had turned sixty-five last year. He was lean, fit, swam his thousand metres every morning in the Grand Hotel pool, could be ascetic for odd periods, always wore a double-breasted suit, had thick, grey hair. When he was eighteen he had a jewel put in his left earlobe, as gypsies, sailors and gay men tended to do. Eight years later he travelled to the Spanish fishing town of Cadaquez and bought a suitcase of lithographs by Salvador Dali – unsigned, it was true – for next to nothing and sold them on to the idle, nouveau-riche jet set along the Mediterranean coast, earning himself a fortune in the process. That was how he got started. Ben, as his closest friends called him – and there were not many of them – had been Peter Wihl's gallery owner for twenty-five years, ever since *Amputations*, his debut exhibition.

'Helene is concerned about you,' Ben said.

Peter sat down again.

'Is she?'

'And when Helene's concerned, I become concerned.'

'I'm just a bit tired.'

'Tired? There are six months to the opening. The following

day you have my permission to be tired. The following day you can die as far as I am concerned.'

Peter filled his glass and drank.

'I'll get over it,' he said.

'Do you realise what's at stake?'

'I know very well what's at stake.'

'You won't get anything for nothing any more. Quite the contrary. They're after you. They'll chuck you on the scrapheap if they can.'

'Thanks, Ben. That's calmed my nerves a lot.'

'I mean it, Peter. That's why you have to show them pictures they've never seen the bloody like of before.'

'That's what I'm intending to do. Here they are.'

'To be frank, you just can't afford to repeat yourself any more.'

'What do you mean?'

'I mean exactly what I say, Peter. Do you know what evil tongues are saying about you now?'

'Tell me, Ben.'

'They're saying that if Peter Wihl paints any more body parts, he'll soon have to start on entrails.'

Peter looked away and laughed.

'And who are these evil tongues?'

'Whoever.'

'Whoever? Who the hell is whoever?'

'Forget it, Peter. What I'm trying to tell you is that you can't allow yourself to be tired now. Do you hear what I'm saying? Are you listening to me?'

'I'll get over it,' Peter repeated.

But Ben would not let go.

'Helene said you looked shaken when you came out of the studio this afternoon.'

'Shaken? Is that what she said?'

'Yes. Shaken. That was the word she used. Had anything happened?'

Peter got to his feet and stood by the tall windows, with his back to Ben. Darkness was drawing in; all he could see was a few lights some distance away, from the houses in the suburb where he had grown up. Rain was falling, but he did not see it.

'Have you heard what's happened to Beckers' titanium white?' he asked.

'No, tell me.'

'The chemist died and the formula was sold to China. Damned if they didn't mix it with soya oil! Now it's unusable. It's lost all its brilliance.'

'Is that why these pictures are so dark?'

Peter swivelled round and could hardly distinguish Ben in the shadow between the pictures.

'You own the walls. I paint the pictures. Shall we leave it at that?'

Ben walked towards him, from a different angle than expected, and raised his glass.

'I'll get you some white from London,' he said.

They drank and Peter knew of course that Ben had not been taken in by this explanation: that Peter was shaken because the chemist, the inventor of his favourite colour, the white base, was dead. Should he not tell him the truth – that he had gone blind for a few moments, even though now he could see again, and this one incident had shaken him in a way he did not have the words, nor even the imagination, to express, that death had sent out feelers six months before the opening, six months before he turned fifty. Should he tell him that?

Helene called them.

They walked through the garden, through the leaves, to the kitchen in the main building.

Kaia helped to set the table. It was covered in small bowls and dishes, containing all that new-fangled food, finger food, which Peter loathed. He did not want to use his fingers; there were implements for that kind of thing.

'Have you made everything yourself, Uncle Ben?' Kaia asked.

Uncle Ben laughed and lifted her in the air.

'I don't make anything, my princess. Everything I have, I buy.'

Ben's friend was already sitting at the table and the moment he saw Peter, he got up, held out both arms and grasped his hand.

'It's an honour to be allowed to come here and meet you, sir.'

'Now, now,' Ben interrupted. 'We use normal forms of

address here please, even though we are in the presence of a genius.'

The man, or boy, would not let go of his hand.

'My name's Patrick.'

With his round child's cheeks, he seemed younger than his twenty-nine years, but perhaps it was mostly because of his clothes: wide trousers, large shoes, T-shirt with Russian letters on the front. Country cousin in town was Peter's immediate thought. Anyway, he did not look like a swimmer, that was clear, but Peter also knew that when Ben picked this boy out, thereby vouching for him, investing in him, so to speak, Peter Wihl became the one on the outside. He would soon be fifty and was not conversant with the codes; the signals were meaningless to him; he no longer knew the difference between the victor's roar and a cry for help; he was, in other words, out of step, a foreign player on home ground and he was fine with that.

Was that what Ben meant by the scrapheap?

'Peter Wihl,' Peter said.

Patrick smiled.

'I'm a great admirer.'

'That's a relief.'

At length Peter got the whole of his hand back from Patrick and they were able to take their places. Helene poured wine or water into the glasses, Kaia drank cider and they ate with their fingers for a while in silence. It was food that required heaps of serviettes and large rolls of paper towels. Indeed, by rights, baths and showers should have followed, and Peter wondered whether to go and get himself a knife and fork as a little joke at the expense of Ben's affected modernism – these exotic dishes that are no more than homely fare where they come from – or perhaps he should just start drinking instead. Of course he did neither. He turned to the boy.

'What do you do, Patrick?'

'Communication,' Ben answered.

Peter filled his glass with water.

'Can't Patrick answer for himself?'

'Communication,' Patrick said.

'Well, don't we all do that?'

Peter noticed that Helene and Ben were constantly exchanging fleeting glances; in other words, they were concerned about him, they had been talking about him and had him under observation.

'What does communication mean?'

It was Kaia asking.

Helene leaned towards her.

'It means understanding each other.'

Kaia gave solemn nods while continuing to look at Peter.

'I asked Daddy,' she whispered.

'It means that soon, when I say you have to go to bed, you have to do it,' he said.

'No!' Kaia shouted.

'Yes, you do,' Peter insisted. 'In simple terms, communication means that I'm right!'

Everyone laughed. A little too much, thought Peter; Helene in particular. After all, he had not been that funny. The dishes were passed round again, past him, always past him, in much the same way as the conversation passed him by, and Peter could not be bothered to follow. He had been uncoupled: he seemed to be in a carriage that was slowing and in time would grind to a halt, in a siding, on the scrapheap, and he had an intense sensation of being on the outside, and that which could be depended on to give him a certain pleasure, his voluntary exile, as it were, where he could do his own thing in peace, wherever he was, which some took to be a charming distraction, gave him no satisfaction, nor any peace, since on this evening he was not master of his own absence; this time it went deeper, down into the terrible darkness that had swept his legs away earlier that day and set him back on his feet with the same rapidity.

'Amputation.'

Peter looked up with a start to see everyone staring at him.

'What?'

Helene placed her hand over his without saying anything.

Patrick bent closer.

'Amputation,' he repeated.

Peter still could not follow.

'Amputation?'

Now they looked at each other, although Kaia continued to look at him; she seemed sad and impatient at seeing her father this way, so out of it, so out of place.

Ben recharged his wine glass.

'Patrick is referring to your debut, my dear friend. Your first exhibition in my gallery. The exhibition which made you what you are. Do you remember it, Peter? It's a mere twenty-five years ago.'

'Is it the wine or this revolting finger food which is making you sentimental?'

Ben laughed.

'And, if you pay careful attention, you'll hear he's very enthusiastic.'

Ben was already loud, as he tended to become at a certain point, by nine o'clock as a rule, not because he was drunk, he was never that, he just wanted to be sure everyone could hear him. It was a bad habit from his youth when most people in his circle whispered, remained silent or lied.

Peter looked at the clock. It was three minutes past nine and he could not remember the time passing; so quick, so long. Had he had a blackout again?

He was terrified, and he laughed.

'How old were you then, Patrick? Three? Or perhaps you hadn't even been born?'

Helene pulled a sheet off the kitchen roll and put it on Kaia's lap.

'Two of the paintings are still in my bedroom,' Ben said.

Patrick looked straight into Peter's eyes.

'Exquisite.'

'Exquisite?'

'Yes. Parts of the body bereft of their functions. Brutal and beautiful. Why don't you paint like that any more?'

There was a moment's silence; the criticism was so apparent, so thinly disguised in the language of polite conversation, in the backhanded compliment, that even Ben looked down, abashed, embarrassed, and he took his time wiping his fingers on what remained of a blue serviette.

Peter looked straight at Patrick.

'Because I've already done it.'

Ben raised his glass and said, in acknowledgement of Peter and as a reprimand to his young, modern friend:

'The answer was a great deal better than the question.'

They toasted, after which there was another silence. By good chance, Kaia broke it; the silence.

'What does amputation mean?' she asked.

Peter set down his glass.

'If, for example, one of your toes hurts and it becomes infected, and there is a risk the infection will spread to the rest of your leg, then they cut off the toe. That's an amputation.'

Helene laughed.

'Don't listen to him,' she said.

Kaia was pensive.

'But what if my head hurts?' she asked, at length.

Helene got up.

'Now it's time for bed!' she said.

Kaia did not protest; she was much too tired for that, and dutifully followed her mother. The three men remained seated. Ben opened another bottle of wine.

'Not long ago I came across a funny thing in an interview with one of these Rembrandt women. She said we always dream in metaphors. Do you?'

Patrick contented himself with a shrug of the shoulders. He was still offended.

'I can never remember any of my dreams,' Peter said.

That was, of course, not true. He could, for example, remember all too well the boy who had asked him the impossible question in the school playground. The entire person, the plump boy, was recognisable, as indeed he, Peter, was, in the peau de pêche jacket, the water-combed hair. In other words, the dream was a metaphor, yet still unrealistic; it was distorted, he could find no other term for it, and in an almost clairvoyant moment it struck him that light comes from the inside in dreams, there are no other sources of light in them, in the same way that Beckers' white can be at the base of a painting, beneath all the layers, and yet make the black surface shine.

Ben laughed.

'Has this female anachronism got a point? Are we just old-fashioned in our sleep? Closet realists, as it were?'

Patrick said, 'I would prefer to call our dreams installations.'

Ben sent Peter a quick glance, almost ashamed for a moment on his young lover's behalf, and they went on drinking for a while instead of talking; that was best, they could hear the rain on the roof, the wind in the trees by the fence, Helene singing to Kaia.

But Peter could not restrain himself.

'So you dream installations, do you, Patrick? Beneath my amputations in Ben's bed?'

'No, there's seldom time for that.'

Ben interrupted them.

'I have some good news, Peter.'

'OK. Let me hear it. Are you going to adopt?'

Ben sighed and turned for a second to Patrick.

'Peter Wihl has his own brand of humour. It takes a while to get used to it.'

Patrick shook his head.

'I think Peter's funny.'

Peter leaned over towards him.

'Do you think I'm funny?'

'I like provocative humour.'

Peter laughed.

'Provocative? I was just trying to be pleasant.'

Patrick laughed too.

'As pleasant as an amputation,' he said.

Peter caught a flash of the boy's fury and fell silent.

Ben placed his hand on Peter's.

'When you've finished this exhibition, there is a portrait waiting for you.'

Peter withdrew his arm.

'Whose?'

Ben played hard to get.

'I can't say until everything has been agreed. But I can tell you this much: we can't go any higher.'

Peter cut him short.

'There are a couple of other paintings I'd like to do first, Ben.'

'Who?'

Peter leaned across the table.

And at that moment Helene returned and took a seat. She looked at the men, sending a smile to each in turn as Ben filled her glass.

'What secrets are you discussing?' she asked.

'Patrick's dreams are installations,' Peter said.

Patrick, who looked more and more like an over-sized child with a soft, smooth face – perhaps brought on by all the wine – squirmed on his chair. It served him right, thought Peter, and

Ben had to come to the boy's aid. He took his hand, turned to Helene and changed the subject.

'Tell us how things are going with *The Wild Duck*,' he said.

'Too early to say. But I think it will be different.'

Ben sighed.

'It's basically an intolerable piece of writing. Ibsen, the niggard, allows everything that can go wrong to go as wrong as possible. And it's unbearable!'

Helene cocked her head.

'What do you think Ibsen should have done?'

Ben's voice grew even louder:

'He is no more than a dramatic poseur. They could have just sorted out all the unpleasantness in the Ekdal family and saved the child's life! Self-centred, middle-aged men must be the most loathsome beings in existence.'

'And then what's left of the drama?'

Ben looked around.

'Isn't happiness dramatic enough? Do we have to have sexual diseases, bankruptcy and violent death in order to create drama? Can't we be content with happiness?'

'Are you after an idyll, Ben?'

'I would at least prefer an open stage. So that the audience can witness Hedvig's suicide with their own eyes. And then I would like some coffee.'

They were interrupted again, this time by Kaia shouting for Peter. He went to her bedroom and sat on the edge of the bed, in the semi-darkness, glad to be with his daughter and glad to slip away for a while.

'Can't you sleep?'

Kaia shook her head.

'Are we talking too loud?'

'Especially Uncle Ben.'

Peter tucked the duvet tighter around her, and could hear the conversation in the kitchen, not the words, just the voices. He would not have been able to sleep with such a noise in the house either; rain was better, on the roof and against the windows. That was the right accompaniment to sleep.

'Yes, especially Uncle Ben,' he repeated.

Kaia took his hand and he was surprised that her small fingers were so strong.

'Who do I look like?' she asked.

And Peter was reminded of his own question in the garden as he came out of the studio, shaken, and Kaia's unease, because she had not come up with an answer. Now it was her turn to ask – for children do not forget; children need to have matters cleared up – and he bent down and passed his finger over her face, in the shadow, on the white pillow.

'Like you, of course. Who else?'

Kaia smiled.

'You do, too.'

She had cleared up the matter and let go of his hand. Now she could sleep.

Peter gave her a light kiss on the forehead.

'What are you going to dream about tonight?'

'I don't know yet.'

He smiled and straightened up.

'Good answer,' he whispered.

But as Peter was about to close the door, her voice was there again.

'Can you leave it open a little?'

Peter turned. Kaia was sitting up in bed, a narrow strip of light falling on her from the corridor.

'But then you'll hear Uncle Ben.'

'I won't be able to sleep anyway, if the door's closed.'

Peter left the door ajar and as he walked back to the kitchen, to the others, he thought with anxiety, almost alarm, about his daughter being just six years old and already knowing the torments of choice, and not being able to choose between two good things like ice cream or chocolate, but having to choose between two evils, between the dark and the noise, between two ways of not being able to fall asleep. He stood by the table: they were drinking coffee, the rain was no longer falling – it sounded as if a veil of sound had been drawn aside. Helene had produced a bottle of Calvados, Patrick seemed bored and Ben was still in a lather about Ibsen.

'Ibsen's life-lies are a hyped-up Norwegian sport! It's not bloody true that life-lies and being happy go together! Just look at me!'

Peter knew, of course, that there was a way to solve Kaia's

problem, to free her from the torment of choice so that she could sleep in peace.

He pointed at Ben and only then did they become aware of his presence.

'Our daughter asks if you would mind lowering your voice. Or else shut up.'

Ben held his hand over his mouth.

Patrick laughed; a high-pitched child's laugh.

'Perhaps it's time you two did the washing-up,' he said.

Peter turned.

'Sorry? What was that you said?'

Patrick looked at Ben, who blushed behind his hand. The skinny, almost elderly, poseur was blushing.

'Don't you have a tradition of doing the washing-up together?'

2

There had been frost during the night.

Peter and Helene were walking arm in arm, slowly, in the low, cold sun. The frozen puddles of rainwater shone like glass panes between the avenue of trees, and Kaia jumped from one pane to the next in cold's very own paradise. They could hear her screams of delight every time one cracked, and it seemed to Peter that some things never change, like the glee with which a child runs through fallen leaves and stamps on frozen puddles.

The park was deserted and bathed in an almost white light. Soon all the rime frost on the grass would thaw and mingle with the sun, forming pale, green shadows.

Church bells rang from somewhere in the town.

It was Sunday.

Peter was carrying a bunch of flowers in his free hand: dried roses.

'What were you and Ben talking about in the studio yesterday?' Helene asked.

'The usual.'

'Oh, just the usual?'

'You know Ben.'

She cut him short.

'No one knows Ben.'

Peter sighed.

'He's already uneasy. About the exhibition. In other words, the usual.'

'Are you?'

'You know very well what I'm uneasy about.'

Helene leaned across to him.

'And I'm not interested in listening to that. You're not the first man to turn fifty.'

'It's the first time I've turned fifty, though.'

Helene laughed and waved to Kaia, who did not see her, so busy was she, dancing from puddle to puddle, further and further away from them, and it struck Peter that their daughter was the only colour in this frost-scarred park: the yellow scarf, the red hat, the green raincoat, gloves and ankle boots. Perhaps that was how he had to paint her, as a contrast, warmth as opposed to cold, colour as opposed to absence of colour, but he rejected this as soon as the idea was thought, or even sooner, while he was thinking it. Kaia did not need any contrast, she was sufficient in herself; she could fill her own picture.

Then Peter noticed something else.

A black dog was running down across the hill from the churchyard.

Helene squeezed his hand.

'What do you think of Patrick?' she asked.

'I don't like people who greet you with both hands.'

'You don't like any of Ben's friends.'

'Friends?'

'Boys. Boyfriends. Lovers. Call them what you will. Couldn't you try to like them for once? For Ben's sake.'

'I've tried. But couldn't do it.'

The dog stopped by a tree, its red tongue hanging out of its mouth and its coat steaming as if it were standing in a cloud of frost and heat.

'I hope Ben's careful,' Helene exclaimed.

'Careful? How do you mean?'

'You know very well what I mean.'

Peter turned towards her.

'By the way, what were you and Ben talking about?'

'The usual.'

'Oh, just the usual?'

'You know Ben.'

'Oh, no one knows Ben.'

Peter smiled and had to close his eyes in the blinding sunshine.

An uneasiness he was unable to put a name to took hold of him.

He no longer heard the dry sound of ice cracking.

'We were talking about you,' Helene said.

'Yes, he mentioned that.'

'You seemed so absorbed when you left your studio yesterday.'

'Ben said *shaken.*'

'Shaken and absorbed. I was frightened, Peter.'

Should he tell her now – as they were walking, his eyes closed to the sun, arm in arm with Helene, the mother of his child, his confidante – that the most important tool available to him, his sight, had failed him, and as he did so, unburden himself but thereby burden someone else and thus double his uneasiness, multiply it by two, or just pass it on to someone else, on to Helene? No, he would keep his uneasiness to himself. He did not want to trouble her. It'll pass, he thought. He said:

'Nothing to be frightened about.'

At that moment Peter heard a scream, close by, yet far away, as though his senses were playing a trick on him. Helene let go of his arm and when he finally opened his eyes, he saw Kaia standing stock-still in the middle of the footpath, her face hidden in her hands, the black dog circling her, slinking closer and closer. Now all he heard was the low, monotonous snarl, like a motor, and he could see the bared jaws, the pink, wet flesh and yellow teeth.

Peter stopped, horror-stricken, rooted to the spot. He tried but was unable to move, he seemed to be too heavy, as though everything was pulling him downwards, down, and for this moment he was no longer a daughter's father, he was no longer a woman's husband, he was a mere witness to what happened one quiet morning in the park at the end of October: Helene runs at full tilt towards the dog, which rears up on its hind legs and plants its heavy paws on Kaia's shoulders. It is bigger than her and sinks its teeth into the cap, the red cap. Helene stops then, without a moment's hesitation, takes slow, measured steps, whispering something as she closes the gap, like a song: it is Kaia's name she is whispering the whole time. Kaia, she whispers, Kaia. The dog pulls at the cap and rips it open, and Kaia lowers her hands to see what is threatening her and who can save her; her face is pale, almost lost from view between the dog's slobbering jowls. Helene then grabs the scruff of the dog's neck, hurls the animal across the gravel with all her strength and hugs Kaia, who now begins to cry, loud and piercing sobs, as if a dam inside her has broken. And the dog, howling, bounds towards a man who comes into view on the slope over by the churchyard.

At last Peter was able to tear himself free, fury drove him free, and he ran too, towards this man; a youngish man with a ponytail, wearing a long, black leather coat and holding a collar, a kind of chain, which he put on the dog lying obediently at his feet.

Peter came to a halt in front of him, breathless, furious.

'Don't you know dogs have to be kept on leads, for Christ's sake!'

The man looked up as though this had nothing to do with him.

'The dog's on the lead now. See!'

'That dog went for my daughter!'

The leather-clad man shook his head, his lips formed a smile, a mocking smile, and there was some truth in the notion that dogs resemble their masters, or vice versa, masters in the end resemble their dogs; they were a match.

'He isn't dangerous.'

'Isn't dangerous? What the hell do you call it then?'

'He was just being playful.'

'Playful! That brute attacked my daughter!'

'Calm down, pal. He's never bitten anyone.'

Peter stepped closer and pointed at the dog.

'That bloody dog should be put down! Do you hear me! Put down!'

'And you can stick those bloody flowers up your ass.'

Peter found it difficult to speak; indignation and terror had dried his mouth. He shouted:

'When I've put these bloody flowers on my parents' grave, I'm going to report you to the police!'

The man tugged at the dog's collar and the dog got up.

'You should take better care of your daughter, you twat,' he said.

Then he left, the dog on the lead, the tail wagging, the ponytail bobbing, back up the hill towards the churchyard.

Peter shouted, he screamed it out:

'It's you who should be fucking put down! You!'

The dog owner turned and gave him the finger.

Peter was about to run after him, without knowing what he would do when he caught up with him: he knew he was capable of doing anything, he was beside himself with fury, but then Helene was at his side, exuding an astonishing calm, and she restrained him.

'That's enough. Kaia will only get more frightened.'

Helene had to hold him, too.

'Is she hurt?'

'The cap's ruined.'

'I could have killed him.'

'They've gone now.'

Peter controlled himself, breathed out and turned to Kaia, who was standing quietly in the cold, wet grass, bare-headed, her dark hair almost covering half of her face, and she stared at him. There was something strange about her gaze, something he had not seen before, and it scared him.

She said:

'Don't be afraid, Daddy.'

Peter lifted her up, he was the one who should have uttered the words *Don't be afraid*, not her, and he could still smell the fusty stench of dog on her clothes.

'We're going home now,' he whispered. 'We're going home now to make cocoa, egg-flip, whipped cream, pancakes and sponge cake and we're going to eat the lot.'

Kaia, earnest, silent, just nodded.

'First we'll go to see the doctor,' Helene said.

Peter sent her a quick glance. Helene turned to Kaia.

'Just to be sure, OK?'

They took a taxi that was waiting at the gate by the main street and went to the duty doctor in the town centre where eight patients were already in front of them in the queue. Kaia was still silent, as if collecting herself, or else in the process of registering this experience, but did not know quite where to place it. She clung to Helene's hand. Peter felt superfluous and went to the vending machine in the corridor, inserted twenty kroner and pressed a button. The machine began to vibrate; it took a while until a bottle fell down, not Solo, the one he had chosen, but a cherry-flavoured Coke, a variety he had never heard of. It would have to do. He took it back to the waiting room. Helene and Kaia were not there. He unscrewed the top, drank and it tasted awful; like spreading glue over your mouth. He ran the back of his hand across his mouth and looked around. The room would soon be full of silent patients, the wounded from the weekend's skirmishes. He sat in the corridor where Helene had left him.

Then Peter spotted one of the doctors by the counter, a

plump man whom he recognised with some difficulty: it was almost an effort of will, a face from another time, his childhood, now bloated and blotched. Finally Peter placed it, the face, in the gallery of class photographs: it was Thomas from primary school, the brutal dux, Thomas Hammer, whom he had not seen since then. Peter turned away, but it was too late. Thomas had caught sight of him, put a few pieces of paper into a folder and gone over to the bench where he was sitting.

Peter stood up, was on the point of proffering his hand, then withdrew it.

'Thomas,' he said.

'Hope it's nothing serious,' Thomas said.

He laughed.

'My daughter was attacked by a dog,' Peter said.

'Ugh! They should be put down. I mean the owners.'

'I said the very same.'

Thomas nodded.

'Given the choice, you would have been happier if the dog had turned on you, wouldn't you?'

They eyed each other. Forty years lay between them. Nevertheless, it felt as if it had been just one long school break that had made them older, middle-aged. It was uncomfortable, like standing in front of a mirror and still seeing a stranger.

Thomas's pager bleeped. Peter hoped he would go. But Thomas stayed put.

'Do you see any of the boys?' Peter asked.

'Yes, I do. You're never at any of the annual parties, though.'

'Never get the opportunity.'

Thomas smiled.

'No, I suppose you've become too famous for us mere mortals now.'

'I've never had the opportunity,' Peter repeated.

'Perhaps you could come this year? I'm the chairman of the party committee. It'll be fun.'

'You'll have to say hello from me.'

Thomas checked the pager and put it back in the breast pocket of his white coat. Most of his face was covered with burst blood vessels, like small, red freckles – the way a face that has partaken of too much drink, too much sun and too little sleep will look; pleasure multiplied by time.

'Did the dog bite her?' Thomas asked.

'No. But my wife didn't want to take any chances. She's a bit anxious by nature.'

Why did he say that? He could have bitten his tongue.

'That's good,' Thomas said. 'Being anxious by nature.'

Peter had to pull himself together. This Thomas, who belonged to the past and to whom he had nothing to say, would have to leave soon anyway. Patients were waiting for him. What was he waiting for? And wouldn't Helene and Kaia also be returning soon? It couldn't be anything serious, even if the dog had bitten her and she had needed a tetanus injection, could it?

Just to say something – he could not bear the silence – Peter asked:

'And you work here, do you? At emergency services?'

Thomas shook his head.

'I have my own practice. But I do the odd couple of shifts here at weekends. When they need people. Pure charity. Makes me feel a better person.'

'Perhaps you need that?'

'Who doesn't? Once in a while, I mean.'

They chuckled at that.

His pager bleeped again. Thomas let it bleep. Someone could be dying while this pointless conversation was going on.

'I've been considering buying another of your pictures for quite some time,' he said.

'Have you developed an interest in art?'

'No. My accountant thinks it would be a good investment.'

'Is that a compliment, Thomas?'

'Indeed.'

'Thank you. You said *another*. Have you got any others?'

'I bought a painting at your debut exhibition, *Amputations*. A hand. Nasty stuff, but wonderful colours.'

'I didn't know you bought something at the exhibition.'

'Yes, indeed. Perhaps I might have a peep at your studio one day?'

'I don't think so.'

Thomas smiled.

'Then I'd better wait until the next exhibition.'

And Peter said, out of the blue – it just came out:

'I dreamt about you yesterday.'

Thomas bent closer, taken aback for a moment:

'I beg your pardon?'

Shamefaced, Peter looked away.

'Forget it.'

'Did you dream about me?'

'Just a stupid dream. Forget it.'

'And then we meet here. There must be some meaning to life after all. What did you dream about me?'

'Forget it! I'm sorry.'

Thomas put his hand on Peter's shoulder.

'Is everything all right, Peter?'

'No, it damn well isn't. My daughter's been attacked by a dog!'

Thomas stood like that for a couple of seconds, with his hand on Peter's shoulder.

'You work too much in bad light, Peter.'

'What?'

Thomas withdrew his hand, looked at the clock.

'Suppose I'd better save some lives now. Hope all's well with your daughter.'

'Thank you.'

Thomas produced a business card, which he gave to Peter, turned and walked towards one of the operating rooms where an obviously impatient nurse was waiting, and the door closed behind him.

Peter looked at the card: *Dr Thomas Hammer. Ophthalmic Surgeon.*

He wanted to throw it away, in the litter bin by the door. What was he supposed to do with the card of a man he had not seen for forty years and would prefer not to see ever again? But now Helene and Kaia were there. He hadn't noticed them – there seemed to be a blind spot wherever he looked – and he put the card in his pocket.

'Everything OK?' Peter asked.

Helene nodded.

'Can you get hold of a taxi while I pay?'

'Of course. Sure everything's OK?'

Helen, with vehemence, whispered:

'Yes, Peter. Outside.'

She went to the counter and handed over the papers.

Peter took Kaia's hand and gave her fingers a gentle squeeze.

'Come on, my little hero. Now we're going home to celebrate!'

Kaia just nodded, without meeting his gaze.

'Mummy's the hero,' she said. 'Not me.'

And Peter repeated these words, to himself, as they left the waiting room:

'Not me. Not me.'

Kaia kept tugging at his arm.

'What did you say, Daddy?'

'That you and Mummy are my heroes,' he said.

There was a taxi free at the entrance. Helene and Kaia sat in the back; Peter had to sit in the front again. The streets were still quiet in this part of the town where the river splits it into two, east and west, and provides place for the homeless, drug addicts and alcoholics along its banks. It had clouded over and when they were in the middle of the old bridge it began to rain; heavy October rain, the way rain is before it turns into snow and which windscreen wipers struggle to clear away.

Helene bent forward between the seats.

'Who was the doctor you were talking to?'

'Old classmate,' Peter said.

'He looked like a nice guy.'

Peter made an attempt at a laugh.

'He sold the answers to maths exercises for a week's pocket money.'

When they arrived at home, however, there was no party.

Kaia was not hungry and wanted to go to her room. Helene was not in a chatty mood, either, and Peter eventually withdrew to his studio to make the most of the last daylight, but the light had nothing to offer him. His hand would not obey, nothing in him obeyed, he was agitated, ill at ease, he was distracted by himself, the fury had burned itself out and laid the foundations for shame in its place. And Peter could think of nothing but the events in the park, of how he had stood still when his daughter had been in danger, whereas Helene had chased the dog away, fearless, without a second thought, except for that one all-embracing notion that excludes all other considerations: to protect Kaia, to save her at all costs. Peter had failed at the decisive moment. He had hesitated. And that was what Kaia had seen, too.

Peter was deeply ashamed.

He would have to make amends.

Restless, he paced between the canvasses, to no avail.

Then he heard sounds in the garden and turned towards the window.

The squall passed overhead and ensconced itself over the mountain ridges and forests in the north where the rain drew a quivering line through the sharp air. And Peter thought: there was always an edge, there was always a line dividing what you see into two, into light and dark, before and after, here and somewhere else, like rivers running through towns.

Helene picked up the fallen fruit and tossed it into a woven basket. Kaia was sitting on the bench beneath the bare, black branch, her hands in her lap, as if they, mother and daughter, had just changed places and nothing had happened between them. But something had happened: the darkness, the dog and, then, Thomas.

Peter opened the door, feeling the cold as he did so, and called to Kaia.

She looked up, but stayed where she was.

Helene took off her large gloves and leaned against the apple tree.

'Kaia,' he called again.

She glanced at her mother – who nodded – then stood up and ambled towards him.

Peter waited and froze. Helene lit a cigarette and followed them with her eyes. Kaia stopped.

'Could you help me with something?' Peter asked.

'What's that?'

'Come inside first.'

She lowered her voice:

'May I?'

'Hurry. So the pictures don't get cold.'

Kaia turned once more to her mother, who nodded, as if giving her blessing, before she followed Peter, who closed the door behind them.

Kaia stood in his studio, filled with a great earnestness, awe almost, it seemed, as she looked around, her eyes shining, her mouth tight-lipped and small in her pale, narrow face.

'Where are the flowers?' she exclaimed.

'Which flowers?'

'The ones we were going to put on the grave.'

'I left them in the taxi. We can go there another day, can't we?'

Kaia nodded, approached one of the canvasses and carefully raised her hand, but did not dare touch it.

'What's it going to be?' she whispered.

'I don't know yet,' Peter said.

Finally she smiled. It was just like a flower blossoming in her face and endowing it with colour, and Peter felt an intense, restless pleasure at seeing this: his daughter was a bouquet of flowers.

Her serious expression returned.

'What do you want me to help you with?'

Peter pointed to the good chair.

'Just sit there and look out of the window.'

Kaia did as he said, sat down on the good chair and looked outside. The sky was deep and clear, blue mixed with black; the rain was elsewhere, behind the mountain ridges and forests. No one was in the garden. There was only the basket of windfalls beside the yellow gloves. Helene had gone indoors. They could hear music from her study, which she must have had on very loud – it was the old Nina Simone album *Old Man Sorrow* which she always played when she was getting down to serious work. Peter, who hated rifts, surprises and irregularities, and preferred to cultivate a routine, with working days and sacrosanct Wednesdays, was reassured that things were nevertheless taking their usual course. The predictable and the unpredictable should be embodied in his pictures, not in his behaviour, not in his own life, and to find this he had to impose strict discipline on himself, an external force which could clear the way for the madness of the paintings. There was no room for more than one form of chaos at a time: the artist is bourgeois; art is free.

And now he had broken his own absolute law and let Kaia into his studio to make amends.

He wanted to make a start on her portrait.

Peter fetched his sketch pad and a pencil, 4b, and sat down

on the bad chair. He observed his daughter sitting there, facing the neglected garden, and drew a few swift lines across the sheet, a curve, an outline, a section; first of all, he had to search for her shape, the unbroken lines of her features, he had to find the centre of gravity in her face and liberate her, and he could feel his hand fulfilling the intentions of his eye and his mind, this fragile sacred triangle, the geometry of creation, an equal distance between each point: the eye, the mind, the hand.

'Now you can look over here,' he said.

But Kaia did not stir; although she seemed to be asleep, the contrary was true: she was awake and alert.

The tall windows, walls of glass, between the studio and the garden were soon invisible; the dusk dissolved edges and borders, and from a hole in the sky night drifted down to earth.

'Look at me,' Peter repeated.

Kaia turned towards him, with that same grave expression, the seriousness particular to models, which makes them resemble each other, as though they are threatened by something in the studio where the artist is a hunter and they are the prey. At the same time they are incapable of concealing their vanity: even Kaia, six years old, wanted to show herself to her best advantage. For, the greatest fear of those who pose as models is that the artist will not finish in time, will not be able to catch their beauty at its zenith.

Such is the gravitas of the model and the lightness of the portrait.

'Why are there no lamps in here?' Kaia asked.

'Because I don't like light bulbs,' Peter answered.

'But what do you do when it gets dark?' Kaia asked.

'I stop painting.'

Peter worked at the sketch for a little longer. He wanted to find the line which encapsulated her. He knew it existed. It would soon be too late. He stood up. Kaia went over to him.

'Can I see?'

He showed her the sheet.

She was silent for a long time.

'Can't you see what it is?' Peter asked.

She hesitated, her lips quivering.

And the answer both surprised and frightened him:

'The dog,' Kaia whispered.

3

The living room was bare, unfurnished; the doors, five in all, were missing; the windows were also mere holes, so that people could come and go as they wished, or look in. When Peter carefully placed a finger on the rear wall, it slipped to the side; behind it was an extended loft, almost bigger than the room itself, and there was a hatch in the slanting roof through which the moonlight fell, casting the rest of the room in deep shadow.

'Ben was right.'

Peter turned. Helene was leaning against the door frame with a glass in her hand.

'Right about what?'

'The open solution.'

'Sure?'

With great care, he slid the wall back into place. She drank the rest of her wine and went over to him.

'Ibsen is so bloody indirect, isn't he? Everything happens somewhere else. Or it has happened before.'

'That's Ibsen's method.'

'So?'

'You want to revisit Ibsen?'

'All he shows is the consequences. That's not just boring, it's also bloody spineless. I want the audience to see everything. They have to see the moment when a damned child takes her life because of her foolish father.'

Helene flicked the wall with her finger, and the room and loft collapsed in a heap.

She laughed.

'Like that,' she said. 'That's how the stage should be when the play's over.'

Peter laid his hand on her shoulder. She stood with her back to him, without speaking.

'Is Kaia asleep?' he asked.

Helene's voice was subdued and tired:

'She's sleeping with me tonight.'

'What about me?'

Helene turned to face Peter, who yet again felt excluded,

sidelined, and he wished she would ask him what had happened in the park when the dog attacked Kaia, while still hoping she would let the matter drop, as all he could say was that he had been unable to move from the spot, he had been rooted to the path between the trees, and that was not a good enough answer.

But this was not what Helene asked. Instead she said:

'I thought you wanted to sleep in the studio?'

Peter shook his head.

'I'd prefer to sleep with you two.'

Helene laid her cheek against the back of his hand and that was enough for Peter, this simple gesture implied a kind of forgiveness, and he wanted to take her in his arms, he wanted to possess her, but she pushed him away, not in a hostile or an unsympathetic way, but with an inordinately tired smile, which was convincing enough, and she walked towards the door.

She turned for a moment.

'You surprised us today,' she said.

Peter looked away, ashamed yet relieved; she could express it in that way too, that he had let them down.

'Yes,' he whispered. 'I surprised myself, too.'

'By the way, what was Kaia supposed to help you with?'

Peter looked at her again. So that was what she meant. The fact that he had let Kaia into his studio was a bigger surprise than the fact that he had not run to her aid when she was attacked by the dog.

'It's a surprise,' he said.

'Surprise?'

'Yes, a little surprise.'

Helene paused a little before saying:

'That's not like you.'

4

November can be sunny, too.

The days were shorter, but the light was still strong and clear for as long as it lasted. Peter got up early every morning, before the night had released its grip, to work in the studio on picture after picture until the light died between his hands and all he could rely on was what his sight could remember. He worked on the portrait of Kaia which she had said looked like a dog; its memory had cast a shadow over everything else, even herself. Peter made a note of an idea he had had on the side of a sheet of paper, perhaps he could use it in the interviews he would have to go through when the time came: *We see what we are.* Then he crossed out the sentence because he realised it was debatable, at worst, untrue, and instead wrote: *When we see, we also see what we have seen.* All the things we have seen merge, our seeing is impure and from the moment we open our eyes for the first time, nothing is ever completely fresh again. At the bottom of the sheet of paper he wrote: *Don't think, see.*

Kaia was playing in the garden.

The dog, she had said.

Peter tore the sketch into pieces and started afresh.

Helene was at the theatre and came home late.

And so these days passed, going faster and faster.

Peter had no time to lose and for Peter time was the same as light: he had no more light to lose.

So, Peter put what he called his temporary blindness behind him, for nothing had changed anyway. Everything was the same: he got up; he worked; eye, mind and hand were in harmony; and it surprised him that the human body was so ingeniously equipped, or perhaps the opposite, that it was created in such a simple fashion that most things pass and he was not just beginning to forget, he even thought he could use this experience as a motif: the light that had disintegrated inside him without any warning and the endless night he had glimpsed for a second, this sea change which through time became connected with another triangle, the geometry of chance: the black dog and Thomas, that nasty boy from his childhood. He found a kind of meaning in this, a construct at least.

Then it happened again.

The light inside him went out.

This time it lasted longer.

When Peter woke up, Kaia was standing outside the glass doors and staring in at him. He was lying on the floor in the corner of the studio. The easel had toppled over. Paint had run across the carpet, yellow or violet. His smock was twisted around his body. She must not see him like that. That was his sole thought. She must not see him like that. He tried to get to his feet, but could not. His left arm ached. He couldn't raise it, either. There was a buzzing in his head somewhere, as though his brain had short-circuited; wires chafed against each other and sudden flashes filled the room with white noise.

Kaia pressed her face against the glass; soon she was hidden in shadow.

How long had he been out?

Peter looked at his watch, the watch face, the numbers, the hands, he could see it all, it was so clear, the points in time, but it meant nothing to him, instead he felt instant nausea, everything was disconnected, the leather strap, the wrist it was attached to, the paint-stained fingers that scrabbled around the floor, just as he too had been disconnected from his habits, his work, his surroundings, and, almost fifty years old, he was striving for the opposite now, not amputation but reconnection, not a fracture but a union.

It was quiet.

He looked at the clock above the door. That did not help, either.

He closed his eyes.

Still he could hear a sound. It would not go away and was close at hand.

He opened his eyes again.

Kaia was beating the glass with the palms of her hands.

Peter struggled to his feet, staggered over to the doors, pulled them open, inhaled a deep lungful of air and was out, by her side.

Kaia backed away.

Peter heard his own voice say:

'There's nothing to be frightened of.'

She stood staring at him as if she, too, was searching for a centre of gravity in his face, and didn't he perhaps wish that? That she could raise him from everything that weighed him down, that tore at him? That lightness could raise a heavy weight?

Peter went closer.

The grass was cold and damp beneath his bare feet.

'Let's sit on the bench.'

They sat down.

Peter took her hand. It was warm. There was something he had to ask. He had to summon up the courage.

'Were you watching me for a long time?' he asked.

Kaia bowed her head.

'I don't know,' she whispered.

'Are you cold?'

She shook her head several times.

The light in the windows, except that of the studio, became stronger and stronger, or so it seemed, but the opposite was true, it was just the darkness becoming denser, making it possible for them to imagine that other people lived there, people other than them, as in a dream, they were sitting on a white bench asleep, and the windows were dreams, and they had gone there to see how the strangers lived, behind the thin curtains, in the rooms behind the walls.

The telephone rang in the hall.

No one answered it. There was no one at home, of course. The house was empty. It soon stopped ringing.

Peter was still holding Kaia's hand.

He was the one who was cold.

'Let's not say anything about this to Mummy, shall we?'

Kaia shook her head again.

Then they went in.

They were the people living in the house.

Peter took a shower, avoided looking at himself in the mirror, changed clothes, noticed a blue, almost black shadow spreading from his elbow to his shoulder, by good fortune not his painting arm, and as he stood with his back to the bedroom mirror it occurred to him that he had not insured his arm, as pianists do for example, he had not insured his hands, and what about his eyes? How much were they worth, how high would the premium be for his eyesight, and what good was a healthy arm if he could not see, or vice versa, what good was it if he could see, but his hand was useless?

Peter thought about this to avoid thinking.

Afterwards he made dinner, he clung to routine, those simple essential chores, repeated at regular intervals, a rhythm of life, the things that prevented chaos, such as the pan of boiling water, the salt, the vegetables, the fish, the knife, while Kaia set the table. She dropped a plate on the floor and began to cry.

Peter had to console her.

'It doesn't matter,' he whispered.

He said it several times: it doesn't matter.

They knelt down and swept up the broken pieces and carefully put them in the rubbish bin.

The telephone rang again.

Peter got up.

'You answer it. It'll be Mummy.'

Kaia ran into the hall and took the call.

And Peter thought that to be a whole person the child has to learn to forget, not to remember but to forget.

She returned.

'It wasn't Mummy,' she said.

'Who was it then?'

'Thomas.'

'Thomas?'

'He wants to talk to you.'

Peter switched off the cooker and went to the telephone. He did not like this, Thomas ringing him; he did not like anyone ringing him, especially not Thomas.

He picked up the receiver and said his name, with alacrity and distance.

Thomas's response was immediate.

'Hi, Peter. Was that your daughter I spoke to?'

'Yes.'

'Kaia is a beautiful name. Bit old-fashioned. I like it.'

'What do you want?'

'How is she?'

'Very well, thank you. What do you want?'

'You owe me an explanation, Peter.'

'Explanation?'

'Yes. What did you dream about me?'

Peter had to hold the receiver in his other hand. His whole arm ached.

'I said you should forget it.'

Thomas laughed at the other end of the line; he seemed drunk.

'Forget it? How the hell can I forget it when an old school pal I haven't seen for forty years says he has dreamt about me?'

Peter put down the receiver. He stood for a few moments, impatiently waiting for it to ring again, even though he hoped it would not. And yet again he was aware, as though he were sensitive, allergic in fact, to these impressions, of the symmetry of events, the darkness, the plate that smashed and Thomas; events which had nothing to do with each other except that they occurred in a particular order during a given period of time, like the dream, the alarm clock and the rain.

But Thomas did not ring again that day.

Peter went back to the kitchen. Kaia was sitting at the table, waiting. He stopped to examine the picture hanging on the wall behind her, as if seeing it for the first time, and he did this with great disquiet: it was crooked, it had been crooked for all these years, and it surprised him that he had not noticed before that this picture, *Arm II*, – painted twenty-five years ago for his debut exhibition, representing an arm, the right one, severed from the body, a lifelike anatomical portrait of muscles, flesh and tendons, in other words, an arm without any significance, a decoration and no more – obviously should not be hanging here in the kitchen.

Kaia was watching him the whole time.

'What is it, Daddy?'

Peter took down the picture and put it in the pantry, behind the empty bottles, and closed the door.

Then he lit a candle.

They ate.

The flame between them on the table rose, high and silent.

The room seemed to have grown larger.

Helene came home when the food had gone cold. It did not take her long to register the change, it was impossible to move an ashtray or a book without her noticing, and she pointed with astonishment, or rather irritation, at the bare wall.

'Why have you taken down the picture?'

Peter stood up.

'It was disturbing.'

'Disturbing?'

'Yes. It was disturbing. Are you hungry? I can warm up the leftovers for you.'

'What were you thinking of hanging in its place?'

'I'm working on it,' Peter said.

He sent a secretive glance to Kaia, who still had not finished her dessert: redcurrants from the garden with custard, red and yellow, colours in the blue bowl which were so clear, so sharp, that he had to shield his eyes, and the thought crossed his mind that that was how it was, either so dark that he went blind or so bright that he was blinded.

'Isn't that right, Kaia?' Peter whispered.

Kaia nodded, without looking at either of them.

Helene had already eaten in the theatre canteen and Kaia went with her into the living room where they watched children's TV and laughed at something on the screen.

Peter washed up, cleared the table and made coffee, all these sacred routines, a powerful rhythm of petty tasks which kept thoughts at bay, which kept him in one piece, which allowed him to carry on.

He left the bowl of redcurrants and custard in case anyone wanted more.

The berries and the custard merged into a particular pattern, still liquid, and made a new colour, somewhere between sweet and blue.

Then there was complete silence and soon afterwards Kaia began to cry softly.

Peter took the coffee in with him. The sound had been turned down. Kaia lay with her head buried in Helene's lap.

'What's the matter?' he asked.

Helene looked up from caressing Kaia's neck.

'There was a dog on television.'

'Switch it off.'

'I have.'

'You've turned down the sound. The picture's still there, isn't it?'

He looked at the mute screen: no dog there now, just the local weather forecast; temperatures were about to fall.

They went to bed early that night.

Peter could not sleep. Helene also lay awake. He could hear that from her breathing and every single movement told of her restlessness. They had shared a bed for more than ten years, sleeping apart for very few nights, when one of them was away or after the odd, infrequent row; sleeplessness was part of their joint estate: if one did not sleep, the other could not fall asleep: that was marriage.

'And what did the great director say about the open solution?' Peter whispered.

Helene smiled in the dark.

'He called it Ibsen's open-plan office design.'

'In other words, he liked it?'

'He was willing to give it a try at any rate.'

They lay silent in the dark for a while, listening to each other.

'Who's going to play Hedvig?' he asked at length.

'Someone in her final year of college.'

'Who looks like she is fourteen years old?'

Again Peter could hear Helene smiling in the dark.

'It's just theatre, that's all,' she said.

They would say that when they did not quite know what to say, or how to say it.

Peter gave a soft chuckle.

Helene leaned against his arm, the sore arm; he winced – it was almost a scream – and she switched on her bedside light and saw the dark shadow over the skin around the elbow.

She looked at him.

'What happened?'

He could have told her now that he had been out cold, or out of himself; that was where he had been, out of himself, which is the greatest loneliness, he had been somewhere else, but now he was back, and once again he did not want to worry her.

'I bumped into the door frame. In the studio.'

'How did you do that? Did you fall?'

'Something like that, I suppose.'

'No, not something like that. Did you fall?'

'I tripped. On the carpet. Have to get rid of that carpet.'

'You tripped on the carpet?'

'Yes.'

'And hit the door frame four metres away?'

Peter could feel enormous irritation welling up, bordering on fury, not because of Helene's persistence, but because he was such a terrible liar.

'It's just theatre, that's all,' he said.

Then Kaia appeared in the doorway. Her face was invisible. She was a thin silhouette, cut out of the dim light in the corridor behind her. In one hand, she held her duvet.

Helene sat up in bed.

'What is it, sweetheart? Couldn't you sleep?'

Kaia shook her head, took one step forward and became visible in the dark.

Helene sighed.

'You can't sleep with us every night, you know.'

Kaia stood there, looking down, but she said nothing.

Helene stretched out her hand, but could not reach her.

'Go back to your own bed now, Kaia,' she whispered. 'And you can leave both doors open.'

Peter sat up, too.

'Just come and lie down with us,' he said.

And Kaia lay down between them, under her own duvet, and she went to sleep the moment Helene put out the light. Peter lay as still as he could, listening. He wished it were possible to hook himself up to the child, to Kaia, to hook up to her calm, regular sleep, her heartbeat in the dark.

Then Helene carefully leaned over towards him and whispered into his ear:

'I don't know what's going on with you at the moment, Peter, but don't you ever, ever, contradict me like that again.'

5

Peter is standing in the studio, in front of the darkest of the canvasses, paintbrush in hand.

Cobalt and emerald.

Pencil and palette knife in the breast pocket of his work smock, the scarf, the sandals, socks on his feet; the floor is too cold.

Peter is ready.

The light seems to be coming from all angles.

He tells himself, aloud: I'm ready.

Yet he hesitates.

It is the fear. It absorbs all his attention, every thought, every movement, every single mood. Fear is not a tool that he can put straight to use and ennoble; fear is a saboteur which undermines, which destroys the holy geometry; fear is an army which invades the body and soul; and in the end it is fear which uses him, and fear does not ennoble; it makes everyone ugly.

Fear is chaos.

Fear is the present tense.

For isn't it the case that fear does not find its expression in art, in the word, in music, or wherever, until it has been traversed, seen, experienced, until the fearer has finally been healed and cured, but is still touched by it?

It must not happen again, it must not happen a third time, what he expects and fears most: it must not happen, Peter thinks.

That is all he can think.

Kaia has gone with Helene to the theatre.

That is for the best.

Peter stands in the studio, raises his hand, the hand with the flat brush, emerald and cobalt, he approaches the canvas, but is still so far away that it is out of reach.

He turns towards the glass doors and sees it now: snow has fallen.

He puts down the brush and the palette, and walks over.

A thin, fine layer of snow covers the garden, the bench and the hidden decomposing, rotting leaves. The trees are even blacker. The last apple, which they left, has released its grip, a red apple on a white cloth and a bird pecking at it. Then the bird flies off and disappears and he sees something else: tracks leading from the gate, which are soon covered by the still-falling snow.

Ben appears outside the glass doors. He is so skinny that the snow does not settle on his shoulders. He is holding a bag in front of him with both hands and seems impatient. Perhaps he is cold. Peter is worried. How long has Ben been standing there?

Peter lets him in.

Ben sits on the good chair, places the bag on his knees and rubs his hands.

'Bloody weather,' he says.

Peter stands with his back to him.

'I like snow.'

Ben points to his sandals.

'And you've started wearing socks. Odd socks into the bargain.'

'Perhaps I should have heating cables laid in the floor.'

Ben laughs.

'Do you know what I really like about you, Peter?'

'Tell me.'

'You *look* like an artist. The paint-stained smock. The scarf. You're unmistakable.'

'Is that another of your compliments? Or are we just having fun?'

'Absolutely. It's a compliment. These days you can't tell who's who any longer. You can't see whether they're stock-brokers, troglodytes or rock stars. You've got style, Peter. Keep it up, please.'

'How's it going with what-the-hell's-his-name?'

'You know very well what his name is. Don't pretend.'

'Patrick, it was. The communicator.'

'Variable.'

'Variable?'

'I'm grateful for what I can get. But I'm sure you don't want to hear any more about that.'

'You mean that at our age we should be grateful for the crumbs?'

'At *my* age, Peter. Dare I remind you about April 6? You remember the date?'

'You don't need to remind me about my fiftieth, Ben.'

'I'm not. I'm reminding you about the private viewing. Friday, April 6 at 7 p.m.'

Peter turns to him.

'What are you trying to say?'

Ben goes quiet and looks around the studio in the slow manner that never bodes well.

At last he says, in a low voice:

'You haven't got any further.'

Peter sits down on the bad chair.

'I've come to a standstill.'

'The pictures have come to a standstill,' Ben says.

Peter gets up again.

'And that's the same thing! I *am* the pictures!'

'But I can't hang you on the walls of the gallery, for Christ's sake, can I!'

The two men eye each other.

Ben opens the bag and empties the contents on to the floor.

The last twelve tubes of Beckers' titanium white.

'Here's that damned winter of yours,' he says.

'The snow makes the light last longer. Thanks, Ben.'

Peter picks up the tubes and carries them over to the table.

Ben is soon on his feet and follows him.

'What's going on, Peter?'

'You know very well. Beckers' white is my compass.'

'I mean with you. What's going on with you?'

Ben rests his hand on Peter's shoulder. There is seldom, almost never, any contact of this kind between them. It has happened three times before: when the first reviews of the debut exhibition appeared in the national papers, when he got married and when Kaia was finally born.

This is the closest they can get to each other, a hand on the shoulder.

Peter leans against the table.

'Lacunae,' he whispers.

Ben does not understand what he says, or thinks he has misheard.

'Lacunae? What do you mean?'

'I passed out, Ben.'

'The day Helene said you were shaken?'

'Yes. And it's happened again'

'Why didn't you say anything to Helene?'

'I didn't want to worry her.'

'Worry her? You worry us all, Peter.'

He has to tell him now, now or not at all, the choice is simple, that's the only thing that is simple right now, for he knows he has no choice, and he turns to Ben, who lowers his hand from his shoulder.

'It's worse than that,' Peter says.

'Worse?'

'I went blind.'

Ben laughs out loud, as if Peter has just told a joke, but moments later he is serious again.

'Blind? Can you see now?'

Peter loses his cool and points to his eyes.

'I lost my sight! Do you understand? My bloody eyesight failed me both times and I hit the deck!'

Ben tries to take his hand, but Peter wrenches it from him and looks away. Ben leaves him alone. Peter hides his face in his hands and cries. He has told him what happened, it has been acknowledged, and he is unsure whether it is fear or self-pity that makes him behave in this way. He stands there crying. And after drying these idiotic tears he can see that Ben has gone out into the garden and is talking on a mobile phone, but Peter hears nothing, nor can he remember Ben opening the sliding doors or going outside, it is as if everything that happens, happens without any connection, the lines are broken, and again he thinks of this one word: lacunae.

His life is full of lacunae.

He needs an overhaul.

It has stopped snowing. It is quieter than before.

Ben's tracks stop at the hedge.

Then he comes back in.

'I'm sorry,' says Peter.

Ben puts the telephone in his jacket pocket.

'You're going to see the doctor.'

'I already feel better. It's not necessary.'

But Ben is not listening, Peter is in his care now, they share a secret and one of them must take charge.

'You're going to see the doctor,' Ben repeats.

'When?'

'When do you think? Now, for Christ's sake. Get your coat on. The taxi will be here any minute.'

6

A lacuna is damage to a picture, or to put it more precisely, a part that is missing or has been lost. It is not caused by general vandalism, as some works of art are subjected to over the years, but rather by time itself: time also ravages the art which transcends the moment and is thereby elevated and regarded as timeless. A flake no bigger than the tooth in the perforation of a postage stamp, almost invisible to the human eye, falls off Botticelli's *Birth of Venus* and turns to dust, blue dust, which is blown along the cold stone floor of the Uffizi Gallery in Florence, to flutter and disappear in the warm winds over the river Arno, thereby changing the character of Botticelli's painting: it is diminished, it is incomplete, it is no longer timeless. Or a crack smaller than half of the nail of an infant's little finger appears in the dry canvas of Van Gogh's *The Sower*; it is an abyss which the picture falls into, and the Arles Gallery in Amsterdam is forced to close for at least three months.

This is the reason why patient restorers sit in the cellars of museums repairing pictures: the timeless art that time has treated so ill. Their task is not to create something new; on the contrary, they just have to evoke the old, they have to close the abysses, they have to find the blue dust and re-apply it, so that time can stand still again.

But Peter Wihl is not timeless: he is caught between the alarm clock and the church bells, made of even more fragile materials than art, namely, blood, bone and marrow, in which time is not just content to form cracks, but in the end to reduce to earth and ashes.

This is the reason he was now sitting in the surgery of Kristoffer Hall, the chief consultant at the private clinic *The Medical Centre* on the outskirts of the town, in the discreetly located area to the west, past the suburbs. The furnishings in the surgery were spartan – a few anatomical charts decorating the wall – and the doctor, Kristoffer Hall, gave the impression of being equally austere, not so unlike Ben, closer to seventy than sixty, about which Peter was very relieved. He could not have tolerated being examined by someone younger, and it struck him, after shaking hands, that he had not been to the doctor's since he was given the Antabus prescription, and that was long enough ago. In other words, it was not before time, possibly even too late, but Peter would have preferred it if Kristoffer Hall had put on a white coat and hung a stethoscope around his neck, and not just sat there wearing a dark suit. That bothered him: a doctor should also look like a doctor, not just like any man in a high position; we must look like what we do, it is our identity, our truest role, so that there is no mistaking us.

The surgery was on the first floor, overlooking a snow-covered, deserted park and behind the trees Peter could glimpse the fjord, like a wide motorway between the mountains.

Kristoffer Hall leaned back in his chair.

'Ben has given me a brief account of what has happened. I would like to hear what you say.'

'Of course.'

And Peter searched for the words, the exact words which could provide a clear description of what had happened to him, but the word was not his medium, the word tended to obstruct what he wanted to say, and he thought that if he had been able to sketch it instead, he would have drawn a thin white line across a black background, horizontal, then he would have inserted a break, a hole, an absence in the picture, a lacuna in other words, and continued the line on to the other side to where the picture finished.

Kristoffer Hall leaned forwards, folded his hands over the table and helped the silent patient on his way.

'You lost consciousness?'

'Yes. Twice.'

'How long between the attacks?'

'Three weeks. Three and a half.'

'And you were unable to see during the attacks?'

'Yes.'

'This is very important, herr Wihl. Did your eyesight fail *before* you fainted?'

'Yes. At first everything went black. Then I passed out.'

'How long did these attacks last?'

'I couldn't say with any accuracy. But the last one was longer.'

'Longer or shorter than five minutes?'

'Shorter, I would say.'

'Was it painful?'

'Yes. It was as if something... how shall I put it?... had burst.'

'Burst? Could you be a little more specific?'

'It all went black. Like receiving a blow on the head. I'm sorry. I can't be any more specific than that.'

'So it was painful?'

'Yes.'

The consultant made notes on a sheet of paper.

Peter also leaned forward. The ensuing silence made him even more nervous.

'What do you imagine it can be?' he whispered.

'We don't guess in my profession.'

'Not in mine, either.'

The consultant looked up, mouthed a weak smile and moved the paper to the side.

'Since I don't have any medical records on you, I am obliged to ask a number of questions.'

'Of course.'

'Have you any other ailments?'

'No. I'm in good health.'

Peter laughed at his own words: he was at the doctor's and claiming he was healthy.

'So you don't take any medicine?'

'No.'

'Or sleeping tablets?'

'I sleep well.'

'What about alcohol?'

'I don't drink any more.'

'Any more? And what does that mean?'

'That I have stopped drinking.'

'Was it a problem?'

'It wasn't a problem after I stopped.'

'Did you get any help to stop?'

'A tub full of Antabus.'

'So you do take medicine.'

'I haven't taken any. I manage without it.'

Dr. Hall nodded and was quiet for a few seconds.

'You're due to open an exhibition in a month or two, if I am not mistaken?'

'That's right. April 6.'

'And I presume you are under a great deal of pressure?'

'That's nothing new.'

'But this time, perhaps, the pressure is greater?'

'It's always greater than the previous time. That's not the problem. Otherwise I would have gone to the psychologist.'

'I see. Have you ever suffered from epilepsy? In your childhood, for example?'

'Never.'

'Has anyone in your family suffered from it?'

'Not as far as I know.'

'Are your parents still alive?'

'They're dead. They died twenty-five years ago. And I'm an only child.'

'I'm sorry to hear that.'

'Thank you. I have got over it now.'

'But I ought to ask how they died. You don't have to answer.'

'It's no problem. Natural causes. Car accident.'

Hall looked down for a moment, as if searching for the next question, and he found it. Peter did not like the question.

'What sort of pictures are you painting now?'

'Has that any bearing on my health?'

'I'm trying to form a picture for myself, if I may express myself in this way.'

'Right. Twelve canvasses. One for every month.'

'In other words, you like a tight framework?'

'Yes. The tighter the framework, the more freedom I have. Could it be a tumour?'

'As I said, we don't make guesses.'

Peter became irritated and impatient at all this precise objectivity, the sobriety of expression and surroundings.

'But we can still use our imagination, can't we?' he said.

Kristoffer Hall smiled.

'You would prefer not to hear my fantasies. It would be better if you told me what *you* think may have caused this.'

'I paint in the dark.'

'In the dark? What do you mean? At night?'

'In natural light. There are no electric lights in my studio. Nothing else.'

'May I ask why?'

'Does it matter?'

'Not per se. I'm just curious.'

'You lose the blue rays of daylight in electric light. That damages my pictures.'

'If the darkness damages your eyes, that's worse, isn't it?'

'I haven't thought about it like that. Until now.'

'It's not definite that the lighting arrangements have anything to do with the attacks, though.'

'But there is something else I've been thinking about,' Peter said.

Kristoffer Hall looked at him.

'Yes?'

'Solvents. Several of my older colleagues have suffered from the effects. Some are in fact disabled and cannot work.'

'Interesting.'

'Interesting?'

'In fact, it has never occurred to me that artists are exposed to this hazard.'

'Painters, please note. And when you begin to behave a little oddly everyone thinks you're drinking too much or you're trying to play the genius. There are many hidden statistics, if you understand what I mean.'

Kristoffer Hall took notes again and nodded.

'Have you started behaving – what was the word you used? – oddly?'

Peter paused for a moment, forced to think about the incident in the park when he just stood watching while Kaia was in danger. Wasn't that odd behaviour?

Nevertheless he said:

'If I behave oddly, I imagine I am the last to notice.'

'Has anyone noticed?'

'You can ask Ben.'

'Have you had any problems with your memory?'

'Not that I can remember.'

Peter imitated a laugh.

The consultant did not react and focused his eyes on him again:

'Since these attacks have occurred twice, perhaps you ought to take certain precautions.'

'You mean it could happen again?'

'Everything that has occurred can re-occur. I'm merely saying you should rest. Take things easy.'

'I don't have time.'

'I can't force you to do anything. But you should stay in the vicinity of your family.'

'My studio is next to the house.'

'Good. Let's leave it at that then.'

Kristoffer Hall stood up and came round the table. Peter followed him with his eyes.

'At that? What happens now?'

'Now we'll give you the full works and see if we are any the wiser afterwards.'

It took close on three hours.

Ben was still sitting and waiting in the foyer when he came down. The secretary called them a taxi.

They walked into the quiet park.

'What did Kristoffer say?' Ben asked.

'I'll get the results of the tests in two weeks' time.'

'Kristoffer is the best there is.'

'You go to him as well, I suppose.'

'Of course. He gives me a check-up every six months.'

'That will reassure Helene.'

Ben chuckled.

'Reassure Helene?'

'She thinks about so many things, you know.'

Peter made a snowball and threw it at the nearest tree. The snow on the branches fluttered to the ground. A squirrel darted across the road, in front of the black taxi that swung in through the gates.

Ben took his arm.

'It's you Helene should be worrying about now.'

Peter turned towards him.

'We won't say anything to her.'

'Aren't you talking to Helene at all at the moment?'

'Don't moralise, please.'

'Don't ask me to lie, Peter. That's all I ask of you.'

'And I'm asking you not to cross the bridge of sorrows until we come to it. Let go.'

Ben let go.

'Until we come to it? I think we've already crossed it.'

'Then I'm asking you to keep your mouth shut. You can do that. All right?'

They sat in the back of the taxi in silence as they entered the town and driving through the low houses they passed a lurid glass mall with a rotating Christmas tree on the roof, at least a month too early, and Peter remembered something:

'Have you thought about the catalogue?' he asked.

Ben turned in surprise.

'Now I think we should take one thing at a time, Peter.'

'Are you afraid I'll die in the interim?'

Ben sighed and leaned his head back against the rest.

'You may not like what I'm going to say, but, actually, I was thinking that Patrick could write the introduction.'

'What are you suggesting? Patrick? That layabout?'

'Patrick has many talents, Peter.'

'Are you using me to do the boy a favour?'

'No, I'm using the boy to do you a favour.'

'Have you talked to him about this?'

'I won't talk to him until I've talked to you. That goes without saying.'

'Thanks. That was considerate of you.'

'And at least one of the pictures should be finished first, shouldn't it? Now, let's get you home.'

'I'm getting out here,' Peter said.

He got out by the university.

The students were sitting on the steps, smoking. Years ago some would have recognised him, but not now.

It did not matter.

Nothing mattered.

Peter continued to wander the streets at will, without feeling any pressure to go to a particular place; a freedom he had not indulged in for a long time. He could not remember the last time he had done this – it must have been while he was still young and went on study tours to other European towns, just after his *Amputations* exhibition, at the time when his colleagues were calling him The Butcher. However, Peter did not content himself with sitting before the works of masters in the Uffizi, Prado, Louvre, Guggenheim, no, he preferred to walk less familiar streets. He could walk for hours, from early morning, before the towns had awoken, before the towns had come to, before the towns had dressed themselves, until well into the night when they, like him, were drunk with light, sounds, smells. He was drunk with all the new impressions and he never tired of it, for he saw something new at every corner: a clothes line strung between windows above him, a churchyard, a bar, a cherry tree in flower, a beggar on a bridge, and sometimes Peter hoped he would lose his way, get lost, yet sooner or later he always turned up at the hotel, as if his pockets were full of iron filings and a magnet drew him back whence he had come. What, in fact, had he done in the meantime, since then? Well, he had tried to piece the parts together. All those years, that had been what he had wanted to do, put the severed parts into one body. Now he was walking as the whim took him in his own town, he thought, and dreaming about the same things he had dreamed about then, in other towns. It amused him to see how the first snow, already dirty in the city centre, created panic and chaos in the traffic, among pedestrians, beggars, street vendors; it always did, townspeople were never prepared, as if this heavy snowfall were a meteorological sensation, something exceptional, even though they lived in a country so far north that half of the nation was without sun for three months of the year.

But amid all this Peter had calmed down, strangely enough he had calmed down: it was a sensitive, delicate balance, even the thought of clumsy Patrick writing about him in the catalogue was tolerable, at least for the time being. He was in others' safekeeping. He was being given the grace to walk here. On the other hand, there was nothing else he could do apart from wait, for two weeks, for the results of the tests: body fluids had been analysed, the pressure in his head measured, his brain X-rayed from different angles, heart rate tracked with jagged or gentle curves over endless rolls of paper, light shone on his retinas and colon examined; there was not an area or cavity in his body that had not been inspected.

It was just a question of waiting.

He would be invulnerable for two weeks; he could not die

before he had been given a diagnosis. They needed him. For two weeks he was indispensable.

It was a wonderful back-to-front logic.

He saw the meagre light fall on a fragment of glass in the gutter, whence it seemed to be cast, or projected, up on to a whitewashed wall, beneath a crooked advertising sign, to land some distance away on a car bonnet that was reflecting the sky in which the clouds finally opened up to release the same light that was shining into the broken green glass.

Never before had he seen them with such clarity, these circles of light in light.

He passed an ironmonger's shop, one of the last of its kind, and bought a gas mask.

Afterwards Peter realised that of course he had not been walking without an aim. His freedom had been restricted after all; how else could he have found the way? He ended up outside The Theatre. That was where he had been going. Helene was his magnet. He went in. But first he had to ring the bell and be channelled through two doors. Then the lady at the reception desk wanted to know his name before she would let him through.

Peter Wihl's heart sank.

'It's me. Can't you see?' he sighed. 'Peter Wihl.'

She checked the screen and turned to him again.

'You're not employed here.'

'No.'

'Have you got an appointment?'

'In fact, I haven't.'

'Then I'm afraid I can't –'

Peter Wihl stooped down and interrupted her.

'For Christ's sake, don't you know who Peter Wihl is?'

The receptionist did not seem to. She just stared at him, frightened, frightened to commit a faux pas, or even worse, frightened of having already done so, committing the unforgivable faux pas, the greatest sin of all in this place, this self-important workplace: not recognising someone who should have been recognised from the very outset, and thus offending someone who should not be offended under any circumstances, such as an actor who had been off sick for a few weeks, or had permission from the theatre to do advertising and a soap series;

and at the same time she was frightened of not doing her job, which was to keep unwanted persons out; failing in this might easily cost her the job, in other words, she had a big problem, which only Peter Wihl could solve.

And he solved the problem by walking straight past her, to the lift where he bumped into the bad-tempered old stage manager, the one person he did like in this building and who had worked here ever since the theatre became famous for its harmless patriotic comedies and crowd-pleasing musicals.

At least they recognised each other.

'Everything shipshape, is it?' Peter asked.

'It never is.'

Peter put his hand on the shoulder of this irreplaceable old sourpuss who also transported the smell of the theatre with him. It was ingrained in his faded clothes, in his braces, his thin hair, the glasses case in his back pocket; he smelled of plush furnishings, sweat, shoe polish, sherry, costumes, tobacco, powder and not least vinegar, which was once used to remove make-up. Vinegar suited him.

'But it can't be worse than last time, can it?'

The stage manager shook his head.

'Can't it? Let me tell you something, young man. It's always worse than the last time.'

'Is that possible?'

'Do you know what little Hedvig said when I gave her the rehearsal timetable yesterday?'

'What did little Hedvig say?'

'Little Hedvig said that she couldn't make the rehearsal with old Ekdal on Wednesday because she had a driving lesson.'

'Is that true?'

'As true as I'm standing here, Wihl. And the paint is flaking off the walls.'

'Are things really that bad?'

'No one wants to be a theatre artist any more. You should paint for us again, Wihl.'

'Don't say that.'

The stage manager let out a deep sigh.

'But do you know what's worse?'

'Even worse?'

'Even worse, Wihl. The scenographer damn well brings her daughter with her to work. It's an absolute kindergarten here.'

Peter laughed and patted him on the shoulder.

'We'll soon put a stop to that.'

The stage manager smiled, a rare occurrence.

'Helene's the best,' he said. 'Helene's the best for all of us.'

'Where are they?'

'They're upstairs in the auditorium.'

Peter took the stairs; he did not feel like standing in the lift that worked in fits and starts, and was so cramped that two people could barely stand side by side. A story that used to be told in the canteen went as follows: During the premiere of the revue *Loose Jacket* in 1956, a title which incidentally was a good description of the theatre at that time, the legendary actor Claussen took the lift in the interval to buy himself a beer and a dram in the bar of the nearby hotel. He was stuck between the second and first floors until the show was over and, the day after, the arts critic – the critic on Norway's biggest newspaper – wrote that the second act had been a particular pleasure to watch, not least because of Claussen's eminent performance.

There was not a sound to be heard anywhere.

He crept past the wardrobes, filled a beaker with water from the dispenser in the corner and stood drinking it in the wings. The top of the stage set would soon be finished. He could recognise the interior of the model, the windows and doors that had been taken away, it was like a kind of peep show on a grand scale and some props were already in position: photographic apparatus, a hat stand, a sofa, a blue curtain, the loft wall which had been shoved to one side so that the scene where Hedvig eventually takes her life with Old Ekdal's pistol would be as visible to the theatre audience as possible. Otherwise the stage was empty, deserted. Peter noticed the bits of tape stuck to the black floor, the positions where the actors would stand at some point and deliver their rehearsed lines, written more than one hundred years ago.

At last he spotted them down in the auditorium, before they had seen him. He stood there like a spy, it was a habit he had and always had had, a bad habit; he was by nature an observer, and had he not had noble intentions, he might also have been called a voyeur, and as he stood there, hidden in the wings, he thought that we are never more attractive than when we imagine ourselves unobserved, when we are unaware, what some call being natural, but it is just a different kind of pose, and yet we are also vulnerable, perhaps most of all at that precise moment, as if the smallest movement, or a glance, can unmask us, turn us inside out, and for that reason his conscience pricked him for standing there like that. He was exposing those whom he observed, so to speak, he was rendering them vulnerable and defenceless, and what had delighted Peter before now filled him with a certain discomfort; this kind of keyhole aesthetics disturbed the fragile calm, despite the fact that what he saw was commonplace and far from dramatic: Helene was sitting in the third row, with a scarf around her neck, studying the model of the stage on a low, makeshift table in front of her, beneath a lamp casting a narrow, almost white light. Further back, in the dark, sat Kaia. She, too, was wearing outdoor clothes, she seemed to be sleeping, but she may have been trying to keep warm. Only now did Peter realise that it was cold in the theatre, terribly cold. There was no one else in the large auditorium apart from them. They still had not seen him.

He crumpled the empty plastic beaker and crossed the stage.

'Are you saving electricity?'

Then, they saw him, too.

Kaia got up; so she had not been sleeping.

Helene straightened up with this quizzical expression on her face, the one which always seemed to be wondering whether anything was wrong, but she did not ask if anything was wrong, she smiled, perhaps she was happy to see him.

'Hi, Peter. Cold, are you?'

'It's warmer outside.'

'Must be. The theatre is saving electricity until the audience arrives.'

'If they can get in. It's a regular fortress down there.'

'The theatre director has brought in new security measures.'

'Oh, I thought it was just to torment the actors a little.'

Helene laughed.

'Shh! They can hear you.'

'Where is everyone?'

'Having a break, Peter. Would you mind putting the wall in place while you're up there?'

'Sure I won't have the trade union on my back?'

'If anyone sees you, say it was on my instructions.'

Peter did as Helene said. The wall was mounted on rails, but he still had to apply all his weight to push it into place. Then he jumped down from the stage and joined her.

'What do you think?' she asked.

'About what?'

She pointed to the stage. 'The colour of the wall. Is it OK?'

The wall, the backdrop, was red, and Peter paused for a moment before answering. How was he to know whether the colour was OK, the colour of an empty room? It was as if it, too, slid open, or dissolved, to reveal not just a loft, but a darkness whose confines no one could imagine and which therefore could be as large as a universe or smaller than a thimble.

He had to hold the worn arms of the chair tight.

'The colour's fine,' he said.

Helene put her hand on his shoulder.

'And when you say it like that I know it is not fine at all. What's wrong?'

'Isn't it a bit gross to paint the wall red?'

'Gross?'

'You might just as well hang up a poster saying something awful is going to happen here.'

Helene sighed.

'The audience already *knows*! The whole world knows Hedvig is going to shoot herself in there. I'm just asking you if you think the colour looks good.'

'It reminds me of the old telephone boxes.'

'Anything wrong with that?'

'Not at all. But I would have preferred normal wallpaper,' Peter said.

They were silent.

Helene pointed to the bag from the ironmonger's.

'What did you buy?'

'A gas mask.'

Helene chuckled – it sounded more like a cough – as she went back to studying the drawings.

'You haven't become a bit paranoid yourself, have you, Peter? Won't be long before the manager thinks the theatre is a terrorist target.'

He looked around.
'Where's Kaia?'
'She's sitting behind us.'
'No, she isn't.'
Kaia was not there any more. Apart from them the auditorium was deserted, and Peter could see that for a moment Helene was panic-stricken, not as in the park, the first Sunday in October, that was not panic, that was panic's foil, namely cold focused fury, but here in the theatre nothing was foreseeable, predictable, it was a death-trap, full of trapdoors, false doors, ropes and mazes. Kaia had gone and Helene sprang to her feet and shouted her name, *Kaia*; her voice was high-pitched, piercing, barely recognisable, and Peter tried to calm her. She resisted, tore herself away and did not want to be, or could not be, calmed down, at least not by Peter, and she continued to shout Kaia's name, even louder. The whole thing lasted no more than a few seconds.
It was Peter who found her.
Kaia was standing on the black stage, in front of the red wall, holding a beaker in both hands, staring at them with a bad conscience and terrified. Their terror had rubbed off on her and so she also had a guilty conscience because she was the cause of it.
'I was just thirsty,' she whispered.
That was all, she was thirsty.
But the revolving stage jerked into action, the theatre's engine had been set in motion, and Kaia stood in the same place as she slowly arced away from them.
Peter ran up to the stage, Helene followed, and together they lifted Kaia down. Peter held her to him, burying his face in her hair, trying to conceal the fact that he was crying, that all of a sudden he could not stop himself.

7

Some paintings consist of countless other paintings, layer upon layer, the artist has painted one picture over another, one under another, to find a way to the right one, to precisely the right one, and only one is visible, the top one, the thin surface which is there for everyone to admire and hides a whole history of art, a wealth of other colours, forms and stories which were never meant to be seen.

But they exist.

A picture begins with the movement, a twitch, a disturbance of the fine geometry between eye, mind and hand.

A picture begins in the unseen.

And Peter Wihl was beginning anew.

He stood in the studio, in the dark, with the gas mask over his face, and spread Beckers' white across the canvas, he squeezed out the last of Beckers' titanium white, started on the canvas once again, he wanted to achieve the impossible, start with white, not ochre but white, and he worked at a furious pace, he launched an attack, he was a soldier, he would hurl this bundle of white light into the dark, a solar hand grenade, and there it would explode like a rainbow in the enemy's eyes.

And in fourteen days' time, no, no more than thirteen, it was well past midnight now, when the tests were finished and the results were available, he would be able to continue with the art.

Peter tore off the gas mask and slumped down on to the good chair, exhausted.

The canvasses around him gleamed, like windows; winter windows.

But he did not yet know what he saw through them.

The darkness he had seen, the non-being, was still unusable, an invalid sight, and another word occurred to him: an amputated sight.

A car drove by, along the road behind the garden: the light from the front headlights swept through the studio, from canvas to canvas and extinguished them, one after the other.

He took out his sketch pad on which he had drawn the first

lines, the curves, of Kaia's portrait. And he thought about the impossible elements of the portrait, of all portraits, those which constitute its paradox: the model ages as the artist works, time becomes the enemy of art, the face changes, the features alter, the skin tightens or hangs in folds, and is covered with blemishes, the mouth becomes narrower, wrinkles appear like small seams or deep furrows, the hair goes grey, the visible person is soon unrecognisable and the artist is working against time, his own time and the model's time, and therefore a portrait must include all ages, the seeds of death in that moment, the worm in the rose.

Then Peter went back to the main building.

He stopped outside Kaia's bedroom.

She was sleeping with the door ajar; her face seemed soft, almost undefined, on the white pillow.

Like that, thought Peter, I will paint her just like that.

Kaia raised a hand in her sleep, as if grabbing at something.

He hurried on.

Helene was pretending to sleep, with the light on.

Peter got into bed beside her. For a while they stayed like that, without speaking, listening to the silence of the house and each other, she with her back to him. Then she turned to face him as he was moving to switch off the light, and only now could she say what her eyes had been asking, ever since he had stood on the empty stage in the theatre, but now it was no longer a question, it was more an acknowledgement brooking nothing less than an explanation.

'I went to the doctor's today,' Peter said.

Helene sat up in bed.

'Why was that? Was your arm still sore?'

'Headache.'

'Headache? How so?'

'I've had it for a long time. A headache.'

'What did the doctor say?'

'He ran a few tests.'

'But he must have said something. Didn't he?'

'They don't make guesses in his line of work.'

Peter did not lie: he just did not tell her everything; he subtracted; lying is the opposite, which is to add or to substitute.

Helene gently stroked his forehead.

'Did you go to your doctor?'

'No. To Ben's.'

She straightened up again.

'So you keep Ben informed, but not me?'

'I didn't want to worry you.'

'Oh, don't give me that. Don't play noble with me.'

'What about you? Is the problem that I told Ben first? Is that what worries you most?'

Furious, Helene leaned over him.

'You can keep your bloody art a secret, but not the rest of you. Do you understand?'

Peter repeated:

'I didn't want to worry either of you.'

'Either? It's out of consideration for Kaia now, is it?'

'It's out of consideration for you both.'

'And how should I show consideration to Kaia if I don't know what's going on?'

'It's just a little headache.'

'And how long have you had a little headache?'

'A while. I can live with it.'

'But, for crying out loud, I can't live with a man who keeps me at a distance. Is that understood?'

Peter pulled Helene down and held her, held her tight.

'Yes, it's understood.'

She put her mouth to his ear and whispered:

'You don't go to the doctor if all you have is a *little* headache. That much I do know about you, Peter.'

He lay silent, then asked:

'Am I behaving oddly?'

'Oddly?'

'Have you noticed any differences? Have I changed?'

She looked at him again, with those quizzical, somehow impatient, eyes.

'What do you mean?'

'For fifty years I have been exposed to damp, heat, light, cold, internal explosions, external influences and God knows what and you ask what I mean?'

Helene laughed.

'You're not hanging in a museum yet.'

'Solvents,' Peter said. 'That's what I mean. Perhaps my brain is like a bloody sponge.'

'So that's why you bought the gas mask.'

'You can't paint with a bloody gas mask on! Gas masks are for those idiots who exhibit dead rats and mutilated cows!'

Helene put her hand on his forehead.

'You always go hypochondriac when it gets close. This time you're starting early.'

'And what's that supposed to mean?'

'You become self-obsessed, emotional, absent-minded, sentimental, nervous and intolerable. In a nutshell, the way you've always been.'

'Thank you very much indeed. You forgot spineless.'

'Spineless?'

'Yes. Spineless. Didn't you dare say it? That I was spineless. In the park. When the dog attacked Kaia.'

She paused, just for a second, no longer than it takes to draw breath, but enough for him to realise that that was what she did think, that he was spineless.

'There are many ways of being brave, Peter.'

'Don't make me less than I am, please.'

'What do you want me to say? That you were contemptible, pathetic, craven? That I don't want Kaia to see you like that?'

Peter said:

'She'll never see me like that again.'

Helene lay back beside him, and once more they were quiet, in the silence all around them.

'I love that smell,' she whispered at length.

'Which one?'

'When you come from the studio before you take a shower.'

'Perhaps you're the one who's been affected by solvents.'

'Mmm. I want you. If your headache is not too bad.'

And at that moment the telephone rang.

It had to be a wrong number, someone ringing the wrong number, because no one rang at this time, no one, and now the telephone was ringing. Helene released Peter and, semi-naked, she ran into the living room. He heard the ringing stop, Helene speaking in a low voice so as not to wake Kaia, if she was not already awake, then she was back, standing in the bedroom doorway, looking at him, pale, worried.

'It's your doctor,' she said.

'My doctor?'

'Yes, Peter. He said he was your doctor.'

Peter walked with all the composure he could muster, past Helene, into the living room, trying to conceal his terror of the bad news that might be on its way. Why else would the doctor call him now? To tell him everything was OK? No, he was calling to say time was running out, that was why he called so late, there was no time to lose, but Peter could not do it, could not conceal it, the terror. Helene saw it. He tripped over the door strip, swore, almost screamed, stood on one leg and held the receiver with both hands and all he could hear at the other end was laughter; he could not understand it, in the middle of the night, and the doctor was guffawing into the telephone.

'Hello?'

'Is that you, Peter?'

'Who am I talking to?'

But he did not need to ask; he already knew.

'It's Thomas from the row by the windows. Was that your wife I just spoke to?'

'Do you know what the time is?'

'She seemed a little, shall we say, impatient.'

'It's nearly two o'clock.'

'Nearly two. Well, I never. What was I going to say now?'

'Forget it.'

'Is that all you can say to an old friend, Peter? Forget it?'

'Yes. Forget it.'

'Forget what, Peter?'

'What you were going to say.'

Thomas laughed again.

'The boys are having a get-together tomorrow. I'll pick you up at six.'

'Out of the question.'

'Not at all.'

'Yes, it is. And you are not my doctor. Have you got that?'

Peter put down the receiver.

Helene was still standing in the hall, no longer pale with worry, but with anger.

'What the hell was all that about?'

'The idiot I met in casualty.'

'But what did he want?'

'The last thing I wanted. A class reunion.'

'When?'

'Tomorrow.'

Peter went over to Helene and placed his hand gently on her breast.

'Go and have a shower now,' she said.

He dropped his hand.

'Oh, yes. I suppose I must have forgotten.'

Helene held him back.

'What was his name?'

'Whose?'

'That idiot from casualty.'

'Thomas. Thomas Hammer.'

'You'll have to get shot of him,' she said.

8

Restlessness.

A morning in black and white.

There are more than a hundred thousand hues, harmonies, shades, pigments no one has yet discovered, in the dust of a fragment of pot in the Sahara sand, in the scales of a snake slithering through ferns deep in the rainforest, in the eyes of a child looking away.

But Peter could not work.

For the first time since he had had the studio built, he did not go there as he had done every single morning, irrespective of whether it was Christmas Eve, a wedding anniversary or a birthday. It was an obsession, an objective obsession, for there was nothing mysterious about it; he was just one of those who had chosen to spend his life searching for the right colour and the right form, even though it was impossible to find the right colour and the right form.

That was precisely why they got up every single morning and continued to do so.

Now he was sitting at the kitchen table in the empty house, beneath the picture he had taken down, which, due to lack of light, had left a faded rectangle on the wall. What should he put in its place? A calendar? Yes, a calendar, that would do, a calendar could hang on the wall in the meantime. He had not had a calendar since he was a child. One Christmas he had been given a calendar by his father, a ridiculous present for a young boy who could barely read or count yet, one of those old-fashioned calendars with pages you rip off when each day has passed, and at the end of the year you have an empty holder. He hated it, he cried; he did not want to tear off the pages and destroy them. Then he began school and had timetables to contend with, but Peter was late anyway because he always dawdled, because he was always detained, as they say, by something or other, something he saw and had to examine more closely, a strange cloud in the sky, a rainworm on the pavement, and he was so often late that he was suspended for two weeks. As a reward, he thought, but his parents did not share his opinion. Being suspended was a disgrace, and that was why they also grounded him for three weeks, with strict instructions to do homework for at least four hours every day so that he would be even better prepared when he returned to school; indeed he might even steal a march on the others in his class. Peter used to sit here, in this same kitchen. He was fourteen years old, pretending to read while in fact he was lost in a dream, far away from the chair he was sitting on, from the kitchen, the house, the garden, the streets and the houses, the school; he left the whole town behind him and he was not alone with such dreams, but this was his dream and hence unique, and he tried to envisage the rest of his life, which of course was not feasible; he could not see beyond the slender hand holding the ballpoint pen; time seemed to have erected a wall in front of him, second by second. From here, though, close on forty years later, Peter could see the whole way back, without a single obstacle, back to the boy bent over his school books pretending to read while sunk in dreams.

Is there a point which stands out from the stream of impressions we are caught in, a stream of offal and gold? Is there an event, an experience, fixed in time and space, shiny and clean, which has made us who we are?

He changed to a new school and made the same wretched mess there, because he had discovered something else, something that drew him in another direction: art galleries. He preferred to go round the town's art galleries, where he could be in peace, where he found peace, that is to say, a different kind of restlessness, and one day he saw a picture by a Belgian artist, de Staël's *The Concert*. He was almost seventeen when he saw it for the first time, one rainy Wednesday in October; he had skipped the last lesson, and later he always said that the colours in this unfinished picture had driven him 'crazy', yes, that was the word he used, crazy; the black piano, the yellowish double bass, the red wall and the white, unpainted squares had sent him crazy. And perhaps this was exactly how it began, when he saw de Staël's unfinished masterpiece, at the travelling European exhibition; perhaps this was the precise point where the line began, the line that would become the rest of his life. At any rate, Peter Wihl crossed the street, to the shop there, and spent all the money he had on a sketch pad, pencils, charcoal sticks, and he kept this to himself, he did not tell anyone; it gave him such a great sense of freedom to keep this to himself, to have this secret; to have divulged it to others might have meant losing this freedom: Peter Wihl did sketches.

He failed two subjects in his school-leaving exams and could not be bothered to do re-takes, as they were known; he preferred to go to sea, he just wanted to get away – to his mother's despair, but with his father's eventual half-hearted consent: if life at sea could knock a bit of discipline into the good-for-nothing, it might be worth the effort. It was a kind of expulsion, he had to be purged, he had to be toughened up and in this way learn discipline and above all fear, first fear and then discipline, in that order, and in the end his father procured him a berth as a galley boy on board the *MS Cuyahoga*, carrying ilmenite to Marina de Carrara. This was freedom, thought Peter, but as soon as they were headed for the North Sea, they hit bad weather – at least that was what it seemed to Peter, he had not realised such weather existed, he could not even hold the frying pan straight, he was seasick, of course, he ate crisp bread and spewed all the way to Gibraltar, apart from a short interval in the English Channel, which in fact only made things worse because during these hours his head cleared enough for him to yearn for home. He had never anticipated that this would happen, that he would be so down, so dispirited that he longed for home, of all places. Then they sailed into the storms again. Peter was eighteen years old and longed for death on board the *MS Cuyahoga*, lying on the deck with nothing to cling to and vomiting blue bile, but no one felt sorry for him, more like the contrary, they were sick of these misplaced, inept maiden-voyage adolescents, sent to sea by affluent parents to be knocked into shape, as if the sea were a bloody institution, no, the sea was a bloody workplace, they should not be given kid-glove treatment, these well turned out good-for-nothings, no, they should be bullied, they should be tormented so they could be signed off as perfect monsters. And thus they dragged him up from the stewards' mess. There was a job to be done, hold the frying pan straight, throw up in the stew and we'll keelhaul you from here to midnight, and tomorrow you'll still be on duty. And Peter staggered to the galley and held the frying pan with both hands and carried the cake dish to the officers' mess every Wednesday and Sunday – he never touched loaf cake again in his life – and he scrubbed toilets and spewed in toilets he had just scrubbed and the fitter gave him a slapping when he knocked the bottle of beer all over his lap, and at long last they passed Gibraltar. It was like walking on to a parquet floor; he stood on the port deck as they sailed into the Mediterranean, and for the first time he felt something akin to happiness, in other words, he was hungry and free. Two days later they docked in Marina de Carrara and unloaded the ore into massive lorries waiting on the quayside, and on the fourth day they had shore leave, and that was when Peter was found out: he was sitting sketching on the mooring bollard, his chest bared, a white handkerchief knotted around his head with the temperature well over thirty degrees. He was sketching the young boys diving off the bridge into the harbour basin, a drop of at least fifteen metres, their supple, brown bodies shining like bronze in the sun as they stretched out, their arms tucked into their sides like narrow wings in perfect flight, seemingly defying all the laws of gravity for a few seconds before they hit the water, without a sound, like golden spears. While Peter was drawing this he sensed someone standing behind him; it was the steward, a tetchy man as a rule, standing and peering with interest over his sunburned shoulders. He even shouted to the others, who emerged from the shadows of the cafe where they had been drinking the thin Italian beer, and Peter hunched his shoulders over the sketch pad and tried to hide the drawings, knowing it was too late anyway: he was found out, unmasked, he had been seen.

Was this that point, one that stands out like black gold in the stream of impressions in which we are forever caught?

At any event, Peter was treated like a king when they sailed on in ballast to Barcelona, where they loaded up with minerals; no one touched a hair on his head, he had risen in status and was beyond criticism as they sat in their regular haunt, the Tequila Bar in Las Ramblas. He knew why. They wanted him to draw them, they had decided Peter would draw them, it was cheaper than photographs, more convenient and, above all, he could draw them as they wanted to appear. And Peter sat in the Tequila Bar in Barcelona and drew them, one after the other, the cook, the steward, the greaser, the stoker, the engineer and the ship's mate, portraits they could send home to their wives, fiancées, girlfriends, parents, sons and daughters. Even the plump saloon girl wanted her portrait done. Couldn't Peter make her a little slimmer? she whispered, just this once – and Peter could, he could turn the saloon girl into a sylph if that was what was desired, and for the first time Peter was of use, and for the first time he drew a sketch of himself, with bared chest and biceps, a bottle in his hand, a smoke in his mouth and a crew cut, signed *Peter W, Tequila Bar, September, 1969.* He put it in an envelope and sent it to his parents without comment, just the drawing, and when he signed off six months later, not as an obedient monster but a young man who finally knew what he wanted to do, he did not go straight home. First of all, he went to see the professor at the Academy and waited outside his office for three hours until he was admitted and allowed to show his sketches. Afterwards Peter was at a loss to comprehend where he had got his boldness, his audacity, from; it must have been something to do with having nothing to lose, but everything to gain. Modesty, false or genuine, comes with age, when success makes you suspicious and you have everything to lose because the more you can do, the more frightened you are. Peter sat in the spacious office watching the professor flick through the sketch pads in what seemed a bored, sleepy way. Then he focused his gaze on the determined, almost irritatingly self-assured young man, gave him a fixed stare, took off his glasses, which were hanging askew from a string around his scraggy neck, and said that Peter Wihl could start on the painting course in the New Year.

Paint a plain surface with madder.

Father tried to persuade son that he needed something to fall back on, a civil title, a proper qualification as he called it, everyone had to have something to fall back on, especially those who, with their eyes open, choose choppy waters. That was how Peter's father expressed it. But Peter did not want anything to fall back on, it would make him lazy, prevent him from giving his all, it would make him an amateur, a wimp, if he fell he should plummet, if he fell it should be with a bang, and that was how it was to be. He rented a bedsit in the city centre and for five years Peter attended the Academy, seldom speaking to his parents, apart from on a few Sundays and at some formal functions he was unable to avoid. Paint a plain surface with madder; don't think, see. He saw and he did not think while the other students, by and large, thought but failed to see. The year he finished his studies, he had a picture accepted for the 1976 autumn exhibition, an oil painting modestly entitled *Exercise 1.20 × 65*, depicting an empty stage, surfaces pieced together to make a room, with no other light than the colours' own suffusion. It was bought by the Riksmuseum and he won the Debutant's Prize. Peter was twenty-four and already the future. He met Benjamin Rav, the somewhat eccentric gallery owner who was always searching for new young talent for his stable; Peter was young, he was new, he was all that an impatient modern age could wish for, he was, as already mentioned, the future. Ben took care of Peter's every need, and the following spring he opened his first exhibition entitled *Amputations* in The New Gallery. Three hours before the private viewing there was a ring at the door of his bedsit. Peter thought it was Ben coming to pick him up; it was not him, it was a priest, accompanied by two policemen: his parents had died in a car accident that morning, the car had left the road, very close to where they lived, landed on its roof, incomprehensible, no oncoming traffic, dry road surface, inexplicable. The priest used the expression several times – it reminded Peter of his father's favourite word *proper* – and in this way the priest did not have to struggle to explain the accident as part of a greater religious design, he was able to dismiss it as what it was, an accident but, unfortunately, it was necessary to go down to the hospital to identify his parents. Peter checked his watch and knew they would not make the exhibition now, which was a triumph, in all ways: there were red tickets hanging under every single painting before the doors closed, those discreet, yet ever such clear, markers that the artist both despises and longs to see, which whisper, no, cry out: *Sorry, this picture is reserved*; *This picture is taken.* There was a buzz of jubilation in The New Gallery that night, champagne, cameras flashing, the history of art, all the radical capital – which is also expected to give a yield: lustre, good rates of interest, enhanced reputations – gathered inside those walls covered with severed body parts; a colouristic slaughterhouse signed Peter Wihl, who said nothing about the accident. It was not until after the viewing, at midnight, while the others were driving back to town, that he took a taxi to the hospital to identify his parents in the mortuary; it was them, they lay there beside each other, each on their own steel bed, covered by a white sheet, they looked real, yes, real, but if you paid closer attention you could see that all their humanity had departed, they were disconnected and did not cohere. Peter thought a clear yet impossible thought as he stood there in the chilly mortuary, under the bright light, next to his parents: Art does not imitate life, it is the other way round; life, and death in particular, imitate art. On the way out, he was handed their personal effects, everything they had on them when they died, apart from their clothes and shoes, placed in a transparent plastic sleeve: watches, wedding rings, his mother's jewellery, his father's wallet, tiepin, a comb and keys. Peter took a taxi home, not to the bedsit but to his childhood home; morning was already beginning to break, the sun rose over the blue ridges in the east and filled the hollow this town lay in with a shimmering mist. He picked up the newspaper on the doormat, let himself in, stood motionless in the sudden silence for a few moments, out of habit he almost called their names, caught himself, sat down at the kitchen table, spread the objects out over the tablecloth: the wedding rings; one small, one big; the old tiepin with the car badge; his mother's plain, austere jewellery; his father's worn wallet. Peter opened it and in the plastic pocket was the drawing he had sent them, the self-portrait in Tequila Bar. His father had been carrying this, so, when it came down to it, he had been quite proud of his son. In the empty house, Peter began to cry; he coaxed out the drawing and slowly ripped it into pieces while reading the excellent review in the paper, the *brilliant debutant.* Now, twenty-five years later, in the same house, he thought of the line he carried with him, the thin line he had once started covertly, in total secrecy. Was this where it ended?

He sprang to his feet, put on his coat, left the house, it was late November, he headed towards the town, in the thick driving snow, not without an aim, for no one walks without an aim, just at random; in the end everyone has somewhere to go, and he stopped outside The New Gallery.

Paint a plain surface with madder.

You can keep going for the rest of your life and never finish.

Peter went in.

All the spotlights in the ceiling were on, the harsh light and the bare walls blinded him, the office door at the back of the room was open, he could not see anyone. In the corner between the windows, which were covered with silver paper, was a pile of bin bags: blue, white, black plastic bags, a whole heap protruding from a bucket and flowing across the floor, where a video camera was positioned on a stand. In the other corner sat Patrick, almost unrecognisable; he was wearing a sharp, dark suit, a purple shirt, tie, polished shoes and sunglasses; the face seemed leaner, perhaps as a result of the make-up. He did not move from the floor.

Nothing of what Peter saw made sense. He did not understand the bin bags, Patrick's new clothes or the silver paper in the windows. Now, whatever he said would be taken amiss, so he might as well be awkward.

'Where's Ben?' he asked.

'At his hairdresser's. Should I pass on a message?'

'Is Ben thinking of changing his hairstyle again?'

'Isn't that what one does at the hairdresser's?'

'Not necessarily.'

'What do you do at the hairdresser's? Stick to the same old style?'

Peter was weary.

'We talk about the golden section at my hairdresser's.'

'Do you really?'

'I see you're clearing up the rubbish. Or are you dreaming installations?'

'Why are you so angry, Peter?'

Patrick sat in the corner, looking up at him with a smile.

Peter took a step forward.

'I'm not bloody angry. Why should I be angry?'

Patrick shrugged.

'I'm not clearing up. I'm just setting up the new exhibition.'

For a few moments Peter stood without speaking in the steep cones of light, the snow was melting and running off his coat, his shoes were wet, discoloured, they must have shrunk, they were tight over his instep and against his heel, one sock had moved forward and collected around his toes, and he had this feeling, no, not feeling, it was not vague, he experienced it as a distinct, oppressive uneasiness, standing on the outside, being the last to be told what everyone else already knew.

'Has Ben promoted you to the post of *curator* as well?'

'Relax, Peter. The exhibition will be over long before it's your turn. Did you say "as well"?'

'He said you had many talents.'

Patrick spread out his arms.

'That's true. What do you think?'

Peter could not be bothered to turn around. He had seen it: the bin bags, the video camera and the blacked-out windows. He did not need to see it again.

'I'm amazed,' he said.

'That's good, Peter.'

'I'm amazed that Ben should allow this muck into his gallery.'

Patrick just smiled.

'You were new once, too, weren't you?'

'New? Are you saying that is a quality in itself?'

'Isn't it?'

'If so, it's a bad quality.'

'Why's that?'

'Because its day is soon over.'

'Yes, I can see that. I can see it right in front of me.'

'I beg your pardon.'

'They still call you The Butcher, Peter. But they say the knife's getting blunt.'

Peter was aware he ought not to say any more, ought to go, leave it at that, but his feet were leaden, he just stood there, in those floodlit, almost hermetic, rooms.

'The rubbish doesn't stink, I'm afraid,' he said.

'Sorry?'

'The rubbish doesn't stink. It's supposed to stink.'

Patrick pointed at him, still smiling.

'Isn't this where you drag up life as an old salt and the hardships of the sea? How you must have had grime under your nails and puke in your hair to produce the genuine article?'

'And you? Where have you gained your experience? In the sauna at the Grand Hotel?'

'No, at the Academy of Art in London.'

Peter was caught on the hop for a moment, he almost

stumbled and there was nothing to grab; he could hear the clear crackle of silver paper, the hum, or the buzz, coming from the video camera.

He said:

'Oh yes, that's where they don't use paintbrushes, just rulers.'

Patrick did not take his eyes off him. His voice was calm, almost friendly. It was perhaps his most irritating feature, this indulgent self-assurance.

'Your pictures are on committee-room walls,' he said.

'So?'

'In foyers. In ministers' offices. Was that your ambition, Peter?'

'I paint. That's all.'

Patrick yawned.

'Knick-knacks for the bourgeoisie. You've become conventional.'

'And who is this shit supposed to provoke?'

'You.'

Laughing, Peter bowed.

'Thank you. Might I ask who the privileged artist is?'

Patrick looked up.

'Me,' he said.

Peter paused, but only for a few seconds, then took another step forward and bent over the boy who was dressed to the nines.

'So that's why you've been sucking Ben off for two months?'

Patrick got to his feet, taking his time, with reluctance, as if the whole business bored him out of his skull, and at length stood face to face with Peter.

'Is this where I am supposed to knock you down?'

'Do you ask before you strike?'

Patrick raised his hand, clenched his fist, Peter closed his eyes, waited for the punch, yes, he even longed for the blow, which would prove he was right about everything, which would justify all his unreasonableness, and they stood there, in the empty gallery, between the bin bags and the video camera, where he had once opened his first exhibition. Peter waited, time passed, but unfortunately Patrick did not strike him. The wonderful, liberating pain failed to materialise. Peter waited in vain and in the end he opened his eyes again.

Patrick's hands were supporting his back.

'Of course, I hope you will be able to attend the opening.'

'When is it?'

'Friday.'

'Friday's fine. What's the name of the exhibition?'

'*Business and Pleasure.*'

'Brilliant.'

'Yes, isn't it? I'm already looking forward to it.'

Patrick was about to go. Peter smiled and held him back.

'But there's one thing you don't mess with. Is that clear?'

Patrick tilted his head.

'What's that if I might ask?'

'Ben.'

And in he walked; Ben. He had had all his hair shaved off; his skull shone like a tight helmet in the steep light. Of course, he smelled discord the second he saw them and put his arm around Peter.

'May I invite you gentlemen to lunch?'

Peter wrenched himself free.

'You certainly may. Then perhaps we can chat a bit about what Patrick Himself intends to write in my catalogue. He seems motivated.'

Ben swung round to him.

'Yes, that was what I wanted to talk to you about as well.'

'Sorry, Ben. I'm going to the pool.'

'The pool, now? And spoil the pretty make-up?'

Patrick kissed him on the cheek.

'The new haircut suits you.'

He fetched a bag from the office, hitched the strap over his shoulder and walked towards the door, then stopped.

'By the way, there was something I learned in London, Peter.'

'Let's hear it. I doubt it will take long.'

Patrick smiled.

'Don't delve too deep. It won't get you anywhere.'

Then he was gone.

Peter and Ben stood in silence. And when the silence had lasted long enough for it to become embarrassing, Peter said:

'That's not a haircut, Ben.'

'No, it's a metamorphosis.'

'Wrong. It's panic. And panic does not become you. Bye.'

Ben followed Peter and dragged him into the restaurant across the street, and they sat down at their regular table, the window table, where the last interview with Peter Wihl would take place, in four months' time. The old waiter bowed and placed the menu on the cloth; Peter swept it off, knocking over a glass.

'For God's sake, don't turn this into a drama,' Ben whispered.

'I'm not hungry.'

'You should eat something anyway. You're wan.'

Peter leaned across to Ben.

'Why didn't you tell me that stripling was going to exhibit his bloody Lego bricks in your gallery?'

'Because you have other things on your mind, Peter.'

'Ah, yes, of course, out of consideration for me?'

'I don't have to consider anyone.'

'Just Patrick, you mean?'

Ben was breathing heavily.

'Haven't I always taken good care of you? Haven't I?'

Peter slumped back in his seat.

The waiter came back with a jug of water and filled their glasses.

They drank. The snow was falling against the window and sticking. It would soon be impossible to see out.

Ben took his hand.

'I apologise. I suppose it's a little too much for both of us right now.'

'I would prefer not to be the person who is told last.'

'Goes without saying. But didn't the doctor say you should take it easy?'

'Do you talk to my doctor, too?'

Ben squeezed his fingers and repeated:

'Have I not always taken good care of you?'

'Yes, you have, Ben.'

'Even when no one else would take care of you, I was there to take care of you, wasn't I?'

'Yes, you were, Ben.'

'Even when you had nothing else to paint except the walls of the theatre, I didn't lose faith in you.'

'I painted the ceiling.'

'What else can you say, other than Benjamin has taken good care of you all these years?'

Peter, impatient, pulled his arm away.

'So this Patrick is going to put me on the scrapheap now.'

Ben looked straight at him.

'It is you who have to outdo all of them, Peter. With one single brushstroke! Now go home and make love to Helene, sing to Kaia and clean your brushes. That's an order!'

Peter stood up.

'I simply do not understand why you had your hair shaved off for that boy.'

Ben stroked his shiny pate and smiled.

'Good for swimming,' he said.

Peter took a taxi home. The clouds hung so low it took them minutes to break through the mist and everything looked beautiful and abandoned: the white roads, the virgin snow in the gardens, the forest beyond the town. The sun drew a pale arc across the sky. At last he unlocked his studio, changed into his work clothes and hooked the palette on to his hand: cadmium orange, madder red and ivory black, cobalt blue; these waves of light that do not exist, that do not take up space, that one can walk through, and yet are all he has, are everything he ever creates. I do not exist, he thought. I have to re-invent myself every time. But the uneasiness was still there, it would not let go, the uneasiness which affects his thoughts first, the thought of uneasiness, and soon becomes visible to the naked eye, concrete and close, at one arm's length, in the hand that quivers in the dark at the base of the picture.

9

And yet this day was to get worse.

Kaia was sitting on the floor in the living room, playing with the model she had been allowed to take home from the theatre. She flipped the door to the side and closed it again, moved the figures representing people around as she talked to herself non-stop: a long-winded, fluent dialogue, or monologue, about who they were and what they were called. She gave them unusual names, she laughed when she made someone enter through the gap in the ceiling instead of through the door, as well-bred people do, but she soon told them off so that there would be no repetition, no visits through the ceiling instead of the door. Only Father Christmas was allowed to do that, if he was unable to find a chimney to climb down, and Kaia laughed again.

Peter stood by the window.

He listened to his daughter's voice and laughter. Her performance was play and reason; he would have liked to be moved around from room to room by those hands.

Helene was lying on the sofa reading her manuscript.

'Old Ekdal is being difficult,' she said.

Peter was standing with his back to her.

'Actors *are* difficult. That's why they are what they are: actors.'

'This time it's serious. He refuses to perform unless he can smoke on stage.'

'So?'

'Smoking is prohibited everywhere in the theatre, Peter. Including the stage.'

'And Old Ekdal still wants to smoke?'

'Old Ekdal has never smoked. It's the principle. There were no anti-smoking laws in Ibsen's time. Ergo, he thinks applying the regulations of our time to Ibsen's universe breaks the illusion.'

'I think I'm beginning to like Old Ekdal,' Peter said.

'Werle, fru Sørby, Relling and Molvik don't. They're refusing to go on stage if Old Ekdal smokes.'

That made Peter laugh.

'Can't he just *pretend* to smoke? He's an actor, isn't he?'

Helene read aloud from the manuscript:

'"Old Ekdal, in a housecoat with a lit pipe in his mouth, emerges from his room."'

'That does it then.'

'Wait for the best bit. If Old Ekdal is not given permission to smoke on stage, he is demanding that the pistol be removed from the play. Keeping loaded weapons in the home is illegal, you see.'

'I'm looking forward to the premiere,' Peter said.

'How are you doing?'

Peter noticed that everything had gone quiet and at first he could not understand where the silence had come from, whether it was just inside him or whether Helene could hear it too. He was afraid and leaned against the window frame. Then he knew. Kaia was not chattering to herself any more. She was talking to him.

'You'll have to paint them for me, Daddy.'

Peter turned towards her. She had an obstinate, even angry, expression on her face, standing there with clenched fists.

'Who?'

'The people who live here, of course!'

Kaia unclenched her hands and dropped the figures on to the floor, sending them everywhere.

Then it was as quiet as before.

'Of course I'll paint them,' Peter said.

And Kaia knelt down and began to gather all the figures together.

Helene went over to him.

'You didn't tell me,' she whispered.

'Tell you what?'

'How you are doing.'

'Fine.'

'Absolutely sure?'

'Yes, absolutely fine. Absolutely sure.'

Helene took his hand.

'I don't think I quite believe you.'

Peter felt a sudden fury, a stab of impatience, which tensed up his face. He put on a smile and asked in the most composed manner possible:

'Have you been talking to Ben?'

Kaia sat on the floor tidying up the figures.

Helene leaned closer to Peter.

'I'm talking to you, for Christ's sake. Who are you talking to?'

Then a car pulled up by the gate and a man stepped out. He left the engine running, lit a cigarette and looked up at the house.

Peter took Helene by the hand as he moved from the window.

'Shit. He's already seen us.'

'Who is it?'

'Thomas Hammer. He wants me to go to the class party. Shit.'

A moment later the doorbell rang.

Helene held Peter back.

'You're not going anywhere. I'm quite happy to tell that insufferable man that you don't feel well.'

'I feel fine,' Peter said.

'Then I'll say you don't feel like going.'

There was another ring.

Kaia stood up.

'Why don't you open the door?' she asked.

Peter turned away and whispered to Helene, as if frightened that Thomas or Kaia would hear:

'If I don't go with him now, I'll never get rid of him.'

And with that Peter went out to open the door.

Thomas Hammer was dressed in a dinner suit. He peered inside inquisitively. The face seemed bloated, from the cold, from alcohol, perhaps both.

'Are you ready, Peter?'

'No.'

'Are you looking forward to it?'

'No.'

Thomas Hammer laughed and tossed his cigarette in the snow.

'The boys are waiting. Are you coming? Or do I have to force you? The choice is yours.'

Peter pointed to his dinner jacket.

'Perhaps I ought to change first?'

'Come as you are, Peter. You're an artist, aren't you?'

Peter was even less partial to Thomas Hammer now. He slung his coat over his shoulders and followed him to the car, then hesitated for a moment, turning to look at the window, and saw Helene and Kaia standing between the curtains. Kaia waved, he raised his arm too and waved back.

Thomas Hammer stopped and waited for him.

'Was I disrupting the family idyll?'

'Don't give it a thought.'

Instead he pointed to the studio.

'Is that the cabin up there where you paint?'

'Yes. That's my cabin.'

The lights from the car – two parallel beams which nevertheless converged and formed an immovable yellow surface, right in front of the glass doors – made one of the canvasses quiver as if hit by a stone, releasing the colours in slow, white waves.

The two men stood looking.

'It's a gift,' Thomas Hammer said in a low voice.

Peter shivered.

'What is?'

'Being able to create.'

'A gift from whom?'

'God. The devil. Ourselves. It doesn't make any difference from whom. Just take good care of it. The gift.'

They drove towards town.

Peter saw his face in the wing mirror; distorted, unrecognisable, it could have been anyone sitting in the passenger seat, but it was him, and the gate and house vanished from view behind them.

Thomas lit another cigarette.

Peter closed his eyes and the sole mitigating circumstance he could come up with was that this evening would also have to come to an end.

'Could you tell me where we're going?'

'Wait and see.'

Thomas parked by the old school they had once attended. Peter followed him out. When the windows were unlit, they made the building look like an abandoned palace. They hurried in. Nothing had changed. The long corridors, the coat pegs, a forgotten jacket, the echo of their footsteps dying away in all directions, the plaster still flaking off the faded walls, everything was as of old, except that they were different and they were trying to converge on a time almost forty years before. Peter's fingers burned and he felt a sudden nausea, perspiration ran, stinging his skin, he had to support himself on Thomas for a moment. Thomas motioned towards the large, empty hall, the stage, the stage curtain and the chairs that had been tidied away and stood stacked against the walls. One of Peter's pictures hung there, an arm, and some pupils, perhaps even a teacher, must have been fiddling around with it and had tried to draw a hand on the severed arm. To Peter it didn't matter, he didn't give a damn, he was finished with the picture and others were welcome to make further additions. Thomas laughed.

'You're represented here, too, Peter! In the school museum.'

They went up the broad staircase – the edges of every step had been worn down in the course of the school breaks, which put together had lasted several lives – and Thomas stopped outside room 7c on the second floor, opened the door and pushed Peter in.

Four men, also dressed in dinner suits, were sitting in the classroom, each by their desk. They stood up straight away. At first, Peter did not recognise them. Soon, however, the young faces shone through, between the wrinkles, folds of skin, liver spots, blood vessels and the fat; young boys disguised in decrepit, overdressed, middle-aged bodies. He recognised them, but did not remember them; they had nothing to do with him any more.

Peter stood by the door.

Thomas took up a position behind the teacher's desk and pulled out the heavy, green register from the drawer. He began the roll call. There were many absences. Only Anders Nilsen, Ivar Hovden, Gunnar Gulden and Preben Sundt put up their hands and sat down, one after the other, behind the desks which long ago had been too big for them, but the desk lids still bore their carved names.

Thomas surveyed them.

'Have any of us gone bankrupt, gone out of our minds, gone from wife and children or gone to the dogs since we last met?'

The skeleton class shouted in unison:

'Like hell we have!'

'Excellent. Our ranks are being thinned mercilessly, boys. We are, if my calculations are correct, two down on last year; however, one disobedient pupil has at last returned after playing truant for all these years. Peter Wihl.'

Thomas shut the register.

'Shall we give him a severe punishment or welcome him back?'

Ivar Hovden put up his hand again.

'Both.'

'Brilliant, Ivar.'

Thomas pointed to Peter.

'You can sit down for the time being.'

And Peter sat down, in his old seat at the back, in the window row. It seemed the right thing to do.

Thomas wrote their timetable on the board in large letters: Hygiene, History and Gymnastics. Then he addressed the class again.

'Before we go any further with today's classes, I would like to announce that our aged P.E. teacher, Mr Holm, has passed away since our last meeting. The funeral was held in the holidays. In other words, there was a very poor turnout. Let us observe twenty seconds' laughter in memory of the old sack of shit.'

Anders, Ivar, Gunnar, Preben and Thomas laughed for twenty seconds.

Then it was quiet.

Thomas raised his hands.

'I also regret to say that Stian Borg who was with us last year, as optimistic and devil-may-care as usual, is down for the count again. And this time I doubt whether he'll be getting up. At present he is residing in three square metres of Thailand. I suggest we make a small financial contribution to his wife so that she can at least buy Christmas presents for the children.'

Thomas put a pile of notes on the register. The others followed suit and then faced Peter. He found some money in his coat, approached the teacher's desk and put it down.

They all shook hands.

'Good to see you again,' said Anders.

Ivar, Gunnar and Preben said the same. It was good to see him again.

'Hadn't reckoned on you of all people becoming famous,' Gunnar said.

'You were always so bloody distant, you were, Peter.'

It was Ivar or Preben who said that.

Then there was a knock at the door.

They rushed back to their desks.

Thomas shouted:

'Come in!'

It was the district nurse. The boys stood to attention. She was wearing a tight, white uniform, open almost down to her navel, so that her pendulous breasts struggled to stay in place, her hair was dyed blonde, her full lips daubed in red. She looked like someone. Who did she look like? An old Italian porn star. And she was pushing a trolley loaded with five Christmas plates, beer, spirits, cigars and syringes. She started with Thomas, did her round and finished at Peter's desk.

'Open your mouth now,' said the sister.

'No, thank you.'

She leaned closer.

'Are you a naughty boy?'

'Yes.'

'Perhaps you'll have to stay in after school?'

'Perhaps.'

'Perhaps I'll have to stick this nasty syringe in places which can be very painful? What do you say to that, you naughty boy?'

The others clapped in time, stamped in rhythm, the floor bounced.

Now Peter could see that her eyes were colourless, distant, sfumato, misty. She was wreathed in a haze, the lines disappeared, the features dissolved, the skin developed cracks and the crudely daubed lips slid over her teeth into a red smile. He whispered:

'Thank you. I'm healthy enough as I am.'

'That's up to me to decide, my boy.'

She laughed and sprayed a pungent green liquid into his face – absinthe, it smelled of absinthe – and Peter pushed her away.

Thomas came to his rescue, gave him a serviette and accompanied the nurse to the door, whence she vanished.

Then the bell rang for the lesson to start, or finish.

The class party could begin.

Peter opened the window a little. The cold hit him like a blow. The sky was black and clear. The yellow moon hung over the town's low shadows and shining circles of ice. He took a handful of snow from the sill. The snow melted in his mouth. He drank the snow.

The sound of cutlery on plates converged into a spike of noise, a burning needle.

Thomas tapped on his glass and stood up.

'I propose a toast with the right hand for all those who cannot be here, whether dead, missing, travelling on business or in prison, and one with the left for us.'

They raised both hands and their glasses.

Thomas looked at Peter.

'Shall I order you a bottle of snow? Red or white?'

Laughter.

Peter just shook his head.

The others toasted and drank.

Thomas stood and opened the register again.

'Since Peter Wihl has been away longest, let's test him first on history. Could you go up to the board, please?'

Peter, reluctantly and slowly, got to his feet and went to the board.

Thomas smiled as he watched the class, the four survivors, draining glasses, bottles, leaning over desks, already drunk, drunk with expectation.

'I haven't done my homework,' Peter said.

Thomas faced him and sighed.

'We don't give a shit what the papers say about you. Life at sea, success, fame, your parents' accident, God bless them, by the way. Tell us all the things we don't know, Peter.'

'Is that the punishment?'

More laughter from the class.

Thomas went closer.

'The punishment? Oh, no, my boy. The punishment and the reward are one and the same. You'll see.'

Peter wanted to leave. He had already made a move to go. Thomas restrained him.

'Would you mind unhanding me?'

The class went quiet. Thomas started to laugh and released him.

'Tell us how you met your wife, Peter. That's the usual test. Our ladies.'

Peter leaned against the board, weary. That was what he thought: I'm just weary.

He began to talk.

'I met her at the theatre. I was painting the theatre. Ten years ago. *The Journey to the Christmas Star.* She was the scenographer. I painted the sky.'

Thomas moistened the sponge.

'Without putting too fine a point on it, could one call that a low point in your artistic career and a high point in your love life? Nadir and zenith at the same time?'

Peter nodded.

Thomas put the sponge on the ledge under the board.

'That's what I told you. Punishment and reward tend to be one and the same thing. And so at a mellow age you fathered a daughter?'

The gleaming moonlight along the window row faded and cast shadows across the floor.

Peter smiled.

'Yes. Kaia. She's six.'

Thomas dried his hands on the serviette.

'And when she's eighteen you'll be well past sixty.'

Peter breathed in.

'How old are your children, Thomas?'

Thomas turned to the class.

'Any questions?'

Ivar put up his hand.

'Why have you always been so bloody distant, Peter?'

Peter was still leaning against the board. The smells of chalk, Christmas food, tobacco and absinthe blended into a vile perfume which almost stupefied him.

'Distant?'

'Yes. You were always inside yourself.'

'Was I? Inside myself?'

Now Anders spoke up:

'Yes, damn it! Bloody distant.'

Peter felt his fury rise – for a few moments it was stronger than his exhaustion – against these old classmates, no, not mates, more like fellow passengers on the voyage of childhood, next to whom he happened to have been forced to sit for as long as it lasted.

He said, 'Perhaps in fact it was me who was near.'

Silence.

Preben put up his hand.

'Near what, if I might ask?'

Peter pointed to him.

'Perhaps it was you who were distant?'

'Us?'

'Yes, you were bloody distant and I was near! Anyone thought about that?'

Ivar shouted:

'Do you mean the whole class was wrong and you were right?'

'Yes, I bloody do,' Peter said.

Preben repeated his question:

'What was it you were so bloody near, Peter?'

He wanted to answer, he had the word on the tip of his tongue, but it escaped him, the word escaped, every time he wanted to say it this word escaped. Instead someone knocked at the door and Ivar interrupted Preben.

'Do you remember the time you got a hard-on when you were being tested on the chronology of Norwegian kings?'

Preben laughed.

'That's not true.'

Ivar laughed even louder.

'Yes, it is. You did. A real boner! The whole class saw it.'

Anders interrupted Ivar.

'What were you near then, Peter?'

Preben interrupted Anders.

'What were you thinking about then, Peter?'

And Peter thought: he had been thinking about Helene whom he had not met yet and was not to meet for many years, under the firmament of the theatre. That was what he had been thinking at that time, standing by the board and being tested on Norwegian kings. It was her, Helene, he had been drawing nearer to; Helene and Kaia. He did not say that, it was impossible to say, of course, it was barely possible to think.

Thomas opened the door.

This time it was the cleaner, wearing a headscarf, a long grey coat, heavy shoes and yellow gloves, and she set to with a will, cleared away the plates, the cutlery, the empty bottles, emptied the ashtrays in a bucket, took the sponge and cleaned the board until it shone, gleamed like water, and then she turned to Peter, tilted her head, smiled, stuck out her tongue and licked her freshly daubed lips, two glistening red snails. It was the same tart, the district nurse, just in a different costume, and she ran the sponge across his face, slowly, his neck, the green stains on his shirt, the belt buckle, opened the buttons, one after the other, wormed her yellow fingers inside and at that moment everything went black. Peter slid down the board and the silence of the darkness enveloped him, where no waves penetrated, and when he came to he was sitting beside Thomas Hammer in the car, parked by the gate outside his house, and Peter thought, that was the third time, it had happened again, it was the third time it had happened.

Thomas shone a torch on him.

'Thank goodness, Peter. You went out like a light back there.'

'How did I get here?'

'Have you been taking anything?'

'Taking anything?'

'Pills. Drugs. Chemicals. Almost thought I was going to lose you.'

Peter shook his head and felt the steady, ponderous beat of his heart, and every beat sent a taste of hot blood into his mouth. Thomas had seen him when he was in the dark; it was an intolerable thought.

'How did I get here?' Peter repeated.

Thomas switched off the little torch and put it in the glove compartment.

'I brought you home, of course.'

'Thank you.'

'Shall I come in with you?'

Peter leaned back in his seat.

'Do you know what I dreamed about you?'

'Tell me. I'm waiting.'

'You came over to me in the big break and you asked: *Would you rather be blind or deaf?*'

'What did you answer, Peter? In the dream?'

'I didn't get that far. I woke up.'

Thomas smiled and put a hand on his shoulder.

'But I remember what you answered. In reality. You answered *deaf.*'

Peter moved Thomas's hand away.

'It wasn't a question. It was a threat.'

'Aren't most choices? Very few people have the privilege of choosing between two good things.'

The light was still on in the house while the studio lay shrouded in darkness.

Peter opened the door.

'Thank you for bringing me home.'

Thomas Hammer repeated:

'Shall I come in with you?'

Peter faced him and said:

'I never want to see you again.'

Thomas merely shrugged his shoulders.

'They all say that,' he said.

Peter got out of the car and remained on the pavement until it had rounded the bend on the slope down into town. Then he sat down on the bench in the garden to rest, to collect himself before going in, but instead an idea occurred to him, an idea he was completely unprepared for, as if someone else had conceived it. He wondered about the darkness he could not escape, if it was the same darkness that had stricken his father and blinded him, causing him to lose control of the car, drive off the road, on a straight stretch with good visibility, that time, one quiet spring evening in May 1977, taking Peter's mother with him to a violent death in the wreckage, in the ditch where they were not found until several hours later, and if that were so, he had inherited this darkness, a multiple darkness. This was what went through Peter's mind on the bench, in the garden, in the cold, beneath the radiant black sky, and he sank to his knees and spewed up over the white snow.

On getting up he saw Ben through the window. He was sitting by the kitchen window, resting his head on his hands.

Helene stood beside him stroking his bald head, back and forth. Peter was unable to make sense of this image. He saw it, and all the elements, every single detail; the image was recognisable: the illuminated window, the kitchen, Ben, Helene. In this context, however, everything he was familiar with became incomprehensible. He did not understand. Had they been talking about him? Why was she consoling Ben?

Peter walked down to the house, let himself in and stood in the doorway between the living room and kitchen.

'What's happened?' he asked.

Ben sat there, with his face in his hands.

Helene turned to him.

'Patrick's dead.'

Peter hung his coat on a chair.

'Dead?'

'He drowned in the pool at the Grand Hotel.'

'Is that really possible?'

Helene, surprised, sent him a quick glance.

'He must have hit his head on the bottom when he dived in. He was alone.'

Ben was weeping, a jerky sobbing, and it struck Peter that he had never heard this man cry before.

'At any rate he's got out of writing my catalogue now,' Peter said.

Helene, furious, disappointed, or both, went closer, raised a hand. For a moment he thought she was going to hit him.

'That, Peter, is the meanest thing I've ever heard! What the hell is up with you!'

Ben lowered his hands.

'Now that was the real you.'

His face was ravaged, he had aged more than his years in the course of this evening, he had caught up with his real age, overtaken it and if he turned around now, for an instant, he would see he was leaving himself behind, faster and faster, transported by grief.

Peter looked down.

'Forgive me,' he whispered.

'You're forgiven.'

Peter rested his hand on his shoulder and they stood like that, without speaking, all three of them, and then Kaia appeared in the doorway, or perhaps she had been there the whole time, watching them, the yellow pyjamas, the thin bare feet, hair messy and black, a child clothed in sleep and yet alert, and he was only one part of what she saw, thought Peter. It would be impossible for her to piece together and interpret this fractured, crumbling composition in the kitchen at midnight.

'Is Uncle Ben sad?' she asked.

Helene turned.

'Yes, darling. Uncle Ben is sad this evening.'

Kaia went over to him.

'Is that why you aren't speaking so loud?'

Ben tried to smile.

'Yes, my sweet. It's not easy to be loud when you're sad. But I must have woken you up all the same.'

'Why are you sad, Uncle Ben?'

Ben paused for a second.

'Because I've lost someone I loved.'

Yes, thought Peter, he had lost youth.

Kaia looked up at Ben and something happened to her face; something crashed, in her expression, in her eyes.

She whispered:

'You've lost your hair, too.'

Ben laughed.

And Kaia immediately burst into tears, silent deep tears and Peter was shaken, but before he could do anything – bend down, comfort and protect her – Helene had already lifted her daughter and carried her back into their bedroom.

Ben said, in a low voice:

'Sorry.'

Peter lit the fire and stood in the heat from the soaring flames.

They could hear Kaia crying, out loud now, it came from another place in her, not where the tears of defiance, grazes to the hand or fear of the dark originated, but somewhere else which had hitherto been untouched, unmoved. Helene hummed and sang to her to dull the pain.

And Peter thought about the black dog in the park.

Then it was quiet, except for the sound of dry wood sinking in the fire.

Peter sat down. Put his hands on the table.

'That's terrible,' he said.

'Yes, it's terrible.'

'How did you find out?'

'His brother rang me.'

'Why aren't you with them now?'

'With whom, Peter?'

'His family.'

Ben looked straight at him. For an instant the flames caught the ring in his ear with a blue glint.

'Because they said it would be inappropriate.'

Ben looked down. Peter gently laid a hand on his.

'You can stay with us tonight.'

'Thank you. I'm fine. Don't worry about me.'

Peter leaned across to him.

'You're not fine. And I may be thinking of myself as much as of you.'

Ben sat up.

'What do you mean?'

'It happened again. My eyesight failed.'

'My God. How did it happen?'

'I faded out. I fade out, Ben.'

They sat in silence. The bedroom had gone quiet. The whole house was still, soundless.

Peter went to the bathroom and prepared for bed. In the mirror, under the bright ceiling light, his face faded layer by layer in the optical shadows until his features dissolved into a grey mass which contracted into one single point: the eye.

Kaia was already asleep in his bed.

Helene spread the duvet over her.

She turned to Peter.

'Did something happen this evening?'

He gave a quick laugh.

'Something happen? Loads of bloody things happened this evening, I believe.'

She did not let him finish.

'I mean, to you, Peter.'

He looked at Kaia – half of her face in profile on the pillow, her arms outstretched as if she were trying to keep her balance in her sleep – and whispered:

'Nothing.'

Helene hesitated before asking:

'Did you get rid of him, by the way?'

And Peter was riven by doubt, a deep shameful doubt. Did she mean Ben or Thomas Hammer?

'Whom?'

'Whom? Don't be stupid. That pest, your friend.'

'Yes,' Peter said.

10

They both sat on a chair, in the dark, in the studio, and tonight neither chair was comfortable.

The canvasses surrounded them, twelve surfaces, leaned against the wall.

The moon drifted behind a cloud, the sky died, the snow in the garden resembled ashes.

Ben poured wine into his glass.

'Since we both have our own preoccupations, it might be best if we say nothing at all,' Ben said.

'That sounds sensible,' Peter said.

Ben sipped.

'Or we could talk about something else?'

'Such as?'

Ben looked around him in the dark.

'The pictures.'

'You can have something to get you off to sleep, if you want. I have a few pills I keep for emergencies.'

'Thanks, Peter. But I would prefer to be centred right now.'

'Centred?'

'Inside myself. I want to know how I am taking it. I want to feel this pain.'

'Do you remember what you said when you brought Patrick here? It was happiness that was dramatic?'

Ben looked down, his shoulders aquiver.

'Yes, happiness is dramatic. Unhappiness is static.'

'It's time spent waiting that is static, Ben.'

Ben looked straight at him. They were two shadows between twelve canvasses in the dark.

'Do you know what I thought at first when that brother rang and said that Patrick was dead?'

'You're going to talk about it anyway.'

Ben smiled; at least it resembled a smile.

'You don't want to talk about your pictures.'

'What did you think?'

'I thought that I had lost my youth. Once and for all. Isn't that pathetic and selfish? Isn't it an outrageous thought to think when you find out your lover is dead?'

'But there's nothing wrong with thinking like that, Ben. For such moments there are no laws.'

Ben took a breath; a dribble of wine ran down from a corner of his mouth.

'From that second on I was an old man, Peter. My jewellery fell off. My clothes no longer fitted. This damned haircut of mine was no longer modern, but the symbol of a dying man. Am I not loathsome?'

'You'll get over it,' Peter said.

'Not this time,' Ben said.

They sat in silence. Ben drank wine. Peter glanced at the clock above the door, the glass was smashed, it had stopped and had been like that for a long time, ten years, he had done it himself, stopped the clock, by throwing a bottle at it, at eight minutes to three, ten years ago. He could not understand why he had ever screwed it to the wall. A clock did not belong in a studio and tonight it reminded him of a station clock on an abandoned platform.

'Do you remember the last thing Patrick said?' Peter asked.

Ben sighed.

'Don't delve too deep. It won't get you anywhere.'

'And then he drowned at the Grand Hotel.'

Ben breathed out, it sounded like a groan, and he projected his voice towards Peter.

'Don't make fun of the dead.'

Peter bent forward.

'It suits you best when you're yourself, Ben.'

'And what is that supposed to mean? It suits me to be lonely?'

'You don't need to adorn yourself with the youth of others.'

Ben smiled again, that sad, fleeting smile, and raised his hand.

'I basked in your youth too, Peter.'

'It might have been more me basking in your experience.'

'And now age just casts shadows.'

Peter took his hand, whispered, for he was unable to say it loud enough:

'We need each other more than ever, Ben.'

Ben nodded. He, too, whispered:

'Do you want me to be there when you get the results of the tests?'

'If you like.'

'No, not if I like, if *you* like, Peter.'

'Then I would like you to be there.'

They were silent as an ambulance dragged its siren through the night.

Then Ben said, 'But they're static.'

'What are static?'

'The pictures. They're static.'

Peter took his hand away.

'They're waiting, Ben.'

'You're waiting.'

'Yes. I'm waiting, too.'

'Then let's wait together, my friend.'

Ben drank the rest of his wine.

Peter placed the sketch pad on his lap.

'Have a look,' he said.

Ben opened it.

'Is it permitted to strike a match in here?'

Peter nodded.

The flame blazed between Ben's fingers illuminating Kaia's face and he sat like that until it went out. The white sheet continued to tremble in his hands.

'The picture's moving,' he whispered. 'My God, it's moving.'

'It will be my present to her,' Peter said.

Ben closed the pad and it was as if he had packed away the only light they had. He undressed. Peter, who was used to working in this darkness, could see the old man's gaunt body, the stepped ribs, the folds of skin on the elbows, the jagged hips like sharp corners, the taut paunch which curved down into the oval crotch, the thin thighs as wrinkled as his arms, and his skin was blue, it seemed, he looked like a Giacometti sculpture who was much too tired to stand upright and therefore lay down on the mezzanine bed.

'Come here.'

Peter went towards Ben, who took his hand and held it tight.

They could hear the wind outside, and further away, a fog-horn, a ship.

'That brother of his asked me to do something,' he said.
'What was that, Ben?'
'To hold a commemoration service for Patrick in the gallery.'
'Do you want to?'
Ben turned to the wall and cried silent tears.

11

The New Gallery was full long before seven o'clock the next evening. Detailed rumours of Patrick's sudden and tragic demise had spread like wildfire throughout the town – in restaurants, academies, clubs, studios, editorial offices, salons and museums. In the course of a day he had died and become famous. And now they were there, those who went by the name of everyone: colleagues, critics, curators, designers, investors, dancers, anchormen and anchorwomen, those who never need an invitation to come, a nobility without titles, a circle of people who slowly mingled, expressing disbelief at the death and admiration of the art, or vice versa, admiration of the premature death and disbelief at the art, but surprise never knocked them off their stools, and they took scant notice of Peter Wihl, who registered no more than a few brief nods, like commas between the slim glasses in the unbroken hushed conversation, not a single word of which anyone was listening to, anyway.

'I can't stand it,' he whispered.

Helene tugged at his arm and smiled.

'Pull yourself together. For Ben's sake.'

Peter smiled too, raised his glass and caught sight of Ben by the door, wearing a light blue suit, turquoise shirt, sunglasses, red shoes, a tight-fitting black leather cap, with jewellery glittering everywhere, around his neck, on his fingers, wrists, his ear lobe; he had taken another shot of youth and the older he became, the bigger the doses, and yesterday Ben had aged, once and for all.

Peter shuddered.

It was too hot in here. The sweat was running down his back. The silver paper covering the windows rustled. He put down his glass and felt alone in this exclusive crowd which circulated without moving its legs. He could not see Kaia. Ben came past, paused for a second, but did not stop, took off his glasses and whispered:

'I know what you're thinking, Peter.'

'What's that?'

'That I'm a whitewashed tomb.'

Helene was back and kissed him on the cheek.

'You're fine, Ben.'

He glanced at his watch.

'For as long as it lasts.'

And Ben had to be off, circulate, keep on the move, stand tall, press the flesh, remember the right names, articulate the right words, but never show his true face; he had done that the night before.

Peter followed him.

'Where's that brother of his, by the way?'

Ben took him aside, his voice even lower.

'He's taking care of the parents. They could never reconcile themselves to – what did they call it? – his nature.'

Ben wanted to move on – some new guests had arrived – but Peter held him back.

'There's something not right,' he whispered.

Ben clenched one hand: the rings looked like a knuckleduster.

'Yes, this evening everything's wrong, Peter.'

'That's not what I meant.'

They were interrupted by Kaia's laughter. She was sitting between the bin bags in the corner and pointing to a monitor connected to the video machine. A few people began to gather there, in front of the screen, thereby breaking the unwritten rule, the choreography of the preview and the commemoration, which is simply two sides of the same activity: to open and close. They stood without moving. Peter made his way towards her, threading through the hot bodies, someone spilt champagne on his jacket, a red ticket on the wall behind Kaia, so the work of art had been purchased, it might as well have been the wall that was purchased, or the people here. Everything can be bought, everything can be purchased, and with increasing indignation Peter thought that art had become senile and infantile at the same time, a game, a toy, there were no more intellectual ideas, there was no craftsmanship, just stunts, building bricks and optics. In other words, art had become a trick, and he wanted to take Kaia away, out, as fast as possible; he had put in an appearance, he had paid his respects, now he could go. Then a young woman stood in his way, obviously a journalist, she was equipped with a pen and pad at any rate, and there was something touching about these old-fashioned accoutrements.

'Have you a comment to make?'

'About what?'

The journalist was taken aback and looked up at him.

'Patrick's death, of course.'

She was even on first-name terms with the dead.

Peter stooped down.

'What do you want me to say?'

Once again she was taken aback.

'Whatever you want to say, of course.'

'My sympathies go to his family. That is obvious.'

Peter made as if to move away, but the young journalist would not let him go yet.

'May I have your name?' she asked.

'Pardon?'

'What's your name?'

She did not know the names of the living.

But before Peter could say a word, not his name – she would have to live in nameless ignorance – but something suitably coarse, a subtle, unimpeachable insult, an excited Kaia shouted:

'You're on TV, Daddy. Hurry!'

Peter turned towards the monitor on the wall and saw himself, in grey, slanting pictures, unrecognisable, but nevertheless clear, it was him without a doubt, Peter Wihl, filmed in the gallery the day before when he was having his minor confrontation with Patrick, but now Patrick had been edited out, removed, only Peter was left, a heated staccato monologue, a whining one-sided conversation, a comical lament repeated over and over again, he was addressing an invisible opponent, Patrick, and his voice was loud and strident: *I'm not bloody angry, why should I be angry, I'm surprised, I'm surprised that Ben should allow this rubbish into his gallery, I'm afraid the rubbish doesn't stink, it's supposed to stink, that's all, and who do you think this shit provokes, and who do you think this shit provokes and who do you think this shit provokes, I'm not bloody angry.* Peter just stood there smiling with his hands on his hips, and at this absurd moment he saw himself, literally, from the outside, and he was another person, he was unrecognisable and defined, he was elevated and downtrodden, he had become an installation. Several people turned towards him, now they knew who he was. The laughter subsided and was succeeded by an almost hostile atmosphere while Peter, still smiling, considered, coldly and logically, what he was to do now, what the most appropriate course of action would be. He could pull out the plug, smash the screen, yell, he could leave – he did none of these things; he just stood there without batting an eyelid; none of them would have anything on him; he would not be provoked. But then he saw that the smile had also gone from Kaia's face, between the bin bags, her mouth quivered and Helene forced her way through from the other end of the room and lifted her up. Peter hears a black dog barking, he hears a black dog barking one morning in a park. Then, at last, Ben, who was as stunned as he, took charge: the picture on the screen became a flicker, snow, as on old television sets at the end of the day's transmissions. He tapped his rings on his glass and everyone directed their attention towards him.

'Ladies and gentlemen, friends, Patrick's friends, thank you for coming at such short notice.'

Ben bowed his head, his voice failed him for a moment, he had to collect himself and the room went quiet, but beneath this silence there was an uneasiness, something disagreeable, a rustling noise, like the gentle movement of the silver paper in the windows. Peter glanced across at Helene. She just shook her head and held Kaia's hand.

Ben's gaze fixed itself on a place where no one could meet it, and continued:

'At such short notice. For death does not give us any time to think. A young life came to an abrupt and meaningless end. Sadly, the history of art is full of those who died young, those who were burnt out at an early age, those whom an arbitrary God stole from us, as though individuals such as these have a special susceptibility to His unpredictable whims. And we are left to imagine what they might have created if their time had not been nipped in the bud. Now Patrick is among them. I remember his last words, here in this gallery: Don't delve too deep, you won't get anywhere.'

Then the door opened and Ben was interrupted. It took the gathering a few seconds to comprehend what had happened, as if there were a time delay, a slowness of the senses. At first they could not believe their own eyes and for a few seconds they were close to being knocked off their stools, falling, taking a bad fall, for had they not been crying real tears just a short time ago?

Patrick walked in.

And he came dressed in a black suit with his face painted white and a cross hanging around his neck.

He raised his arms in the air like a victor.

'I'm back. It was much too boring being dead!'

Ben took a step back, as amazed, as dumbfounded as everyone else.

Then the assembled crowd burst into laughter, there was enthusiastic shouting, applause, Patrick had risen from the grave, from the pool at the Grand, shaken the soil and water off him and returned, in triumph, he was embraced, kissed, raised aloft, perhaps he had dreamed himself into an installation and now it had become a reality, and purchased by death, thought Peter. That was all he thought: everything here had been purchased by death; they all had red tickets pinned to their skin and were waiting to be taken to the Great Museum.

But when Patrick turned to Ben, to receive homage from him, he was disappointed. Ben just stared at Patrick, for one embarrassing, mortifying moment, rent asunder, and then he sank to his knees and hid his face in his hands.

To open and close: two sides of the same activity.

The assembly moved aside, expectant, as if making way for Peter, and left Patrick standing alone, in the middle of the floor. Peter approached Patrick and stood in front of him. He smiled.

'But I won't ask first,' he said.

And Peter did not punch him for the audience, Ben, art, the darkness, nor for himself; he punched him for Kaia's sake, the punch that had started in the park, on that Sunday morning when a black dog appeared. He clenched his fist into a hard ball of fingers, punched with all his might and split Patrick's white face.

12

Even though Peter knew that he had heard what Dr Kristoffer Hall had just said, and that he had heard him correctly, he nevertheless leaned forward in his chair, in the silence that followed, at this moment which would upend everything, turn his existence inside out, not that he saw his life passing before him in a series of lofty, sad and banal tableaux, what he saw was rather the darkness approaching from the other side, a wild runaway locomotive coming straight at him, and in this one moment resided a heavy silence, and so he leaned forward, almost cheerily, and broke the silence with a tentative question:

'What did you say?'

'I'm afraid you're going blind.'

Kristoffer Hall closed the folder containing all the papers, folded his hands and glanced at Peter, but he soon shifted his attention to Ben, who, sitting in the chair beside Peter, gave a loud groan, a sudden delayed gasp from between his lips, then he pinched his mouth shut and laid his hand on Peter's shoulder.

But the words still had not struck home with Peter, those fateful words, *I'm afraid you're going blind*, they slipped by, eluding all meaning, and became mere sounds, discordant notes, acoustic clinker, like the rain which continued to fall against the windows, washing away the snow, making a hole in winter. It almost made him laugh.

'Going blind?'

The X-ray pictures of his eyes were on a white viewing box whose glare both lent their faces a wan sheen and cast them into jagged shadows, the way children look when all the lights are off and they press a torch under their chins to frighten the others.

Kristoffer Hall looked back at Peter.

'I am indeed sorry to have to be so brutal. But neither of us benefits from beating about the bush.'

Peter cut in:

'So brutal? You've just pronounced my death sentence!'

'I know what this means to you, herr Wihl, but let me stress that this ailment is not fatal.'

'But I can't live if I can't see!'

Peter made as if to stand up; Ben held him back and addressed the doctor.

'Is this diagnosis final?'

'Yes.'

'My God, is there no hope at all?'

'You mean doubt? No.'

Dr Hall took a pair of glasses from a case and polished them on a corner of his white coat, which fortunately he had put on today, at last he looked like a doctor, and he took his time, rubbing with force, perhaps to allow these words to sink in so that some form of meaning could emerge from the hard ground where they fell.

Nevertheless, Peter stood up and gesticulated with his arms as if someone had told a bad joke or played a monstrous practical trick on him.

'I don't believe you,' he said.

'Lots of patients say that when they are told something of this kind. It's natural.'

'You can be brutal, but you don't have to be patronising.'

'I apologise if that is your perception.'

'And nothing is natural in this situation.'

Hall continued to polish the narrow gold-framed glasses.

'I can understand your despair.'

'Can you? Do you, in fact, understand my despair?'

Dr Hall let go of his coat and stood looking at the glasses he was holding in both hands, and answered in his own time, as though the words were being painstakingly created as he formulated them:

'No. Of course, you're right. The despair is yours. My understanding is confined to the diagnosis.'

Ben, gentle and incisive, intervened.

'And you should be bloody happy about that, Peter. Kristoffer is the best. And now let's stick to hard facts.'

At last Dr Hall put on his glasses and pointed.

'Can you see this,' he said.

Reluctantly, Peter bent down over the light, over the X-rays of his eyes, and he just saw black cavities, the outline of the cranium, the back of the face, diffused in shadows and bones. It showed him nothing, this too was impossible to decipher, his insides were abstract, he shied away, nauseous and giddy, and again Ben had to support him.

Dr Hall pointed to a darker area and began to speak, factually, dispassionately, as though reading from a manual:

'We have found a rare form of infection on the retina, what is known as *retinitis pigmentosa*, which is either congenital or acquired at a very young age. This disease causes, amongst other things, enormous pressure on the eyeballs, which become so hard that the membranes do not even yield to finger pressure. In other words, the sensitivity in the eyes is lost. And, at the same time vision is restricted. The pathology is, to a certain extent, reminiscent of a cataract, but unlike with a cataract this process is irreversible. Eyesight gradually deteriorates and culminates in total blindness. I regret to say there is nothing we can do.'

Dr Hall took off his glasses, regarded Peter and added:

'Except make the best of it.'

'The best of it? What is that?'

'Minimal pain, herr Wihl.'

Peter looked away. He had to ask:

'Why has my eyesight failed me three times? If you say it happens gradually.'

Hall switched off the light of the viewing box where the X-rays were and the room was engulfed in shadow.

'In the last phase of the disease patients may experience such violent pain in and around the eyes and the left side of the head that they lose their sight for a brief period.'

Peter faced Dr Hall again.

'Patients? Do you mean me?'

Dr Hall hesitated, then said, 'Three times? Has it happened again?'

'Yes. It's happened again. The third time.'

'Then there's not a lot of time left.'

Peter sat down.

Ben remained standing, staring down at the light, this inverted light in which the shadows shone.

'Is that all you can say?' he asked.

'I'm afraid so,' said Kristoffer Hall.

'Is there no chance that Peter could be treated abroad?'

'No. It's too late.'

'So there's no hope?'

'No, Ben. He will go blind.'

Peter listened to the conversation, he heard his name, but still the conversation did not seem to have anything to do with him, they seemed to be speaking about someone else, a stranger who happened to have the same name, Peter, and who also suffered from this rare eye disease which would make him go blind before very long.

'How much time is there?' Ben asked.

'A month. Maybe six months. Maximum.'

'Will it be painful?'

'Not necessarily. He can take medicine along the way. The crucial thing is that he makes preparations. For his new life. And those closest to him also make preparations. That they work together on this. Of course, we'll give him all the back-up he needs. And his family.'

'And that means?'

'I would recommend that we take him in when his sight has gone.'

They turned towards Peter, who jumped to his feet.

'I don't believe you,' he repeated.

Kristoffer Hall paused before speaking:

'I hear what you say. You can see another doctor. That's your right. But he will give you the same verdict.'

Peter laughed.

'Verdict? Have I done something illegal? Am I being punished? Darkness for life?'

'I apologise. That was thoughtless of me. Of course, I meant to say: the same diagnosis.'

Dr Hall fetched a printout. It was a colour picture of his eyes, glowing balls with a ramified network of black stains. They looked like planets.

'You can take that with you, if you like.'

'I don't bloody want it.'

Then Peter changed his mind, stuffed the sheet in his pocket and walked towards the door. Once there, he turned. A thought had crossed his mind, and these thoughts frightened him more than the diagnosis itself.

'You said this disease was congenital?'

Kristoffer Hall nodded.

'Yes. That is probable.'

'And that means it is also hereditary?'

'Not necessarily. But I cannot rule that out.'

Peter was reminded of his father again and the time he lost control of the car on a straight stretch of road one quiet, dry spring evening, for no known reason. What was the last thing his parents saw before they died? Was it each other, or just darkness? He thought of Kaia, of Kaia's green eyes, and everything she had not yet seen.

'I have a daughter,' he whispered.

'We can examine her, too. To be on the safe side. But you should think about yourself for now.'

'Me? Right now I'm thinking about everyone else except myself, Dr Hall.'

'What I'm trying to say is that you shouldn't worry yourself unduly. The chances of your daughter suffering from Daniel's Syndrome are very slim.'

'But there is a chance?'

'There is always a chance, herr Wihl.'

'Are you trying to reassure me or scare me?'

'I am trying to be as truthful as possible.'

'Thank you.'

'You'll be called in for regular check-ups. And you can ring or contact me whenever you wish. Is there anything else you need right now?'

'I'd like to book an appointment for my daughter. As soon as possible.'

'I'll send you an appointment card. As soon as possible. But, as I said, you don't need to concern yourself.'

'I do concern myself.'

Peter proffered his hand; Kristoffer Hall took it, looked at the plasters over the swollen knuckles and gave a quick smile.

'I read about the incident in the paper. May I say that so-called artist got what he deserved?'

Ben answered.

'Yes,' he said. 'He got what he deserved.'

They left and stood in the chilly rain, in the little park between the clinic and the main road. The grass that appeared from under the shrinking snow was stuck to the ground, flat and slippery; a thin layer of ice would soon freeze over it, perhaps as soon as tonight, a shiny invisible film of frost, and accidents would probably follow.

Neither of them knew what to say.

Finally, Peter said, 'How is Patrick, by the way?'

'For me he's dead, regardless,' Ben answered.

Peter shook his head.

'You've been unlucky with your current selection of artists.'

'Don't think about your exhibition now, Peter.'

Peter leaned over towards Ben.

'I'm not bloody blind yet!'

'Sorry.'

'And the exhibition will go ahead as planned! Do you hear me? As planned!'

'Of course. And now let's take a taxi back to yours.'

'You take one. I'd rather be on my own.'

Peter walked towards the gate, through the hard, persistent rain that was still falling, reverberating around him.

Ben followed and shouted:

'We need each other now, Peter. Wasn't that what you said?'

But Peter just kept walking, out of the gate, away from the clinic, along the road to the town, without looking back, and everything drew nearer, in magnificent detail, the shiny impenetrable surface of the world, the raindrops on the black tarmac, the trees in the grove, the dry patches by the roots, a bird with a red breast alighting from the branches, it was as if the muscles of his eyes were summoning up all their strength for one last great effort, as he carried his light, his fading electric light, towards the darkness, to show him this, random and beautiful, the raindrops rolling across the black tarmac, the gnarled roots, a bird with a red breast and he thought of the eyes he had once seen in the Metropolitan, in New York, the Egyptian eyes in a showcase, all alone, moulded from iron and wood, with brown pupils, green eyebrows, and it was just as though these eyes had come to life in the artist's hands, 2,500 years ago, and now they were staring at you, in the few seconds you were present, and they would continue to see long after you had gone, and these words struck Peter as he was walking in the freezing rain, and they struck him with such force and precision, it was so overwhelming that he had to sit down at the edge of the road, on the kerb, and rest his head in his hands: eyesight is my view of life; without eyesight I am nothing.

Peter Wihl stayed sitting like that. For how long he was not sure. Then a car pulled up in front of him, an old black Mercedes with shiny bumpers and hubcaps. The driver rolled down the window and peered out.

It had stopped raining.

Peter looked up.

It was an elderly gentleman with an imposing yet gentle face. A woman, most probably his wife, leaned across his shoulder, at once curious and shy.

'What is it?' she asked.

'We have to help him.'

'Why?'

'Can't you see he's ill?'

'Perhaps he doesn't want any help.'

'At least we can take him home.'

The man opened the rear door and Peter got in.

They drove off.

Peter was freezing, but soon it was warm in the car, which smelled of leather, tobacco and perfume. The rain coursed down his clothes.

'Sorry,' Peter said.

The man craned his neck, smiled.

'Oh, that doesn't matter.'

Peter looked down. The floor was covered with faded, yellow newspapers, years old, dating from his childhood.

The woman said in a sharp, stern voice:

'Watch the road, Father! Watch the road!'

In her lap she was gripping a small bag with both hands. Now and then she would stamp her foot as if she were braking.

The man was wearing driving gloves.

The mahogany dashboard shone; a green gleam, light green, as if under water. The thin needle of the speedometer quivered over the speed limit.

Peter sat in the middle of the back seat, as he always did, so that he could follow the road through the windscreen.

'Don't we have anything we can give him?' the man said.

The woman let go of her bag, opened the glove compartment

– a little lamp lit up – and located a box of liquorice lozenges, which she hurriedly passed to Peter.

'Please help yourself.'

He took one, sucked it and leaned forward, between the seats.

'You're very kind,' he said.

'Shh,' the woman whispered. 'Don't disturb Father.'

No one said anything for a while.

It became darker as the clouds drifted away, at mercurial speed, they disintegrated and the scattered light from the deep blue sky fell in bundles between the tall, stooped trees, and then all of a sudden an animal, a fallow deer it was, sprang into the road, no more than fifty metres away, paused for a second and turned towards them. Its coat was smooth and wet, its breath hung like smoke, a mist around the muzzle, it stood motionless, staring as the man braked for all he was worth. The woman screamed and the Mercedes aquaplaned over the slippery tarmac, then the animal vanished with long, slow bounds into the woods on the other side. There was a bang under the car, everything shook and, with one front wheel perched on the edge of the ditch, at last it came to a halt.

The woman was clutching her bag, her shoulders were trembling and her voice was stern and frightened:

'You'll have to get out now,' she said.

The man was breathing heavily. He rubbed his tight driving gloves together, met Peter's gaze in the rear-view mirror and nodded.

'Can you push?'

Peter crawled out, closed the door and went behind the car, placed his hands on the lid of the boot and shoved. The wheels spun and spun, sending a wave of mud over his trousers and shoes. Finally, the wheels of the car caught hold and Peter stood watching the black Mercedes drive away, the man with his hand raised in salute, the woman facing the front.

13

The frozen grass cracked at every step Peter took on his way down to the house.

Helene was standing on the patio with a shawl over her shoulders, in the shadow between the outdoor lamp and the kitchen window, smoking a cigarette. Peter had not seen her smoking for several years. She dropped the glow into the dark and came towards him, stopped, and let Peter walk the last part. She had been crying. In the dark Peter could see she had been crying and he knew straight away that Ben had already been there and told her everything.

'Ben's been here,' he said.

She gave a swift nod of the head, as if she were freezing, her teeth chattering.

'Yes.'

'Then you know.'

She nodded again.

'Yes, Peter.'

'I'm going blind. It's terrible, isn't it?'

'Yes, Peter. It's terrible.'

He laughed.

'Couldn't I have gone deaf, eh? I wouldn't have minded going deaf. That wouldn't have bloody bothered me.'

Helene put her arms around him.

'Where have you been?' she whispered.

'Just walking.'

'We were worried about you, Peter.'

'Sorry.'

She laughed, too. Her voice was low, with clear intonation, a long flow of air, the way she spoke to Kaia when she needed comforting.

'It doesn't matter, because you're here now, Peter. You're here with us now, aren't you?'

'Where's Kaia?'

'Kaia's asleep.'

'You haven't said anything, have you?'

Helene cut him short.

'Of course not.'
'What did Ben say?'
'You know.'
'Tell me anyway.'
'The doctor said you're going blind.'
'When?'
'Please, Peter.'
'When am I going blind?'
'In a year. Six months.'
'Was that all he said?'
'Or a month, Peter.'
He cut her short.
'Didn't he say the exhibition was going ahead as planned?'
Peter walked on, towards the studio. The grass cracking under his shoes was the only sound he heard, not the wind; he could only see where it bent the black tips of the trees, like a comb grooming the woods.
Helene held on to him, surprised, seemingly disappointed.
'Where are you going?'
'I just want to be alone for a bit.'
She clasped his arm tightly with her fingers.
'You're not going to be on your bloody own now.'
'Let me go, Helene.'
'We're not going to be on our bloody own now. None of us! Do you hear me!'
Helene would not let go of Peter and they walked together into the studio and before she had time to look around, to see the twelve unfinished, recently begun, canvasses, he had pulled up her skirt and whipped down her panties, and he took her with her back against the glass doors, as if there were nothing between them and the night outside, between the night outside and the artificial darkness of the studio, just a hard invisible membrane which could be smashed at any time, splintered; her lips smelled of tobacco, her tongue was stiff and cold, then her mouth melted and he came, in passion and pain, wanted to scream, but could not produce a sound, withdrew from inside her, caught his tender part on the zip, felt blood flowing between his fingers, hot blood and semen, and Helene sank to the floor and sat gasping for breath as Peter put her shawl around them and they said nothing until everything had settled down again.

'Do you remember the surprise I mentioned?' he whispered.

'Was that it?'

She looked at him, not the pictures, the unfinished pictures, and put on a smile.

He shook his head, without quite managing a smile either, and passed her the sketch pad.

'This is the surprise, Helene.'

She flipped the cover and sat hunched over the wide paper for a long time.

'You can see better in the dark than I can,' she said.

'Can't you see her?'

'Who?'

'Kaia.'

Peter took Helene's hand and guided her fingertips with care along the lines until she had also drawn Kaia's face.

'It's going to be good,' she whispered.

'I'm frightened.'

'Me too, Peter.'

'Don't be. There's only room for one person to be frightened in a family.'

Helene bent forward and kissed Peter.

'We have to go to Kaia.'

'Don't say anything to her.'

'We'll have to tell her when the time comes, won't we? Come on.'

But Peter did not move and said, out of the blue:

'I saw my parents today.'

'What did you say?'

He gave a short laugh.

'My parents. I saw them today.'

Helene held his head in both hands and tried to look into his eyes.

'Peter, please.'

'It's true. I met them.'

She let him go and gave up.

'Where did you meet them?'

'It was shortly before they died.'

'Did they say anything?'

'They asked me to push their car.'

'Their car?'

'Yes. Typical of them.'

'Did you?'

'Certainly bloody did. Look at my trousers. And my shoes. Ruined.'

Peter hid his face in his hands. Helene ran her hand through his hair.

'Never mind.'

'I don't think they recognised me.'

Helene hesitated, then stood up and said:

'Kaia may have woken up.'

He looked up.

'I'll always recognise Kaia, won't I?'

'Of course you will. Why shouldn't you?'

Peter stood up too, dizzy, exhausted, his crotch smarting, his head burning and any pains were welcome rather than the thought of what was approaching.

He pointed to the clock above the door.

'It needs fixing. It hasn't moved for at least ten years.'

Helene took his hand, impatient, insistent.

'Are you coming? Kaia is on her own.'

Peter said, 'I have to finish off here.'

'Sure?'

Peter, just as impatient and insistent, said, 'Yes, I have to finish.'

Helene looked at him, nodded, wrapped the shawl around her shoulders, opened the doors and was gone.

Peter did not move.

He could hear her swift footsteps fading away in the cold.

Then he set to work on the canvasses.

He scraped at the base and added, added and scraped, he built up and tore down, tore down and built up, at a furious tempo, until the colours were textures you could touch, light and heavy, thin and dense, he inhaled the darkness, he was at work, he was at one with his work, body and art connected with the electricity of his fingertips in a circle of light, and everything he laid his fingers on resembled Kaia.

A restless shimmer filled the studio.

The day made a narrow, dazzling incision into the night, an ochre-yellow border around the high, black sky.

And Peter thought, yet again, that it was up to the shiny, impenetrable surface that he had to go: there, nowhere else.

He carried all the canvasses into the garden and stood them there, working until his fingers were a useless ball of cold.

He left the canvasses, went inside, lay down on the mezzanine bed, shivering, closed his eyes for a moment and when he awoke he heard sounds, quick light footsteps, or skating, not far away.

He opened the doors.

It was Kaia. She was running in and out between the pictures. Peter watched her. Kaia in a red cape, long green scarf, black gloves and black cap, running between the pictures on a morning made of glass, thin fragile glass.

She pulled up sharp and turned towards him. She seemed afraid, unhappy.

'You didn't forget, did you?' she said.

'No. What was that, sweet?'

She looked down.

'You have forgotten, haven't you!'

Peter went a step closer.

'Tell me what I've forgotten.'

Kaia peered at him again.

'To paint my figures.'

Peter nodded.

'Of course I'll paint your figures. I haven't forgotten that.'

And Kaia, an angel in red, continued to run through the labyrinth of canvasses.

Helene was standing on the doorstep, hair dishevelled, wearing a jacket and a dressing gown, holding a cup of coffee in both hands, also surprised at what she saw, a garden full of pictures.

The light rose relentlessly and erased the yellow border.

And Peter saw all that was unfinished, unseen, on this morning of glass which had not yet cracked.

Helene waved to him. He raised his hand in response.

Then Peter went back into the studio and closed the doors.

The coat he had been wearing on the Sunday after the first frost, when the dog appeared, was hanging on a nail beneath the clock. The card was still in the pocket. He took it out: *Dr Thomas Hammer. Ophthalmic Surgeon.*

14

The painting hung in the waiting room, a hand, a left hand, 120 cm × 90. The surface is red, monochrome; that is why the hand seems to be hovering, or floating in blood, detached from its human owner, and it was painted with meticulous precision: the crooked fingers, nails, the yellow edges, the wrinkles on the knuckles, the veins like blue arcs under the skin, the brown stains on the back of the hand and slender, black hairs, the white stripe left by the wristwatch, and then, all of a sudden, the crude cut, the gash, the shreds of flesh, as if a reckless butcher has been at work. It is a man's hand, an old man's hand at the time it was painted. Today it looked like his; he was approaching his motif, so to speak, and Peter was disgusted at seeing this painting again. There was a kind of posturing about it; it was contrived, seductive, a sort of virtuoso pain intended to arouse revulsion and admiration at the same time. He felt disgusted, and all he wanted to do was to heal the rupture, attach the arm, the shoulder, the neck, the torso, the face and painstakingly make the human body whole. It was like a conviction, indeed a calling, and Peter had never had a clearer feeling or idea: he should finish the man. And he remembered the price: the painting had cost 4,000 kroner twenty-five years ago, a price which Ben considered golden for the artist and the market. And now it, *The Amputation*, was hanging here in Thomas Hammer's waiting room.

Thomas was opening the door while putting on his coat, one sleeve was inside out, he swore, and then he noticed Peter, the only person sitting in the waiting room. He started in surprise, the long coat hanging at an angle off his shoulder and dragging along the floor, but it only lasted a second before, as though bored, he grumbled:

'Have you got an appointment?'

'No.'

'We work on an appointment basis only.'

'Then I'll make an appointment. If that's possible.'

'It's past four o'clock. I've shut up shop.'

Peter got up, with relief in fact. He should never have come, he already deeply regretted coming and it was not too late to go.

'I'll have to ring tomorrow, then.'

Thomas Hammer, breathing heavily, finally got his arm into the coat. His forehead was moist with sweat; droplets were running down the bloated cheeks. You would think he was crying if you did not know any better. Then he quickly passed his hand over his face and grinned.

'Oh hell, what are old friends for, Peter?'

'I can phone tomorrow,' Peter repeated.

Thomas Hammer went back into his surgery. Peter hesitated and followed. They sat down, face to face across an empty table. The walls were also bare, apart from the obligatory wallchart with letters which get smaller and smaller until they merge and lose their shape in the last line.

'Did you like the art out there?' Thomas Hammer asked.

'No,' Peter said.

'That's what my patients say, too.'

'Why did you hang it up there?'

'To distract them. Give them something else to think about while they're waiting. Isn't that a good enough objective for art?'

'I don't paint for waiting rooms.'

'But isn't life itself one great big waiting room?'

'Now you disappoint me,' Peter said.

Thomas Hammer laughed and folded his hands on the table.

'During the Spanish Inquisition the best artists were executed while the mediocre ones were allowed to live. They were allowed to work. They were not dangerous. Which would you have preferred, Peter?'

'Out of what?'

'Being the best and dying or being mediocre and surviving?'

'Being mediocre.'

Thomas Hammer leaned closer, as though to hear better.

'What did you say? Did you say mediocre?'

'Yes. You heard correctly.'

'That was a bloody mediocre response.'

Peter was tired of the game. He asked:

'By the way, do you have many patients?'

Thomas Hammer sat up.

'I have a few stalwarts. I'm the last doctor everyone comes to. As you have.'

Peter was unable to take his eyes off him; his pale, fat hands; his face caught in a network of burst blood vessels.

'Why do you say that?'

'Have you decided to come for a drink with the old boys after all?'

Peter looked over at the window. The blinds were down; one of the pulleys had broken. From another room, perhaps underneath, or on the floor above, it was difficult to tell, music could be heard. Someone playing the violin stopped and went back to the beginning. Otherwise no sounds intruded. It was one of those rather aged buildings in the town centre from the nineteen-thirties, functional and mysterious, no one knew exactly what it had been used for. There was a smell of linoleum and pungent furniture oil here; there were long corridors, broom cupboards, firms of solicitors without clients, accountants without accounts, musicians without orchestras, doors without names and Thomas Hammer was here, the ophthalmic surgeon with loyal patients.

'I've come because I'll be blind within six months,' Peter said.

'Blind? Who on earth told you that?'

'My doctor.'

Thomas Hammer smiled and pointed.

'What did I just say?'

'What?'

'That I'm the last doctor you come to.'

All of a sudden Peter felt weary, tired of all the repartee. He had to stop himself slumping in the chair and falling asleep, wishing he would wake up somewhere else, in another time, in another body. He said:

'You're the second doctor I've seen, Thomas.'

'And now you want to hear something different.'

'Or a confirmation.'

'Or shall we say a miracle, a minor miracle.'

'I don't believe in miracles.'

'Oh, yes, you do. The sicker you are, the greater your belief in miracles. The place is swarming with patients who spend fortunes on finding a doctor who can tell them they are healthy.

Even if they have to be wheeled into the surgery with an oxygen mask and drip. We are strange creatures, aren't we?'

'You're only the second doctor,' Peter repeated.

Thomas Hammer laughed.

'I know what you want to hear. That you won't go blind, you'll go deaf.'

Peter stood up.

'I'm going. I should never have come.'

Immediately, Thomas Hammer stood up too, and stuck out his hand.

'I'm sorry. I went too far. Please, take a seat.'

Peter stayed on his feet. He could have gone. He did not go. He could have turned his back on him and left. Instead he stood looking at Thomas Hammer's broad hand, the rigid, stumpy fingers, and it was impossible not to think of these coarse fingers, which were better suited to repairing a tractor, handling sensitive systems in the body, the muscles of sense organs, the eyes, but Peter did not go. He did everything he was loathe to do because he thought he had nothing to lose.

He said, 'All right.'

Both men hesitated before seating themselves.

'May I ask who your first doctor was?' Thomas Hammer asked.

'Kristoffer Hall. At the clinic.'

Thomas Hammer no longer seemed amused.

'I regret to say he is usually right.'

'Thank you. Was that the miracle?'

'It was a fact. What was Hall's diagnosis?'

Peter placed the X-ray in front of Thomas Hammer. He studied the star-shaped, black patches on the retinas, leaned forward, pressed his thumbs gently against his eyelids, twice. Then he sat in silence, his hands in his lap, without smiling.

Peter became impatient.

Thomas Hammer pushed the X-ray to one side and looked at him.

'Glaucoma. The famous ophthalmic surgeon Von Gräfe discovered the first remedy for this disease in Berlin in 1856, an iridectomy, cutting out a piece of the iris.'

Peter rolled up the X-ray and put it in his pocket.

'What is glaucoma?'

'Damage to the optic nerve,' said Thomas Hammer.

'So you're saying I've got cataracts?'

Thomas Hammer smiled.

'No, I'm not. You're not that fortunate. *Retinitis pigmentosa* may well be closer to the truth. An infection of the retina. The name doesn't help anyone. The fact of the matter is there is no way back.'

Peter interrupted him, tired of hearing all this.

'You say I'm going blind, too?'

Thomas Hammer nodded.

'You went to the first doctor too late. And came to the second even later.'

'Is there no form of treatment?'

Thomas Hammer placed his elbows on the table and clasped his hands together.

'So that was what happened to you that evening? You lost your sight, temporarily.'

'That was the third time it had happened.'

'Then I'm afraid it is getting closer.'

'Kristoffer Hall said the same.'

Thomas Hammer looked at Peter.

'Are you disappointed? Did you think I would be able to say anything else?'

Peter shook his head.

'It's good to know where you stand. Before you fall.'

'Are you hungry?'

'Hungry?'

'Let's go and eat.'

Thomas Hammer was already on his feet and Peter joined him.

They took the lift down, inching from floor to floor, through the deserted building where a sole violinist was practising Bach's *Sicilienne* and came out into the gaudy, restless lights of the wet, noisy Christmas streets, walked to the nearest crossroads, into the dingy cafe there and found a seat in the corner, in the drab gloom between the bracket lamps which just provided sufficient light for customers to see the glass, the ashtray and their change.

Peter kept his coat on. He was not hungry. He had to go soon, anyway.

Thomas Hammer hung his coat over the chair.

'I can recommend the Christmas platter.'

'No, thank you.'

'Or cod in lye. It's tender this year, just right.'

'I have to go soon.'

An old waiter in a stained white jacket came over to their table.

'I'll have the same as my friend,' Thomas Hammer said.

'And what will Thomas Hammer's friend have?'

'Mineral water. With lemon.'

The waiter looked back at Thomas Hammer.

'Mineral water?'

'You heard what he said.'

'With lemon?'

'Yes, for Christ's sake. Two mineral waters with lemon. And give Olsson a refill. He'll soon be dehydrated and sober, won't he?'

Thomas Hammer passed a few notes to the waiter who walked back to the counter, taking his time. On his return he placed a beer and an aquavit on the table in front of an emaciated old man nursing an empty glass between both hands. A thin, yellow smile lit the gaunt face as he exchanged grips and raised the tot, filled to the brim, with such care and so slowly that he could well have died before tasting it, but better that than to waste a single burning drop of it.

Then they were served the mineral water with lemon.

Peter nodded towards the thirsty old man.

'A good deed,' he said.

Thomas Hammer smiled.

'I'm trying to be... what shall I say?... a good person.'

'Isn't everyone?'

Thomas Hammer ignored the question, took a sip from the acidic mineral water that gave off a slight fizzing sound, as if the glasses were sighing, and leaned across the table.

'What was the first thing you did?' he asked.

Peter didn't understand.

'The first thing I did?'

'When you found out you were going blind.'

Peter put his hand inside his jacket, just to make sure that he had not forgotten his wallet.

'I went home.'

'And what did you do when you got home?'

'Why are you asking?'

'I like to know as much as possible about my patients.'

'I'm not your patient.'

'You came to see me.'

'And you couldn't help,' Peter said.

Thomas Hammer clinked his glass against Peter's.

'I only wanted to know if you went to your daughter or your studio first.'

Peter studied him.

'I went to my studio and there I fucked my wife and I worked for the rest of the night.'

Thomas Hammer put down his glass.

'What would you have preferred to be: a blind artist or a blind father?'

Peter took out his wallet.

'You're unbearable.'

'I'm paying, Peter.'

'I don't need your miserable bloody charity.'

'I can help you.'

Peter paused, looked up at Thomas Hammer, who sat there with an earnest expression and a smile on his face, and for the third time Peter did not leave.

'What do you mean?' he asked.

'There is a way to save your sight.'

'You said the diagnosis was final.'

'But there's always a way, Peter.'

'What kind of way?'

'Not everyone acknowledges it, nor deems it official.'

'Meaning?'

Thomas Hammer leaned closer, across the white tablecloth, in the gloom between the orange lamps on the wall.

'It requires a journey, a certain amount of capital and some discretion.'

Peter was quiet for a time.

'Has this way been used before?'

'Several times.'

'With success?'

'Complete success. The patients regained their sight. No one has complained.'

'Risk?'

'Even a headache pill carries a risk, Peter. The only thing which is a hundred per cent sure is to do nothing. Then you will go blind.'

'What does this way involve?'

Thomas Hammer looked him straight in the eye. It was a few seconds before he said:

'You won't want to know.'

'I have to know.'

Thomas Hammer shook his head.

'Give it a bit of thought before you make up your mind.'

Peter opened his wallet. In the plastic pockets there were photographs of Helene and Kaia, taken in the garden outside the house. Kaia is a newborn baby; she is asleep; Helene is holding her in her arms, looking at him, smiling; they have just returned from the hospital; it is spring and the tree in the background is in blossom. He sat looking at them, closed his wallet and eyed Thomas Hammer.

'I've made up my mind,' Peter said.

Thomas Hammer shrugged his shoulders.

'All right. At least I tried to help you. But you were always a little wimp, you were, Peter.'

And Peter leaned over to him.

'Let's go for it.'

15

This is the base of the picture: in an office in the Kremlin, at the Ministry of Agriculture, during the winter of 1960, it is decided that the same corn from the lush fields of America that Party Leader Khrushchev had seen with his own eyes when he visited Eisenhower should also be grown in the Estonian Socialist Soviet Republic, so that the crops could also germinate and grow there with the same vigour and discipline and ultimately yield what was expected. Prior to spring soldiers transported this alien seed grain to the largest collective farms in the areas around Tallinn where, even though the order came straight from the Party Leader, the farmers simply shook their heads at this latest caprice from the Kremlin: Estonia was not America, East could never be West and this grain would never grow on chalk and stone where the temperature seldom rose above nineteen degrees in June. But those who dared to speak up and say this were soon despatched to dig peat instead, for it had already been decided in a Kremlin office that the cornfields of Estonia should billow as they do in America, and the loyal farmers, who had no choice, sowed their fields with these potent, alien seeds, and when the autumn came only a few thin ears of corn were visible in the black furrows. The bureaucrats and, not least, the Party Leader in the Kremlin, were furious: it was the farmers' fault, if it grew in America it was bound to grow in Estonia. That was definite. And the following spring the farmers were sent more seed to sow, but the same thing happened. The fields lay barren, there was famine, families starved, dissatisfaction spread, it smouldered, and in the end the Party sent along men from their own ranks to the largest collective farm in order to discipline these rotten, idle farmers. They arrived in their long coats, black shoes and grey gloves, accompanied by a whole company of soldiers; they cast their eyes over the cornfields and the man in charge took off his gloves, picked up a fistful of earth, which just ran between his fingers, looked at the sterile stalks remaining in his hand, turned to the farmers and said: 'I knew it, you idiots, you planted the seed upside down!'

The three men sitting in the cellar restaurant of Hotel W in Tallinn burst into laughter. They were waiting for the Captain and no other guests were present. There never were, when they were waiting for the Captain. And while they were waiting, the oldest of them – he was almost old enough to remember that far back – told them this story. He was drinking beer and leaned across the table.

'My grandfather heard that one. With his own ears! You planted the seed upside down!'

The other two were younger, well under thirty, and they were amused even though they had heard the story before.

'And do you know what my grandfather said to the men from the Kremlin?'

They knew, but wanted him to say it anyway.

'What did your grandfather say?' asked the youngest.

The oldest man took out a comb and dragged it through his hair, milking the moment.

Then he said, in a loud voice:

'I thought so. You idiots. It's you who are standing on your heads!'

Again they roared, but not for long.

'What happened to your grandfather then?'

'What do you think? He was sent to Narva to dig peat for the electricity board until he died.'

All three men shook their heads and the oldest man pointed to a scar at the corner of his mouth which pulled his lips upwards so that he seemed to be always smiling – a crooked smile, it was true.

'And that's where the damned soldiers hit me with the fork when I tried to hold on to my grandfather!'

The television was on, with the sound turned down, the colours as garish as the shiny balls on the Christmas tree in the corner. The walls were bare, white. They called the waitress. She returned promptly with more beer. She could not have been more than twenty years old. A red apron tied tightly around her waist. She collected the dead glasses.

'Do you know what crushed communism, Ewa?' the oldest man asked.

Ewa shook her head.

'Have a guess!'

'Gorbachev?'

The men laughed. Ewa flushed.

'Don't you mean the Americans?'

'I don't mean anything,' she hastened to say.

Ewa wanted to go back to the kitchen, but the oldest man caught her arm.

'You don't need to be frightened,' he said.

'I'm not interested in politics.'

'Are you interested in wages?'

'Yes.'

'Are your grandparents still alive?'

Ewa nodded.

'Are you interested in whether their house is heated on Christmas Eve?'

Ewa lowered her eyes, close to tears.

'Yes.'

'Then you're interested in politics, Ewa.'

He let go of her.

She whispered, 'Thank you.'

'And now, I'm sure you would like to know what put paid to communism, wouldn't you?'

'Yes. Of course.'

'A grain of wheat from the Black Sea, Ewa.'

At that moment the Captain came down the stairs, together with his henchman. The men stood up. Ewa made a deep curtsey. The Captain slipped her a few banknotes. She curtseyed again and hurried into the kitchen. They sat down. The henchman stood between the bar and the toilets, staring at the mute television screen.

'You haven't lit the table candles?' the Captain asked.

The youngest man pulled out a lighter and lit the thin stub of a candle.

The Captain looked down and smiled.

Then he blew out the flame.

The henchman turned up the volume. A girl was singing *White Christmas* in a reedy voice.

'Peeteli Church will soon be full,' the Captain said.

Ewa returned with four cups of coffee.

They added sugar and waited for her to go.

The henchman turned up the volume even higher. Now a choir was singing.

The Captain stirred his coffee slowly and leaned across the table.

'Some will have to stay in the old transformer station in Kopli.'

The oldest man sighed.

'They'll be cold there.'

The Captain stared at him.

'And that's why we have to hand out some Christmas presents. There are two containers in the harbour. Shoes. Games. A plough. Beds. Medicines. Seed grain.'

The youngest man laughed.

'Seed grain? From Norway? We won't risk it!'

The Captain turned to the oldest man.

'Have you been talking politics again?'

The oldest man shrugged.

'We were just talking.'

The Captain scanned the faces at the table.

The youngest man breathed in and held his coffee cup with both hands.

The room fell quiet.

The henchman pointed the remote control at the screen, pressed the buttons again and again, but it made no difference. All you could see was soundless, electric snow.

The Captain lowered his voice.

'And we need to pick up a Christmas present.'

The two youngest men said nothing.

The oldest man wiped the back of his hand across his mouth and sighed.

'Is that necessary?'

The Captain turned to him.

'What do you mean?'

'I just don't like it.'

The Captain placed his hand on his.

'Everything is politics, my friend.'

'I don't like it,' the oldest man said.

The Captain leaned closer.

'What colour are your eyes?'

The oldest man looked down and fell silent.

The Captain's voice went lower.

'It's best if you find one in Kopli.'

He put a photograph on the cloth between them.

The men said nothing.

The men bent closer.

'Who is it?' asked the man who said least.

The youngest breathed out in relief when the Captain smiled again.

'It's the doctor and his friend. From a very long time ago.'

The oldest man shook his head.

'It's not even in colour. What are we supposed to do with it?'

It was a fragment of a photograph, torn off a larger picture, a class photo, taken on the stage in what must have been a school hall: two pupils, boys, one seems shy, eyes downcast, the other spirited, self-confident, his face raised in an obstinate, almost mocking expression, and yet they have their arms around each other as friends do. At least it looks like that on this torn scrap of a class photo lying on the table in the cellar of Hotel W, in Tallinn. It is Thomas Hammer and Peter Wihl.

16

Kaia had to undergo the same tests as Peter.

She did not cry, but she was taciturn, reserved, evasive; she looked down, she looked elsewhere when, on December 14, a Wednesday morning, they drove to the clinic, Kaia in the front beside Helene, who was driving with caution on the slippery roads, Peter in the back. Light snow was falling, an uneven white shimmer that merged into the dark. They assured her that it was not dangerous, that it did not hurt, that she was not even ill, this was just something they had to do, to be on the safe side, and when they said this, to soothe her fears, with quasi-enthusiastic smiles, they could hear their words did not sound as they should, the way they were intended, more the opposite, the words made it worse. And they decided to talk about something else, about presents, what she wanted for Christmas, whatever she wanted she could ask for and she would get it, but Kaia had no Christmas wishes. She just shook her head, ashamed somehow, it seemed. Peter saw that when he tried to put his hand on her shoulder and she twisted away. She was ashamed, apparently ashamed that she had caused them worry, trouble, as if it were all her fault, and it was worse than that. Pain and fear are open sores; shame is a scar. And Peter realised that she had understood more than they had told her; their well-meant covert language had betrayed them, it had unravelled, word for word.

A Christmas tree stood illuminated in the middle of the small roundabout in front of the entrance.

Dr Hall received them.

They went up to the first floor, to the X-ray department.

Peter had never seen Kaia like this; vulnerable, exposed. When she raised her arms in the air and Helene helped her off with her vest, it was as though everything he saw he was seeing for the first and last time: her narrow back, her smooth skin interrupted by vertebrae, a soft ridge arching up to her thin, erect neck, before her hair cascaded down over her shoulders, which trembled for a second, an almost imperceptible movement, a twitch, gone before you could see what it was, and yet an earth tremor which had a devastating impact on the gamut of Peter's nerves. He had to look away, to avoid tears.

Blue light floated into the room as a nurse opened the door. Helene took Kaia by the hand and they followed her. The door slid to without a sound. The blue light covered the floor like a frozen pond. The time was twenty-five minutes past nine.

Peter sat down.

And he had this gnawing feeling, there was no other word for it, gnawing, everything converged in this one word, the gnawing spread through his body, and there was only one consolation: if Thomas Hammer could save Peter's eyesight, he could also save Kaia's.

But this consolation, this meagre, bitter consolation gnawed at Peter even more, for what was it that Thomas Hammer did not want him to know?

It was twelve o'clock.

Kristoffer Hall came in, folder in hand.

Peter rose as if he had been awoken, giddy from the sudden movement.

'How's she doing?'

'Just fine. She's brave and patient.'

Peter held the back of the chair and breathed out.

'Thank you.'

'Does she take after her father perhaps?'

'No, I wouldn't say so. She takes after her mother.'

Dr Hall took his arm.

'Let's sit down.'

'Thank you,' Peter repeated. 'Thank you.'

Dr Hall studied him.

'How are you doing, herr Wihl?'

'Me? I don't notice any difference. On the contrary. I might even say I can see better than ever. So, maybe I do notice a difference after all.'

Peter knew at once that he was talking too much, too quickly, he held his tongue, felt his molars crunch as he clenched his teeth, as though his mouth were full of dry sand.

'You haven't had any more attacks?' asked Dr Hall.

Peter shook his head and turned to him.

'Is it true that blueberries are good for your eyes?'

Dr Hall chuckled.

'Where have you heard that?'

'My mother used to say that. English pilots always ate blueberries before going on bombing raids in the Second World War.'

'Yes, that's an old story. Blueberries could well be good for your eyes.'

'So my mother was right?'

'And blueberries are very good for the digestion. They prevent diarrhoea. I would think that is important for a pilot, too.'

'Then I choose to believe my mother was right. The country was saved by blueberries.'

Dr Hall smiled.

'Have you consulted another doctor, herr Wihl?'

Peter checked his watch. Soon it would be half past twelve.

'Of course not.'

'Close your eyes, please.'

Peter closed his eyes and could feel Dr Hall pressing a finger against each eyelid, as Thomas Hammer had also done, harder and harder. It took a few seconds, then he stopped and Peter could see again. At first it was just a narrow strip of light, like looking through a keyhole, afterwards his field of vision widened, in fits and starts like an umbrella with broken ribs, and finally he saw, at last, that the blue pond on the floor had dried up.

'What was that about?' he asked.

'The eyeballs are hardening.'

'Hardening?'

'It's part of the process. When the optic nerves fail.'

Peter faced Dr Hall.

'I hope you use different language with my daughter.'

'Of course I do. I apologise if I unsettle or offend you.'

'I'm not talking about me, Doctor. I'm talking about my daughter. What do you say to her?'

'As little and as much as possible. If you understand me.'

'Do you have children of your own?'

'No.'

'Then I hope you know that children also hear what we don't say to them.'

Dr Hall produced a few pamphlets and brochures and gave them to Peter. It was information from the Institute for the Blind.

His voice was measured.

'And that's why complete openness is crucial when the time comes.'

On the front of the glossy brochure there was a picture of a family: a mother, a teenage boy and girl, a father and a dog, a golden retriever. They were out walking by a small lake in the forest, but the father was obviously blind, at any rate he was holding a white stick, and everyone was smiling, overblown smiles, as if the unpleasantness should be submerged in a tawdry idyll. It was cynical and nauseating, an advertisement for blindness, a subscription to the great darkness. Peter could not look at it. He put down the brochure, and said with indignation:

'If you think I'm going to get myself a guide dog, you're very much mistaken.'

Dr Hall gave him more papers. At the top was the name of a psychologist.

'As I said, you will face not only practical but also psychological challenges.'

Peter almost had to laugh.

'Practical challenges? You can say that again.'

'Especially psychological challenges,' Dr Hall reiterated. 'With a profession like yours.'

Peter cut him off.

'You don't have to explain that to me.'

'I am nevertheless obliged to mention it because it concerns, to a large degree, your family. I recommend that you also start going to therapy together.'

'We are used to coping.'

'But this time you will have to get used to a very different lifestyle.'

Peter turned to Dr Hall.

'Have you ever heard of Thomas Hammer? An ophthalmic surgeon.'

Dr Hall hesitated long enough for Peter to know that he had heard of Thomas Hammer and that what he had heard was not favourable.

'I know of him.'

'What do you know about him?'

Dr Hall struggled with himself.

'Sadly, in every profession there are black sheep.'

'Black sheep?'

Dr Hall observed Peter.

'If you've been thinking of going to this Thomas Hammer I would warn you against doing so in the strictest possible terms.'

'Why's that?'

'He was banned from the Norwegian Medical Association five years ago. I assume I need say no more.'

'Why was he banned?'

Dr Hall sighed and shrugged his shoulders.

'He was running a little practice tricking patients into thinking they had cataracts. Each operation earned him a fortune. Now the quack, excuse the word, finds it difficult to get permission to do the dusting in the casualty ward.'

'The quack?'

'I wouldn't even send my dog to Thomas Hammer. Why do you ask?'

'We were in the same class at school.'

Dr Hall scrutinised him and lunged forward with a menacing grimace on his pinched face:

'If you go to Thomas Hammer I can no longer take any responsibility for you as a patient, Peter Wihl. In other words, I am no longer your doctor. Have you been to see him?'

Peter remembered what Thomas Hammer had said, that Kristoffer Hall was usually right.

'He asked me to go to a class reunion,' Peter said.

'I beg you to keep this conversation between ourselves.'

'Of course.'

Dr Hall rose and proffered his hand.

'Read the material I gave you thoroughly,' he said.

Peter also got to his feet and shook his hand.

'When will the time come?' he asked.

'What do you mean?'

'You said complete openness was crucial when the time comes. When is that?'

Dr Hall released his hand.

'When we have received the results of your daughter's tests.'

17

Helene and Kaia were decorating the house.

They hung up the old mobile in the kitchen window. Helene was holding Kaia as she stood on a stepladder tying the thread on to a hook above the windowsill. The long thin spirals of silk with tiny bells soon began to move, to whirl, to quiver in a random yet fixed pattern, slowly spinning round and round although no one was nearby, the way the wind makes its presence known when snow falls off a branch.

Helene lifted Kaia down.

They stood watching the mobile.

Peter saw them from the garden.

They did not see him.

He was frozen.

Peter was carrying the pictures back into the studio. He scraped off the ice, the rime frost and the leaves. Nature is a terrible artist. Nature is a scrap dealer. The pictures were motionless. The clock above the door was motionless. He stood motionless. It was a state of emergency. It was a period of waiting. Kristoffer Hall had not rung yet. And he had not heard from Thomas Hammer, either. And once again Peter had to return to this word *gnawing*, it was gnawing at him, it was as if the word itself was tormented, it was at one with its meaning, and he thought – he had often thought this of late – that people do not get better with age, experience was no guarantee, you did not learn from your mistakes, you did not rise through the ranks, surely the opposite was the case, his best work lay behind him, he had given his best, he had scaled the heights, he would be fifty in three months and from then on things were sure to go downhill, unrelentingly downhill, all that was left was to paint and sink into mediocrity and obscurity, embarrassment and sentimentality, brown sauce. Would it not be better to give up, take the rest of his life off, be quite frank about it? His best work lay behind him, there you are, there it is, behind me, in the wake known as the past, overtaken, imperfectum, praeteritum, passed, yes, that was better, it was respectable, and yet he could not do it, he could not let go, could not stop trying to paint, because every time he dipped his brush in the paint and raised his hand he was a master, all-powerful and undisputed, a wild dispassionate dreamer, but as soon as the thin sticky marten hairs came near the canvas, near the sketch of Kaia, he was a fool again, everything dissolved between his fingers, vanished into thin air, into nothing, and that was when the next thought joined the queue, a chain reaction, cynical, logical and blasphemous, becoming blind would be a heroic way of concluding his career, such an end had depth, a touch of tragedy, and if furthermore he bore his fate with fortitude, with dignity and style, this darkness might cast a new, almost boundless light over the pictures he had succeeded in painting and so lend the virtuosity content, the technique humanity, his dead eyes would have a retrospective effect, as it were, and be seen in his amputated life's work, making it complete.

Peter bent over the sink and threw up.

When he straightened up he could hear the thin, restless tones of the mobile all the way to his studio.

Or was it just inside him, this sound, the sparks from his nerves, the echo of the darkness?

He no longer knew.

And when he ran his fingers along his temples he could feel the blood flowing just under the skin, he felt the intense, heavy throbbing and for a while he was afraid his head would not stand the pressure and simply crack open and everything would spill out in a deluge of brain matter, blood, fluid, mucus, eyes and tears until he was drained, empty, and the skin over his skull collapsed like a rubber mask and it was as though his vision was being constricted more and more, the shadows were pushing him from all sides into a narrow strip of light.

He could still see.

Mosaic artisans at the Vatican were capable of distinguishing between more than 30,000 different hues.

Peter turned his back on the pictures and painted the figures instead, the figures Kaia had been playing with; he painted half in warm colours and the rest in cold; that was all he could manage: warm and cold.

Then he fetched the axe, went to the clump of trees behind the studio and felled a spruce tree. It landed without a sound in the snow and he stood wreathed in green and white particles.

For a moment he thought he could see an animal disappearing through the trees, the shadow of an emaciated, starving animal that had ventured close to humans in search of food, household refuse, but there was nothing, just the wind and a branch being gently swayed. His vision expanded again, his visual angle, in elastic light, and he carried the tree down to the house.

They decorated that too, from star to base.

It was Christmas Eve.

Ben joined them, as usual, but on his own this time. His hair had begun to grow again and lay like a thick black lid over his scalp. He put the gilt walking stick, his winter walking stick, in the corner and lifted Kaia off the ground. She turned away, unable to look at him.

Ben attempted a laugh.

'Beautiful princess, I'm not that hideous!'

Kaia did not answer, she looked away, and Peter was stunned, but nevertheless proud, though for the most part stunned, by this resolute earnestness which they all shared, and how she nursed this earnestness, with such attention.

Dr Hall's words: when the time comes.

The time had not yet come.

Ben gently lowered Kaia and glanced at Helene, who just shook her head and put her finger to her mouth.

Peter gave him a glass of wine.

'Happy Christmas, old frog,' he said.

Again no one laughed.

They put their presents under the tree and went to the table in the kitchen as usual.

But nothing was as usual.

When on the rare occasion they said something, they did not say what they wanted to say; language took detours in a fragile conversation.

And between the words they could hear the thin, restless tones that did not finish and never stopped.

'How's it going at the theatre?' Ben asked.

Helene topped up his wine glass.

'The premiere has been postponed till February.'

'February? Well, I never.'

'The joiners are on strike again.'

'I thought old Ekdal was the problem,' Peter said.

Ben turned to him.

'What's the problem with old Ekdal? Prostate?'

Helene sighed.

'He wants to smoke a pipe on stage. As Ibsen wrote.'

Ben laughed out loud.

'Can't the idiot *pretend* to smoke?'

Peter passed round the dish.

'I said the same. Isn't that his bloody job? To act with such conviction that the audience thinks he's smoking? Even if he's sucking a stick.'

Helene helped herself.

'He probably won't remember his lines then. There's too much going on at once.'

Peter would not let go.

'When Hedvig shoots herself, we don't expect her to die, do we? We just expect her to make a good job of acting dead.'

Helene sent him an accusatory glance.

Peter went quiet and lowered his gaze.

Ben raised his glass.

'I think the theatre should invite the audience to the rehearsals.'

They toasted.

It was quiet again.

Except for the mobile in the window.

Peter was at cracking point, he could not stand the constant sounds, which were barely audible but relentless, like wind and ice, a piercing and false synaesthesia which filled the room with sharp, violet tones.

And then they saw that Kaia was sitting with her eyes shut. She was squeezing them, hard. And she must have been sitting there like that for quite some time because her thin eyelids were quivering. A deep furrow over her nose divided her wan forehead into two; her mouth was pinched, a mere line. She had dirtied the white cloth and hidden her hands under the table.

Peter breathed in, almost knocking over his glass, because for one second he could not recognise his daughter.

Helene leaned over to her.

'What are you doing, darling?'

Kaia did not answer.

'Are you tired?'

Kaia shook her head. Her face was knotted hard in concentration.

Helene caressed her cheek as though wanting to loosen it, to loosen the knot, open up her face.

She whispered:

'You have to open your eyes now. You mustn't sit like that.'

But Kaia just squeezed harder and bowed her head.

Helene turned to Peter. There was a kind of bewilderment in her eyes he had not seen before, and it scared him, just as much as Kaia's thin, quivering eyelids and her unfamiliar face. It scared the wits out of him and he didn't know what to do.

He tried to find Kaia's hand.

'Look at me,' he said.

But she refused to look at anyone.

'Look at me,' he repeated.

That did not help, either.

Kaia just knotted her face in a painful, stern grimace and shut them out.

Without making a sound, Ben put down his cutlery.

Peter looked at Helene.

Helene looked imploringly at Kaia.

And Kaia looked nowhere, inwards, downwards.

All they could hear was the mobile, a carousel propelled by a draught, heat, breath.

And now Helene could stand it no longer. She grabbed Kaia's arm, as though to shake her.

'Now stop playing around! Do you hear me?'

But Kaia became even more determined, fixed, and wrenched her arm away.

And then Peter could not stand it any more.

He got up, went over to the window and snatched down the mobile.

At that moment Kaia opened her eyes and looked at him.

'Sorry,' she said.

Her eyes were large and dry.

Peter stood by the window, with the thread, the bits of silk and the bells in his hand.

He tried to smile.

'Sorry? You don't need to apologise for anything.'

Kaia's mouth trembled.

'Sorry,' she repeated.

Peter let go of the mobile and it hit the floor without a sound.

'Why do you say that, Kaia?'

But she did not answer.

Helene, stroking the nape of her neck, smoothing it out, whispered:

'There's nothing to apologise for. It's we who should say sorry.'

Peter stood behind them. Everything was disintegrating, that was how it felt, he was destroying everything, and he did not know how to repair it, what had been broken, what he had destroyed. He was the one who should say sorry now.

Helene straightened Kaia's hairclip. Her forehead shone, smooth and white, as if she had a temperature.

'Do you hear me, pet? You have nothing to say sorry for.'

Kaia, bowing her head, whispered:

'You are both telling lies.'

Helene bent closer.

'What did you say?'

'You are both telling lies.'

'Lies about what, Kaia?'

Kaia pushed Helene away. Her voice was angry, obstinate. Peter looked down at them, and it felt as though the whole room was tilting: the remains of the mobile fell on to the ceiling, Kaia was rotating the room, she had turned it on its head with five words, from shame to accusation: *You are both telling lies.*

'About everything,' she said. 'You're both telling lies about everything.'

Helene had to hold her still.

'We're not lying.'

Kaia tried to shake herself free.

Helene looked up at Peter with the same bewilderment, the same panic.

Peter crouched down.

Kaia refused to look at either of them.

'We're not lying,' Peter said. 'Because we don't know anything yet.'

Kaia swivelled round abruptly to face him.

'You know.'

'What do I know, Kaia?'

And just as abruptly the knot in her face loosened, her features softened, became tired and soft. She put her hand next to his on the cloth, over the stain, and for a moment she resembled the child she had been.

'Don't you know?' she asked.

Then Ben stood up and was as loud as usual.

'I can't wait any longer! Let's open the presents now!'

They went into the living room. And as soon as Peter saw the shining tree, the glittering green tree he had cut down himself and carried into the house, as his father had done for him every single Christmas, he was reminded of his grandmother who thought the electric candles were real. She could not come to terms with the notion that the candles were not genuine, or perhaps she did not want to. That was why there was always a bucket of water beside the tree. She had demanded it whatever they said, in case of an accident, a fire. And once Peter had seen his grandmother; she must have thought she was alone – he had been hiding behind the door, as he often did – and she bent down to try to blow out the candles, the electric ones, again and again, this defiantly stubborn individual. She became more and more furious. Soon her face went blue from all the blowing, and then Peter crawled along the wall to the corner and pulled out the plug. The tree lights went out and his grandmother clapped her hands in triumph.

At that time, when he was a boy, a surprised spy with ready laughter, he was unsure whether she was play-acting – and if she was, perhaps she was doing it for him, which meant she also had to know that he was spying on her – or whether she was just very old and stupid.

But this evening, a Christmas Eve close on forty years later, in the same house, in the same room, he was again being plagued by this gnawing suspicion that was pursuing him, perhaps it was the gene he carried within him, the darkness, and which he might already have passed on to Kaia: Could Grandmother really not see the difference between a real and an electric candle?

They no longer kept a bucket of water beside the tree.

Peter began to hand out the presents.

Ben got an Italian straw hat; he laughed, tried it on and performed a deep bow.

Helene got a shawl and crampons to wear under her shoes She pretended to be offended.

'Am I that old? Am I?'

Peter got a dressing gown and a mobile phone.

Kaia got a watch.

Helene put it around her wrist and had to use the last hole, and still it was too loose. They had to make another hole with an awl in the new, slim, blue leather strap because she was so thin and when the watch was on Peter set the correct time – it was twenty to nine – but he was unable to work out whether she was happy, surprised or disappointed about this present. Her facial expression was neutral, or worse, indifferent, and it struck Peter that she might have thought she was going to get the portrait, the picture of herself, that that was what she had been expecting, and he was about to say something, that it was not finished yet, that it would soon be finished, soon, but he dropped the idea. And Peter was deeply ashamed when he gave her the last present, which was not a present at all, just the figures he had painted in nothing but cold and warm colours.

Kaia left them in the small box and thanked him, politely.

Peter thought: she was waiting for someone to say she was healthy and there was nothing the matter with her, but no one could say that yet.

Afterwards she sat in the chair by the fire and went to sleep.

Peter watched her head loll forwards, several times, until her body settled, and there was a kind of comfort in that: she was not indifferent, disappointed, neutral or angry; she was tired.

She was tired of being frightened.

And no one could console her.

Helene carried Kaia into the bedroom.

Peter and Ben went into the kitchen and did the washing-up. Peter washed, Ben dried, it was a ritual they had, a tradition, Peter and Ben took care of the washing-up, but this time Peter could sense some unease. Ben seemed uncomfortable, perhaps he thought it was a strain to be on his own with Peter the way things were. He even dropped a fork on the floor, picked it up with alacrity and continued to dry it. Peter said nothing, he felt like a drink, no, not one drink, he felt like several, this wonderfully impossible yearning, like an old sting that starts to itch. Instead, he drank a glass of water; he was like his grandmother, always keeping a bucket of water within reach in case of fire, you can never know.

Ben said, 'Time you got yourself a mobile phone.'

'Time? Do you think so?'

'Yes, I do. It's very handy.'

Peter laughed.

'Oh, I know. When I'm blind you can just ring and ask where I am.'

Ben opened the cognac, poured a generous portion into his glass and raised it. The dark, heavy aroma filled the room, then he paused.

'Does it bother you if I drink?' he asked.

Peter was furious.

'For fuck's sake, are you starting to be considerate too, now?'

'I was only asking, Peter.'

'You haven't asked before.'

'Apologies.'

'And it doesn't bother me. Drink. Drink, for Christ's sake!'

Ben drank and checked the doorway to see if Helene would be back soon.

Peter listened. He could not hear her singing to Kaia. Perhaps they had both fallen asleep.

'The straw hat suited you,' he said.

'Thanks. Made me think of *Death in Venice*.'

'You're talking about the film, I take it?'

'Yes. I'm afraid I haven't read Thomas Mann's short story.'

'What was the name of the Swedish boy who played Tadzio?'

Ben refilled his glass with cognac.

'Bjørn Andersen. Who can forget him?'

'Please don't talk so loud, Ben.'

Ben lowered his voice.

'An old chump like me would not forget blonde Tadzio, would he?'

They both chuckled at that.

Helene had still not returned.

Peter pulled out the plug and watched the dirty water, along with a film of grease and foam, slip down the drain, in a spiral, which became ever narrower and in the end was no bigger than a black coin, before it disappeared too, at an angle, down the drain where the leftovers had got stuck – a bone from the meat, a few stones from the prunes – and he thought: these movements, this pattern, they are the same as the forces that heavenly bodies are subject to, the sink is no more than a symbol of the universe, and at the same time, or as a consequence of this, another thought struck him: who the hell was God, then?

Ben hung the tea towels up to dry.

Peter said, 'There was something in the book that unfortunately did not appear in the film.'

Ben turned to him.

'Tell me more.'

'Mann writes something to the effect that readers would be deeply disappointed, or confused, if they got to hear where artists discovered the sources of their inspiration.'

'Why's that?'

'Because the sources are often banal, pathetic, dirty, sordid and random.'

Ben shook his head.

'But, I assume that a sunrise, a flower or a star may also provide inspiration, hmm?'

'I'm afraid those are the exceptions,' Peter sighed.

'And so?'

'And so? In all probability Mann considers it smartest to keep his cards close to his chest and let art do the talking.'

'That's true of most things in life, isn't it?'

'Your words.'

Ben put his hand on Peter's shoulder, and for a while they stood like this, without saying anything, until Ben said:

'The washing-up went fine after all.'

Peter nodded.

'Yes, almost like the old days.'

Ben looked around.

'And nothing broken as far as I can see.'

'Just a fork on the floor.'

Ben gave a tentative smile.

'How are you really, Peter?'

Helene was standing in the doorway – she might have been standing there for some time and have overheard parts of their conversation, the end at least. She interrupted them.

'He carries pictures into the garden and leaves them there for several days. As if that would help.'

They turned. Her face was pale; she was wearing the new shawl over her shoulders, black silk, perhaps that and the light from the ceiling emphasised the whiteness of her skin, making it seem like marble, particularly her forehead.

Peter attempted a laugh.

'Don't give away my secrets, Helene.'

Helene went closer and she was the one who was laughing.

'Do you know what the neighbours say? That screwy artist's up to his tricks again.'

Ben laughed, too. Ben laughed loudest of all.

'It gladdens my heart to hear that. I hope the frost didn't damage them.'

Peter interrupted them.

'Is Kaia asleep?'

Helene picked up the smashed mobile and put it in the bin.

They sat down at the kitchen table.

Ben poured a glass of cognac for Helene.

'Is Kaia asleep?' Peter repeated.

Helene looked at him.

'Have you said anything to her?'

Peter shook his head.

'Not yet.'

Helene said, 'I think she knows most of it, anyway.'

Peter took her hand in his.

'Whatever happens, sooner or later we'll have to tell Kaia the truth.'

Helene shook her head.

'Christ, how I loathe that word!'

Peter let go of her hand. Ben leaned over towards him.

'Did it help?'

'What?'

'Carrying the pictures into the garden.'

Peter looked down.

'It's brown sauce,' he said.

Ben guffawed.

'That good?'

'Yes, real brown sauce. Like looking at mire.'

Ben turned around and stared at the empty space on the wall over the table.

'Perhaps we should postpone the opening,' he said.

Peter got up.

'Postpone? What the hell do you mean by that? Postpone till when?'

'At some point we will have to make a decision, Peter.'

Helene put her arm around him.

'Ben's right,' she said.

Peter sat down. He was breathing heavily; he had to have water, more water.

'The decision's already been taken,' he whispered. 'The exhibition's opening as planned.'

Ben nodded, pointed to the bare wall, the faded square.

'What are you planning to hang there in its place?' he asked.

Peter smiled.

'In its place? I'm very happy with what's there now,' he said.

Ben glanced at him.

'Sorry? What do you mean?'

'Can't you see? Classic still life. All that's missing is a little skull near the light switch. Vanitas. Everything is a void.'

Helene brought her glass down hard on the tablecloth. Her cognac slopped over.

'At least give your self-pity a rest. It doesn't help anyone!'

Peter looked away.

'Sorry. It was just a joke.'

'A bloody awful joke!'

Ben, ill at ease, cleared his throat.

'What did Hall say?'

Helene sighed.

'We get the results of Kaia's tests some time after Christmas.'

Peter poured water into his glass.

'I'm going to hang Kaia's portrait there,' he said.

Ben looked at him again, smiling, as though meaning to say that there was some inspiration it was unnecessary to hide, the exception that shone with such power it overshadowed the rule.

'And what does our friend say about you?'

'He says we should go to therapists and psychologists and dog trainers and God knows what! To hell with him!'

Ben turned to Helene.

'But isn't that sensible?'

Peter interrupted them again.

'Going blind is quite enough to deal with on its own. Is that understood?'

At that moment the telephone rang.

Helene was up and off into the hall.

Peter and Ben sat listening, heard the ringing stop, Helene's low, tremulous voice as she said her name, then it was sharp, enraged. She slammed down the receiver.

She came back, sat down, out of breath, on the verge of tears.

'I thought it might have been Dr Hall,' she whispered.

Ben filled their glasses.

'Kristoffer doesn't ring on Christmas Eve,' he said.

Helene hid her face in her hands.

'My God, I was so frightened.'

'Who was it?' Peter asked.

Helene dropped her hands, lifted her glass and turned to him.

'It was that damned childhood friend of yours. Thomas.'

'Thomas? What did he want?'

'He just wanted to say "Happy Christmas". He was drunk.'

Peter went to see whether Kaia had woken up. She was sleeping with her face on her arm. The luminous watch face shone in the dark. Ten minutes past eleven. He could see that from where he was standing. The second hand slowly ticked round. He stood watching her. The model of the theatre, Helene's workplace, was on the windowsill. Then the telephone rang again.

This time Peter answered it.

'Happy Christmas,' Thomas Hammer said.

'What do you want?'

'Did you get something nice?'

'A mobile phone.'

Peter immediately regretted saying that, he did not quite know why, but he regretted it from the bottom of his heart, as if he had betrayed a secret and in doing so bound them closer together.

'Congratulations, old friend. Don't forget to charge it.'

Helene came out of the kitchen, looked at Peter – he just shook his head – and went over to him.

'Could you give him my regards and tell the idiot never to ring here again.'

She went on to the bathroom and slammed the door after her.

Thomas Hammer was impatient and drunk at the other end of the line.

'Are you there, Peter?'

'My wife sends her regards and says you are never to ring here again.'

'Yes, I heard.'

Thomas Hammer laughed.

'What do you want?' Peter repeated.

'I've got a present for you, too.'

'Have you?'

'It's arranged. The treatment has started, so to speak.'

'What do you mean?'

'We'll be travelling within two weeks.'

'Where?'

'Have you got a lot of candles at your house?'

'Candles? Why?'

'There are children in Estonia who need candles, Peter.'

Helene came back from the bathroom in her nightdress, her face exposed, defined, tiny wrinkles by her mouth and under her eyes, standing out like rifts in the pale skin. She sent him a quick glance, of resignation, irritation, and said:

'I'm going to bed now.'

Peter waited until she had gone.

'Estonia?'

'I'll give you more details soon. And don't forget the candles. That was all I wanted to say.'

'Thomas?'

'I'm still here.'

Peter whispered again.

'If this treatments works for me, can Kaia have it, too? My daughter, that is.'

'I see. Has she inherited her father's ill-starred eyesight?'

'We don't know yet. Can she?'

'If it works for you, it'll work for her.'

'Thank you.'

'No problem, Peter. Go to Helene now.'

Peter was on the point of slamming down the telephone.

Then Thomas Hammer's voice was back.

'Just one more thing, Peter.'

'Yes?'

'I had this old class photo of us, you know. Where we're standing in the hall. Do you remember it?'

'No.'

'It's a black-and-white photo.'

'So?'

'What colour are your eyes?'

Peter hesitated.

Finally he said, 'Blue.'

Thomas Hammer rang off first.

Peter stood with the receiver in his hand, the house was quiet, only the dialling tone, the engaged signal, could be heard. He put the receiver down beside the telephone and went into the kitchen.

Ben was still there. Peter sat down. With the bottle on the table between them.

'Do you miss it?' Ben asked.

'What?'

'Drinking.'

'No.'

Ben filled his glass, then drained it.

'Was that the pest from the old days?'

Peter nodded.

Ben got to his feet.

'Fortunately I have no pests from times gone by. Apart from you, of course.'

He laughed.

'I'm scared,' Peter said.

Ben placed his hands on Peter's shoulders.

'I know. We're all scared.'

Peter pointed to the tablecloth, to the dark stains where Kaia had been sitting.

'Do you know what I was thinking, Ben? I was thinking that that's why everything has gone wrong. Because of those stains. It's the stains' fault. And if we send the cloth to the cleaner's everything will be all right. That's a bloody stupid thought, isn't it?'

'Do you want me to stay?'

'You don't have to. Thanks.'

'Sure? I can sleep in the studio.'

Peter chuckled.

'It's impossible to sleep surrounded by brown sauce.'

Ben did not laugh.

'I have to ask you again, Peter. Will you be able to make the deadline?'

'I will.'

'What about pulling in a few old lithographs? Ones you haven't exhibited before.'

Peter did not answer; it was unworthy of an answer.

But Ben would not let go:

'Or a retrospect? No problem tracking down paintings in private ownership.'

Now Peter responded:

'I am not blind yet, or dead.'

'I'm serious, Peter.'

Peter straightened up with a start.

'Shall I ring for a taxi or show you the door?'

'Thank you, I prefer to go of my own accord, my friend.'

They both laughed. But it was not a laughing matter.

'Thank you for coming,' whispered Peter.

Ben bent down and planted a cursory kiss on his forehead.

'And it's exactly three months and fourteen days to the opening.'

Then he put on his new straw hat and walked out with his gilt stick, into the wintry night.

Peter remained in his chair. The bottle was on the table. There was still some left. He whipped off the cork. The aroma burst out, like an invisible black bouquet, and anaesthetised him for a second. That pleasure was over. That thirst was quenched. He put back the cork and headed for the studio. It was bitingly cold. He did not feel it. He rummaged through the drawers: old brushes he had not had the heart to throw away, notes, a review, boxes of matches, the gas mask, a postcard of Nicolaes de Staël's unfinished picture *The Concert*, knives, a faded watercolour, a Filofax and finally he found them: the pills. There was no expiry date on the label, only the day they were prescribed, ten years ago. They were for ever. He took two pills, washed them down with a glass of water, felt nothing, just a kind of calm he knew was a figment of his imagination, but that was fine, too.

Peter had to press his head against the mirror to be able to see his eyes in the dark.

They were blue.

He had no more Beckers' titanium white. Tubes squeezed flat lay strewn across the floor. There was no more Beckers' titanium white in the world.

Then he cut the canvasses out of their frames, tore them to pieces and shoved them into the wood burner, sprinkled white spirit over them, lit the fire, sat down and watched the strips of flax fibre folding up and relinquishing their hold on their own material, so to speak, as the colours dissolved in the flames, boiled and went up in black smoke.

It took several hours.

Afterwards, when it was over, still hot and dirty, on his face and hands, he stopped by the door, exhausted and at peace, beneath the clock where time stood still, and that was when the thought struck him, it was so sudden and obvious: he should not be at one with his time, in step with his time, he should withdraw from it, as far away as possible, that was what to do, so as not to be either ahead of or behind his time, nor out of step, for being out of step is just another discipline, but on the outside, somewhere else.

A simple, impossible insight: no such place existed.

But that was where he had to be.

And yet he could not escape this nagging thought: Would he finish on time?

In the end, everything was about time.

Peter remembered the words of another artist and he made them his own: You never finish a work of art, you forsake it.

Then he went back to the house. Kaia was sleeping in the same position. Ten minutes to five, it would soon be morning. A ripple ran through the curtains, and then they were still again. The model had fallen off the windowsill and lay in pieces on the floor; the walls, the floor, the ceiling were knocked flat. He left it where it was. He did not want to wake anyone. He got into bed beside Helene. She was awake. He caressed her bare shoulders with his hand. She kissed it and moved away, surprised.

'What have you been doing?' she whispered.
'Tidying up the studio.'
'You smell of burning.'
'I've made a new start.'
Helene went closer.
'You're always saying that.'
Peter shut his eyes.
'I had to take a pill,' he said.
Helene was quiet for a moment.
'Are you drinking again?'
'No.'
'Sure? Because I haven't got time to rush about and keep an eye on you now. I have a premiere around the corner. Do you remember?'
Peter gave a nod of the head.
Helene put her arms around him.
'Speak to me, Peter.'
'I'm going away for a while.'
'What do you mean?'
'I'm going to try a new treatment.'
'What kind of treatment?'
'I can't tell you.'
Helene took her arms away.
'Can't tell me? Why not?'
'Because I don't know what's involved.'
'And yet you're willing to try it?'
'I have nothing to lose, Helene.'
'What does Dr Hall say?'
Peter hesitated.
'He knows nothing about it. And he had better not find out. All right?'
Helene sat up in bed staring at him.
'Has this Thomas Hammer put you up to it?'
'That's irrelevant.'
'Has he?'
'He can offer me treatment which is not available in Norway, Helene.'
'And why can't Dr Hall offer it?'
Peter looked away. The draught made the curtains tremble; soon they would be still again.

'Perhaps Dr Hall hasn't got that far yet,' he said.
'And you believe that?'
'It can save my sight. Isn't that enough?'
'And you don't even know what kind of treatment it is?'
Peter said, 'I don't want to know.'
Helene just shook her head, got up and went into the corridor. Peter stayed in bed, he heard her stop outside Kaia's room, stand there for a while before going into the kitchen and opening the fridge. And he thought about what he had just said, that he didn't want to know. It was true, it was a lie, it was both, it was his double cowardice, it was the black dog baring its teeth once again, pulling at the leash, and he was the one who did not move, did not do anything, who just shut his eyes, a coward, yes, a fearless coward was what he was. At last she returned and sat down on the edge of the bed with a glass of water full of ice cubes clinking against each other.
'You've already made up your mind,' she said.
'I don't have any choice, Helene.'
'What you said was you had nothing to lose. That's not the same.'
Peter whispered, 'If the treatment works for me, it could also save Kaia.'
Helene interrupted him.
'I'm going with you, Peter.'
'That's no good.'
'No good? Why not?'
'Because I have to do this alone.'
Helene, helpless, snorted.
'You should have heard yourself just now,' she said.
'Do you perhaps imagine I don't? Do you perhaps imagine I don't hear myself all the time, do you?'
Helene looked away.
'When are you going?'
'Soon. Within a couple of weeks.'
'I don't like it,' she said.
'I need your support, Helene.'
'I've always supported you.'
Peter pulled her down and, reluctantly, she submitted.
'I'll do it for Kaia's sake. Do you understand? For Kaia's sake.'

Helene was quiet for a long time.

At length, she said:

'And if Kaia is fine? Who are you doing it for then?'

'Us, Helene. Us. Who else?'

She did not answer.

When it was already morning, they fell asleep.

Peter had time to dream, or perhaps it was another night he dreamt it, a dream that persisted and would not let go, and it's the light in the dream – a light that exists nowhere else apart from in this dream, as though the low, lustreless December sun is shining in May – that he remembers best and not the fat, pushy, well-dressed boy who asks him an impossible question in this same impossible light: If you could choose? If you could choose, Peter?

Then they were woken up.

Kaia was standing by their bed.

'The snow's black,' she said.

They sat up in bed.

Helene put out her hand.

'What's that, my love?'

Kaia stayed where she was.

'The snow's black,' she repeated.

Peter and Helene went over to the window, opened the curtains and looked out.

It was a clear day with a high sky, the moon still visible in the west.

A magpie was sitting on a branch, pecking at a rotten apple.

And spread across the garden, from the studio to the house, there was a fine layer of soot and ashes.

18

Beneath the base of the picture there is something else, which is also part of it and yet remains hidden, not the sullied sources of the inspiration, but the subject matter: two people will soon wake up, two children, they are only children, in the shed on the disused, tumbledown collective farm. The boy wakes first. He is freezing. The skin on their hands has cracked in the course of the night, forming deep fissures. There is snow in here, too. It is minus fifteen degrees. It is Christmas Eve. He turns to his sister. He lets her sleep a little longer. She is lying under a sheet of cardboard. She has tied plastic bags over her feet. It is his little sister. Her name is Samara. His name is Vova.

Vova and Samara.

He looks around him:

Rusty machinery, broken tools, a carcass, perhaps of an ox or a cow, skeletons, nothing to eat, nothing to drink, nothing to sniff. The cold is worse than hunger. The wind is worse than thirst. Sleeping is better than staying awake.

He puts snow in his mouth, chews the black snow.

Then he wakes her.

They have to go on.

They scramble over the snowdrifts behind the open door, which bangs again and again in the wind, and walk out over the grimy, lifeless fields. When they look back they can barely see the slanting cluster of abandoned buildings in the drifting bands of mist. It is still morning. It is still dark.

It is Christmas Eve.

They come to a road. They follow it. A bus drives past without stopping. A red star flashes in the rear window and is gone. Samara lags behind. Vova has to wait for her. He takes off his torn shoes. She can wear them instead. He ties the plastic bags around his bare, almost blue feet. They continue. They walk all day. Samara weeps quiet tears. Vova comforts her. They are going to Peeteli Church. He has heard it is open. He has heard they have beds there. He has even heard they also have presents there; other children they have met have told them: chocolate, boots and candles.

The sky turns white.

Vova holds his little sister's hand, or perhaps it is the other way round, Samara holding on tight to her big brother so that he doesn't leave her behind.

He does not leave her behind.

They follow the railway line for a while, a disused line between Tartu and Tallinn. A rail tricycle stands frozen to the rails. It is impossible to move. So they take the road again. They approach the town. They can see the outline, the surrounding outer walls, the cupolas, the cranes and the spires.

A cold, wet wind blows in from the sea.

Vova smiles.

He knows where Peeteli Church is.

It is just a question of heading for the tallest spire.

And that is where Vova and Samara go.

The streets are narrow and the cobbled stones slippery. There is an illuminated cross in the market square. It is already dark again.

It is Christmas Eve.

The sky over Tallinn is soon invisible.

They stop outside the broad door.

Vova knocks.

Samara hides behind him.

It takes them time to open up. Vova is close to losing heart. Perhaps everything he had heard was lies. And he has lied to his little sister too, and dragged her all this way for no reason.

Nonetheless, the door is then opened.

A nun appears in the doorway and looks down at them: her black headscarf is tied tightly around her head, her long white cloak flaps like a sail, her hands are small, almost pink, she smiles, but she does not step aside and let them into the church, into the warm, where they can hear music: an accordion, a flute. No, the nun just stands in front of them, and her smile is full of despair and resignation; it is the most frightening smile Vova has seen on anyone. And he shows her a photograph, a tattered photograph, almost ripped to pieces. He holds the picture in his hand and shows the nun, but she only shakes her head and starts to talk. It is full, they cannot come in, they do not have permission to let in any more, many before them have been turned away, there is too much suffering and not enough room, the nun says, before disappearing for a moment and returning with a bag which she gives to Vova. Happy Christmas children, go in peace, go to Kopli, the old transformer station, and ask there. And with tears in her eyes the nun shuts the heavy door of Peeteli Church.

Vova puts the photograph in his pocket and looks in the bag. At least it was true there were presents here: a cuddly animal, like a rabbit, a bar of green soap, a tallow candle with a black wick, chocolate in silver paper. He breaks off a piece and gives it to Samara; she is greedy and wants it all. He advises his sister to eat slowly, but she cannot and Vova has to hold her while she throws up into the snow.

Then they go on, to Kopli, the disused transformer station.

No one to ask there.

Vova takes Samara's hand and they walk into the building.

They cannot see anyone, but they can hear, faintly, a long way away, or very close, it is impossible to say, breathing, crying, sounds. They find a place in the dark where they can sit down, by a wall. Anything is better than nothing. In is better than out. A roof is better than the sky. A floor is better than the ground. The dark is better than the wind. Nothing is better than anything. And someone touches Vova's shoulder. He clenches his fist and swings; he hits nothing, just thin air. Someone laughs, brief reedy laughter, and straight after a bottle is thrust in his hand. He takes a hurried gulp, it is the sediment, a thick grainy spirit, and he can taste the bitter yet pleasant onset of intoxication, which is like sleep, but a different kind of sleep, not the sleep where you rest. And he pulls out the bar of soap. It gives off a strong smell in his hand, quite delicate, and he passes it round; he received something, so he will give in return; it is important to have friends and as few enemies as possible. And the smell goes from hand to hand, filling the old transformer station with perfume, a dirty perfume, and now it is converted, into song, as though the room is high tension once again. Someone begins to sing, a boy's deep voice in the dark, and the singing spreads, from mouth to mouth. Vova sings, Samara sings, there is a whole choir in the cold darkness. Then it is interrupted, the song finishes in mid-verse, everyone immediately seems to sense that something is going to happen, something good or something unpardonable: three men appear in the doorway, three shadows, one stays put, ill at ease, the other two come inside, towards them. There is total silence except for the sounds of their footsteps; they throw something on the floor, a sack, or a bin bag. A pile of things resembling parcels tumble out, but no one moves. One of the men comes even closer, continues slowly past them, stops, and stoops down again. The other man comes to where he is standing, switches on a torch; the men are invisible, those shining the torch are hidden, in the dark behind the bright light, and they see the emaciated girl sitting there, with her hands clutching a cuddly toy, and the filthy-looking boy beside her, who pulls her in to him. Vova's eyes are brown. Samara's eyes are blue.

19

Kaia's eyes were green.

Helene did not want to drive in the morning. They took a taxi instead. She sat in the front. Peter and Kaia sat in the back. She slept against his arm. There had been a sudden shift in the weather. It was mild, there was rain in the air, wind, a rare föhn, which like a monsoon, a sirocco, was not native to northern climes and was regarded in southern latitudes as the cause of madness, famine and divorce. The snow subsided and melted away, leaving ice, mess and mud. Flooding swept away bridges. Avalanches blocked roads. It was more like early spring, March, April. It was like no other season in the calendar. It was December 28. The results of Kaia's tests were ready.

The clock on the dashboard showed sixteen minutes past ten.

Peter, circumspect, leaned forward and whispered:

'What did his voice sound like?'

'His voice?'

'Yes, Dr Hall's voice. *You* spoke to him.'

'He asked us to go and see him, Peter.'

'Did it sound different?'

'I couldn't hear any difference. His voice was normal.'

'But if everything was fine, he could have told you on the phone, couldn't he?'

Helene glanced at Kaia. She was still asleep.

'I suppose he wanted to talk to us. Not on the telephone. Isn't that normal?'

'I don't know what normal is. Nothing is normal.'

'Let's wait and see, Peter.'

'I could ring him now.'

'Yes, go on, you do that. Ring him from the taxi.'

'I've got my phone with me. Which you gave me. I can ring him now and ask.'

Helene became impatient.

'Don't make me more nervous than I already am. All right?'

'Am I making you nervous?'

'Pull yourself together, Peter. Otherwise you can just get out here.'

'Dr Hall is making us nervous.'

Helene turned to him.

'Perhaps you think meeting him will be uncomfortable, do you?'

Peter forgot to whisper.

'If Kaia was fine he could have just told you, couldn't he!'

Helene, exasperated:

'Shh!'

Peter sat back.

The taxi driver switched on the radio. Long queues by Østre Bridge, an articulated lorry had overturned. That was of no concern to them, thought Peter. It would not delay them; it was the other side of town. A meteorologist said the wind, the fickle wind, could increase to gale force over the course of the day, possible storms in exposed areas. People were advised to stay at home. Peter thought: that was of no concern to them, either. Headlights, flickering, yellow, floated past and disappeared, an interminable swishing, far away, tyres on wet tarmac, rain, music, it was like a piano piece by Satie, the windscreen wipers were not in rhythm.

The driver lowered the volume.

Kaia woke up.

'Where are we?' she asked.

'On the way to see the doctor,' Peter said.

Helene craned her neck.

'Not long now, sweetheart.'

Kaia looked out of the side window. There was little to see. Raindrops flowing upwards, thick streaks, as if everything had been turned on its head. Everything *had* been turned on its head.

Who should console whom now?

Peter clung to the thought – his one fixed point in this shifting terrain – that everything he was doing, he was doing for Kaia's sake.

Kaia did not make mistakes.

She put her delicate, white hand between Peter's rough, stained palms.

They sat like that as they drew closer.

'It'll be fine,' he whispered. 'It'll be fine, Kaia.'

Soon afterwards they swung in through the gates and pulled

up in front of the clinic. Peter asked the driver to wait. A nurse accompanied them to Dr Hall's surgery. The doctor greeted Kaia first. She curtseyed. Peter tried to read his face. It was impossible. It was blank, neutral, could have been any face at all, it gave nothing away. Three chairs had been put out in readiness. Kaia was given the middle chair. Peter held her hand. She held his. The X-rays lay gleaming on the viewing box. One of them was crooked. Dr Hall meticulously pushed it into position, sat down, flicked through some papers and looked up.

'Kaia is in the clear,' he said.

Peter thought: Yes, she has inherited her mother's eyes.

Helene leaned forward and asked to hear it again, as if she were frightened she had misheard.

'Is that true?'

Dr Hall smiled.

'She has a clean bill of health. Isn't that right, Kaia?'

Kaia just stared at her lap and nodded.

Again and again Helene ran her hand through Kaia's hair.

'We knew that, sweetheart, didn't we? Everything's fine. Nothing wrong.'

Dr Hall switched off the viewing box. The darkness rose from the base, as when you fill an aquarium with water.

Helene straightened up.

Peter let go of Kaia's hand and looked at the clock. It was a quarter past eleven.

Dr Hall said, 'As you know, we have carried out the most detailed, thorough examination, and the conclusion is beyond doubt. There is nothing further to add. Kaia's sight is flawless. Do you understand what I'm saying, Kaia?'

Kaia nodded again.

Peter stood up.

'Why didn't you say that straight away?' he asked.

Dr Hall was taken aback.

'What?'

'Why didn't you say that when you rang this morning? That Kaia was fine?'

Unruffled, Dr Hall turned to Helene, who was looking up at Peter.

'Do you mind,' she said. 'Not now.'

But Peter did mind. Something inside him exploded. There

was an indignation that he had to vent. It was justified and he had to vent this indignation. He pointed to Dr Hall.

'For over an hour, to be precise one hour and twenty minutes, you have subjected us, not least Kaia, to unnecessary anxiety.'

'I apologise, herr Wihl, but –'

Peter interrupted him.

'Apologise? Was it your intention to torture us? Or didn't you think the time had come this morning?'

Dr Hall folded his hands under his chin. If he was ill at ease, he did not show it.

'We are not in the habit of giving diagnoses over the telephone.'

'Diagnoses? All you had to say was one single word. Fine. Fine! Fine is not a diagnosis!'

Then, out of the blue, Kaia asked:

'Will Daddy be fine, too?'

Everything went quiet for a moment.

Peter's indignation evaporated in an instant. And now it was he who was ill at ease. He placed a gentle hand on Kaia's trembling shoulders. Helene put an arm around her.

Dr Hall closed the folder he had in front of him and looked at them.

'That was in point of fact why I wanted to speak to all of you together.'

And he waited for a second before adding:

'Won't you take a seat, Peter?'

Peter did not move.

Dr Hall addressed Kaia again.

'So you know your father has an illness?'

Kaia continued to stare down at her lap.

'Yes,' she whispered.

Helene just shook her head.

And Peter sat down.

Dr Hall said, 'This illness is not dangerous, Kaia. He can live a perfectly normal life with it. The difference is that he won't be able to see.'

Peter could stand it no longer.

'Is this necessary?'

'What do you mean?'

'We have a taxi waiting.'

Dr Hall turned to Helene.

'What is happening to Peter affects all three of you.'

Helene nodded.

'We know.'

'And that's why it is crucial that you are as well prepared as is humanly possible.'

Peter repeated, 'Is this really necessary?'

Dr Hall looked at him.

'Yes, it is. It's my duty.'

'Is it your duty to place this burden on my family?'

'It is a burden which you will all have to carry.'

Kaia interrupted.

She said, 'Will we get a dog?'

Peter laughed. Everyone laughed. With her transparent innocence and childish honesty Kaia released them from the tension, but when Peter, relieved and grateful, bent down to kiss her, he was struck by the child's utter seriousness beneath the innocence. And he realised it was not expectation; it was fear which had made Kaia ask as she had. He was ashamed, he was deeply ashamed.

He said in a soft voice:

'No, Kaia, we will never have a dog.'

Afterwards, Dr Hall accompanied them down to the taxi. Kaia wanted to sit in the front seat. Helene helped her to put on the seat belt, but she could not do it up either and in the end the driver, a young and obviously very patient man, had to press the belt into the buckle between the seats.

By the steps, Dr Hall took Peter aside.

'You are under a great deal of pressure.'

'I'm glad Kaia is healthy.'

'I didn't like what I observed upstairs.'

Peter buttoned up his coat.

'We're getting wet,' he said.

'You're out of kilter.'

'It's over now.'

Peter wanted to go, but Dr Hall held him back.

'It's far from over, herr Wihl.'

Peter stopped.

'It strikes me that you have this nasty habit of alarming people instead of consoling them.'

Dr Hall took his hand away.

'I simply tell the truth.'

Peter smiled.

'That must be why,' he said.

Then he got into the back seat with Helene, and the car drove off.

Soon the clouds were drifting past, going in the opposite direction. Everything seemed to be happening at a different speed; the sky raced while they stood still. The low, dull sun blinded them for a moment and tinted the rain and oil on the tarmac blue, almost green. The stormy weather which had been predicted had not materialised; not yet.

Kaia kept tugging at her seat belt as they approached the town with its white suburban houses on the other side of the park, where the tall hedges between the gardens stood without foliage, unable to conceal anything.

The driver slowed down and leaned back.

'I think your daughter's going to be sick,' he said.

Hardly had they got Kaia's seat belt off and the door opened, than she knelt into the kerb and vomited. Peter saw some objects fall out of her coat pockets. He moved closer and picked them up. It was the figures he had painted in warm and cold colours. Then Kaia was better again. Helene wiped her face and mouth. Peter passed her the figures. He did not know what to say.

'Did you bring them with you?' he said.

Kaia looked away.

'They don't have anywhere to live.'

She put them back in her pockets.

Peter looked at Helene, who was crouching down beside her.

'Yes, they do.'

Kaia shook her head.

'Their house is ruined.'

A telephone rang.

The driver, who was waiting outside the car, leaned in and took the handset on the dashboard. It was not his. He pointed to Peter and laughed.

'It's yours,' he said.

It was Peter's mobile ringing. It was the first time it had rung and he was unused to these sounds. Helene stood up, holding

Kaia close to her, and looked at him. Peter moved away. It had stopped ringing. He took the phone from his coat and after some fumbling managed to press the right button. It was a text message: date, departure time, the name of a hotel, a sum of money. And finally: *Don't forget the candles. Delete this message.*

20

Flying time was one hour and forty-five minutes.

Peter had a window seat. Apart from clouds, mist, there was nothing else to see. He left the food untouched. He drank water. It was lukewarm. Then the plane dipped and sank. He checked that his seat belt was fastened, tightened it, and when he looked out of the window again, he caught sight of fields, dirty snow, scattered and abandoned huddles of houses, and further away, the coast, the sea, before the plane flew into another low bank of clouds, tilted, and the next time he looked out he only saw the sky, a deep and blue, almost black sky, he could not ever remember seeing such a sky, a colour that was boundless, and he was not thinking this was the last thing he would see, but whether it was the last thing he would remember seeing, the sky over Tallinn.

Then the plane landed.

Peter had only hand luggage. He was stopped at customs and taken into a cubicle, behind a curtain, where there was another man dressed in civilian clothes who proceeded to put on a pair of rubber gloves, and Peter feared the worst, but yet without fearing it, they could do what they wanted, it was no longer any concern of his. He had to take off his jacket and shoes, empty all his pockets and they examined every item in detail, those common objects which immediately become uncommon when laid out on the narrow steel table: the pencil, the bunch of keys, the watch, the mobile phone, some toothpicks from the plane, the box of pills. They opened it, smelt, studied the label, smiled and screwed the lid back on. Then they spent a long time flicking through his passport and finally they peered into the bag, rummaged through the few clothes he had brought with him, and Peter had this wonderfully strange feeling that everything was happening in reverse order, that events had started at the wrong end, and that when they gave him back his passport and bag he would have to board the plane again, fly home and it was all over.

They found something.

The man in civvies held a white candle in his hand and

showed the others, who had also found a candle, a purple advent candle, half burnt. Both smiled and turned to Peter. The one in civvies removed the thin rubber gloves and welcomed him to Tallinn. The other one replaced everything in the bag and wished him a happy New Year. Peter could go.

He hurried out. No one was waiting for him. The wind stung his face. He took a taxi to the hotel, checked in and enquired about Thomas Hammer. No one staying by that name, so he asked if there were any messages. There were no messages. He thanked them, was given the key and went up to his room on the second floor, locked the door and sat on the bed. It could have been anywhere, any hotel in any town: TV, minibar, a basket containing chocolate and nuts, a narrow writing desk under a mirror, otherwise bare yellow walls. He had a look at the bathroom: shower, green curtain, small bottles of shampoo on the washstand, plastic beaker and a bar of soap. He had a pee, flushed, washed his hands, went back and opened the minibar: three shelves of spirits. He found a bottle of water, unscrewed the top, swallowed two pills, held his breath for a couple of seconds, switched on his mobile phone – no messages there either – and rang home.

Helene answered at once.

'Just me,' Peter said.

'How's it going?'

'Haven't heard anything yet.'

'Perhaps he's tricked you.'

'Is that what you're hoping?'

Helene was quiet.

Peter stood at the window, peering out between the curtains. On the corner, directly below, there was a cinema. He could see the poster in a display case by the entrance: *Girl with a Pearl Earring.* A dog ran across the cobblestones in the middle of the deserted street.

He told her.

'*Girl with a Pearl Earring* is on here. The one about Vermeer.'

'Are you thinking of going to the cinema?'

'We can see it when I come home.'

'Actually I have enough on my mind, Peter. The rehearsals

are chaotic, Kaia is difficult, it's New Year's Eve and my husband is in Estonia.'

'We can rent it and all see it.'

Helene lost patience.

'What shall I say to Ben this evening?'

Peter let the curtains fall back into position.

'Tell him I needed a bit of time to myself.'

'And do you really think he'll fall for that nonsense?'

'You don't have to say anything, Helene.'

'Are you asking me to lie to our best friend as well?'

Peter sat back down on the bed.

'What's Kaia doing?'

'She's already gone to bed.'

'Don't wake her.'

'You didn't answer, Peter. Shall I lie to Ben, too?'

'Do you remember what you said on Christmas Eve?'

'We said a lot on Christmas Eve.'

'You said you couldn't stand the word *truth*.'

'That doesn't mean I like lies.'

'No one's lying, Helene.'

'What do you call it then?'

And Peter said what he usually said when things got tough and the world became unmanageable and awkward.

'It's only theatre, isn't it?'

And he immediately heard how hollow and false it sounded. That line no longer worked. It was out of place. It was untrue. The words left an unpleasant taste.

Helene's voice, tired as well as sharp:

'Have you been taking those pills?'

'I love you.'

'You didn't answer my question, Peter.'

'Yes, Helene, I did.'

There was a knock at the door.

No more was said.

Peter went to open up. It was Thomas Hammer. He slipped in and stood between the bathroom and the bed. Peter shut the door and turned to him.

'Hungry?' asked Thomas Hammer.

'No.'

'Good. You mustn't eat anything for the next twelve hours.'

'What's going to happen?'

'You're going to the workshop to have a few rusty parts changed.'

Peter took a step closer.

'Tell me properly, for fuck's sake.'

Thomas Hammer checked his watch.

'The operation takes place tomorrow, at ten o'clock sharp.'

'Where?'

'At a hospital out of town.'

'What kind of hospital?'

'Before, it was a military hospital. Now it's private.'

'How long will the operation take?'

'Usually a couple of hours. Then you'll have to be under observation for a couple of days before you travel home again.'

'And you'll be operating on me?'

'Of course, Peter.'

Thomas Hammer put his hand on his shoulder.

'If there's anything else you want to ask about, do it now.'

Peter vacillated. They stood without speaking for a few seconds, facing each other. Some music drifted in from the streets, soon it died away too, all they could hear was the inner workings of the hotel, the generators, the lift, the ventilation system, a metallic pulse which after a while you do not hear either, because these sounds merge with the noises of your own body and become part of the guests' headache, heartbeat and sleeplessness.

Peter took a drink of water, closed his eyes and asked:

'Will anyone suffer as a result of this?'

Thomas Hammer laughed.

'You get a full anaesthetic and I get full payment.'

'Answer me, Thomas.'

Thomas Hammer sat down on the bed, keeping his coat and gloves on.

'What does it matter actually?'

'It matters.'

'You're here, Peter. You've already made up your mind. It no longer matters.'

'You didn't answer, Thomas.'

'Can I have a little water?'

Peter gave him the bottle. Thomas Hammer drank. Then he smiled as if something had occurred to him and said:

'Don't you use an *écorché* at the academy?'

'Yes, in drawing lessons. Why?'

'Actually it means *skinned*, doesn't it? *Écorché*. We used it too. When we had anatomy. But we called it the muscle man.'

'Muscle man?'

'In the old days executed prisoners were used in our studies. They were skinned and laid on the table in the autopsy rooms so that students could familiarise themselves with the splendours of the human body.'

Peter, weary of this chatter:

'Fortunately that time is past.'

'But wasn't it a wonderful thought that even the lowest and basest could be of some use?'

'What are you trying to say?'

Thomas Hammer looked up.

'I'm a kind of artist, too, Peter. Just like you.'

'Just like me?'

'Yes, we make minor amendments to reality, don't we? And to make progress we have to experiment a little. Isn't that so?'

Peter went to the window and drew the curtains tighter.

'You didn't answer my question,' he said.

Thomas Hammer lobbed the empty bottle in the basket under the desk.

'The sum total of suffering will decrease. Is that answer good enough?'

Then he got to his feet again, buttoned his coat and lit a cigarette.

'Did you remember the candles by the way?'

Peter pointed to the bag.

'Bring it with you,' Thomas Hammer said.

'Where are we going?'

'The children will be pleased, Peter.'

They took the lift down.

It was already dark, but there was almost no one on the streets. A few youths sat drinking beer on some steps, sheltering from the wind. One of them shouted something. Thomas Hammer threw the packet of cigarettes to them. The cobblestones were slippery. The wind gusted round the corners. It was raining. They walked across the town hall square, Peter a few paces behind Thomas Hammer. A stage had been rigged up.

Eight musicians, all wearing folk costumes, were doing sound-tests. A microphone blew over, letting out an electric wail which drowned the wind for some minutes. It crossed Peter's mind that the same stormy weather had now moved here. He had been following the storms or they had been following him. Then the streets became narrower. They passed a church and arrived at the other side of the town. Thomas Hammer came to a halt in front of a massive building. It was like a mausoleum, an unlovely architectural commemoration of communism. It was the old transformer station, blacked out, disconnected, out of service. They went in. Inside it was even darker. Peter could hear sounds, faint, as though the cold, damp hall was full of animals crawling around. Thomas Hammer took a candle from Peter's bag, lit it and held it forth in the darkness. A face appeared, in the restless yellow glow, a child's face. Then the candle was handed round, another face stepped forward in the dark, another child, they lit more candles, the flame went from hand to hand, like a fire spreading, and in the end they could all be seen sitting alongside the walls, each with their own candle, a tallow candle. Now Peter could see them, their emaciated faces, the ancient faces of children, blinded and begging.

'Who are they?' Peter whispered.

'Whoever you want,' Thomas Hammer answered.

One of them stood up, raised the candle and waved. Peter went closer. It was a boy, barely fourteen years old, maybe younger, it was impossible to say. In his other hand he held a soft toy, a teddy bear, with two loose shiny buttons above the nose; they looked like buttons off a uniform. The boy dropped it. Peter wanted to bend down to pick it up, but instead the boy took hold of his arm and showed him a photograph, a tattered photograph, in the light of the restless flame that made the ragged picture glint: a young woman with her arms around a young girl standing in front of her, probably her daughter. The girl is smiling, her face is thin, lively, her hair dark, reaching down to her shoulders; she is looking in front of her, with open, undaunted eyes, radiant blue; the sun casts jagged shadows. In the background there is a glimpse of a Ferris wheel. The picture must have been taken at a funfair, or an amusement park. The boy pointed to the girl, to the girl's smiling, innocent face while interminably repeating a name. Samara it sounded like, Samara. Peter just shook his head and retreated. But the boy pushed closer and would not stop saying this name. Peter tried to get away. The boy would not let go. The boy clung to Peter and wanted to give him the photograph. Peter refused to accept it. In the end, he had to shove the boy away, kick, punch him, and the boy stumbled against the wall, lost the candle, which went out in the dark and fell on to the floor in the empty space beside him.

Peter, breathless, ran over to Thomas Hammer and whispered:

'I want to go back to the hotel.'

Thomas Hammer pointed to the candles.

'Can you see how little it takes to make them happy?'

'For fuck's sake, I want to go back to the hotel.'

'We have a car waiting,' Thomas Hammer said.

They left. A driver opened the door for them. They sat at the back and were driven through the town, which was full of people now, on the pavements and in the streets, hordes coming towards them, full of life, drunk. The car inched its way forward, two girls sat on the bonnet and stayed for some distance, already drinking champagne, laughing. They seemed so carefree, almost weightless, sitting on the bonnet; the driver beeped several times, the girls pouted at him and jumped off. The driver turned, sent Peter a look with an apologetic, almost embarrassed smile, but then Peter discovered that the man was simply like that. A deep scar from one corner of the mouth pulled his lips upwards and gave him this crooked smile, as if it had been tacked to his cheek, because in his eyes there was no apology or embarrassment, just contempt, coldness, and Peter looked away.

They pulled up in front of the hotel.

Thomas Hammer followed Peter out.

They stood in the stream of loud, excited people pushing past.

'Do you need any company?' asked Thomas Hammer.

'No, thank you.'

'Anything else you need?'

Peter shook his head.

'Where are you going now?'

'To get everything ready for you, Peter.'

Thomas Hammer got back into the car.

Peter went up to his room.

He was standing by the window when the first rockets exploded between the church spires, making white circles and spraying a myriad of colours over the town.

The wind had dropped.

Then the whole sky was torn apart in a crackle of patterns and shapes.

But he was unable to get the girl's face in the photograph out of his mind.

Samara. That was what the boy had called her: Samara.

Peter knew what he was going to do soon.

He could see it in his hands.

He could taste it on his palate.

The pills flowed like dust in his blood, but it no longer mattered, he had made the decision.

The poison that was meant to protect him had to be put aside to make way for more poison.

Poison against poison.

He took the fruit knife into the bathroom, cut off a piece of the soap, put it in his mouth and swallowed it. He did it again. Then he knelt by the toilet bowl and spewed up. Afterwards he sat in front of the minibar, opened the door and started on the top shelf, from the left, Chivas Regal, Beefeaters gin, vodka. He drank systematically. He wanted to work his way down. Brief flashes of fireworks lit the room as the sounds receded and died. The sounds in the hotel receded. All the sounds receded except for his heart hammering away in a wild, unsteady rhythm. He could see his heart beating. It was pounding him to pieces. He drank more. It did not help. His blood raced through him. His hands became swollen. The skin around his head tightened. His fingers fused and he lost his grip. He went to the bathroom and was sick again. The vomit was blue. Poison cannot withstand other poisons. Looking into the mirror, he saw a different man. The face was suffused with red. He was a stranger. He did not belong here. He went on drinking. It did not help. The hotel receded. The room receded. His heart receded. Six bottles of VSOP and two of Bacardi were on the lowest shelf. He drank until there was nothing left. He drank until he receded. He was out of function. He had receded. But it did not help. It did not recede: the girl's face in the tattered photograph.

They fetched Peter Wihl the next morning and drove him to the hospital outside town.

21

Peter sat in the taxi looking down at the house.

He saw no one in the windows. No one saw him.

Smoke rose from the chimney, a vertical, grey column. It calmed him down. Helene had lit the fire.

A story she often used to tell went like this: when a colleague, a famous, eccentric and ageing scenographer died a few years ago, all his personal possessions went under the hammer at an auction run by the town's most distinguished art dealer. His home was already well known to most, having featured in periodicals, magazines and newspapers; its opulence was unparalleled both in Norway and beyond, and there had been programmes about this unique stage-like property on TV. In a time noted for its disunity and arbitrariness, as he put it, his goal and rule of thumb, his religion as it were, had been to create harmony and beauty. He was dubbed colourful and a bon viveur. His motto, which he repeated ad infinitum, was that you create the path as you go along. As mentioned before, he died. He had no heirs, no family, just debts, it would also transpire. And his beautiful home, his stage, now in darkness, was split up and portioned off and sold bit by bit to the highest bidders. The catalogue of his effects alone ran to two hundred pages. Helene went to the art dealer's public viewing. There was hardly room to stand. Everyone wanted to see the famous man's even more famous home. But this home no longer existed. It had been taken apart. The objects he had collected over a long lifetime were displayed over three floors, numbered in random order: Persian carpets, stuffed birds, candelabra, the double bed, an Olivetti typewriter, a grand piano, butterflies, a photograph of Matisse, a Baroque mirror, Japanese embroidery and Moroccan lamps. You could even bid for his gilt walking stick, hat and white suit. Helene found being there difficult. It was as though the individual items had lost their lustre, she used to say. Torn from their natural environment, detached and transported, they became frail, forlorn, common. If his life had been a stage, his death was a flea market.

Sitting in the taxi and staring at the quiet house where he

had grown up and lived the whole of his life, apart from the autumn and winter when he was away at sea and the two years he lived in a bedsit before his parents died in the accident, Peter wondered what had made him think about this story which, furthermore, he loathed. He had not been thinking. He had just been letting his mind wander and stumbled over this story. At any event, these thoughts served to postpone the inevitable. He needed time. He was at home. He was relieved. He was frightened. Now he could not sit there any longer. He put on his dark glasses, which had side protectors, paid the driver and began to walk down to the house, this path he had walked so many times, between the gate and the door, the door and the gate. Black frost, no wind, January, the New Year, the remains of a rocket on the bench, probably let off by the neighbours, drawn curtains in the studio, in three months he would be fifty. He could have found his way in the dark. He smiled, a flitting smile, it hurt, he was not walking in the dark, he could see, through the dark glasses which cast a soft shadow over everything he saw, and he saw Helene coming out on to the steps and behind her Kaia, and Peter had only seen Helene's face like this once before. She stepped to the side to make way, or to avoid him; he didn't know and did not want to know, either. He dropped the bag and lifted Kaia in the air and she pressed her forehead against his shoulder. Was he able to cry? He hadn't asked about that. He did not cry. He held his arms around Kaia, her forehead against his shoulder, embarrassed or timid, he was not sure; he put her down again. Helene took his bag, surprised at how light it was, and they went indoors. Peter put his scarf on the shelf and hung his coat on the stand. The Christmas tree had been taken out. He saw a few spruce needles on the carpet, green tinder; he picked them up. He felt a wall of heat. Kaia stood by the fire, with her back to them. Peter followed Helene into the kitchen. She turned to him.

'Can't you take them off indoors?'

'What?'

'The sunglasses.'

Peter contemplated the bare, faded gap above the table, and this void filled him with a terrible impatience.

'No,' he said.

'Not even if I switch off the light?'

'I need to wear them.'
'For how long?'
'A bit.'
'Does it hurt?'
Peter shook his head and threw the spruce needles in the litter bin. They stuck to his skin and he had to shake them off.
'I don't feel anything.'
'Nothing?'
Peter turned on the tap and rinsed his fingers.
'It stings a little.'
Helene went closer.
Peter was uncomfortable.
'What is it?'
She breathed in sharply:
'You've been drinking again, haven't you?'
Peter found a towel and dried his hands.
'I missed you on New Year's Eve.'
'We missed you, too.'
Helene caressed his face and he leaned his forehead against her shoulder, as Kaia had done.
'It's over now, Helene. I'm back home.'
She whispered, 'What happened to you in Estonia, Peter?'
Kaia stood in the doorway, behind Helene, and the moment Peter caught sight of her, she turned away, faced the window.
'Are we going to eat soon?' she said.
Peter released Helene, relieved, relieved at the normality of these words, which said no more than the meaning they carried, these words were sufficient in themselves, this question *Are we going to eat soon*? had an answer, and it was as though a secret dream was realised in these few seconds, a dream he had never dared or wanted to acknowledge, his bourgeois dream, the magnificent grey dream that embedded him in normal life, it was his father's foreshortened dream.
But then he realised that not even Kaia's question was unambiguous and normal, for now he saw she had already put on her pyjamas.
'Are you hungry?' he asked, even so.
Still facing the window, she shook her head.
'I want to go to bed.'
Peter, confused and persistent, went over to her.

'Go to bed? You just asked if we were going to eat soon.'

Kaia ran into her room.

Helene raised her hand to Peter in an admonitory or perhaps an apologetic gesture before following her.

Peter stood there, bewildered, he could hear Helene talking, soothing, singing, and her voice became quieter and quieter until it too disappeared in the great silence of the house.

Then he fetched his bag. He had nothing with him except for the pills. He had thrown everything else away; the shirt, the shoes he had been wearing and the underwear. He wanted nothing left from Estonia on him. He had even thrown away the mobile phone. The bag smelt of tallow. The only thing he wanted to do was forget. He wanted to forget the smell of tallow. He threw away the bag, too. He wanted to forget the smell of soap. He wanted to forget Estonia. He wanted to forget the three black days there, about which he remembered nothing until he came round from the drink and the anaesthetic in a green room in the old military hospital. It wasn't long before Helene was back.

'You'll have to say goodnight to her,' she said.

Peter went in to Kaia and sat on the edge of her bed. She lay with her face to the wall and did not make a movement. She might have been asleep. Peter didn't know. She should be allowed to sleep. Carefully, he tucked the duvet over her shoulders, stood up without a word, switched off the light and left the door ajar.

Helene was standing outside.

'You scare her,' she whispered.

'Scare her? What do you mean?'

'The glasses. You frighten her.'

Kaia still had her back to him. Peter sat down again, without switching on the light. He was not sure if she was asleep. Perhaps she was awake. He started speaking.

'Do you know what I did in Estonia, Kaia?'

Peter hesitated for a moment. His mouth was dry. These words did not come easily. He had to say them.

Helene was still standing by the door.

'I went to the workshop for repairs.'

Kaia did not say anything, nor did she stir.

'And now I'm just fine,' Peter whispered.

He put his hand on Kaia's arm and could feel her heart beating, racing, it could have been his own, intertwined with hers, perhaps she was sleeping after all, but then she slowly turned. Her face was tranquil, her eyes still closed, her mouth shaped in a little smile and he let her lie like that.

In the same soft voice, he said:

'This is our little secret, isn't it, Kaia?'

And he stole a glance towards the door.

'Isn't it, Helene?'

Afterwards, Peter went up to the studio. The weather had turned cold in the days it had stood empty. He was freezing. He did not have time to light the stove. He would have to freeze. It was unimportant. It would do him good to freeze. The unused canvas stretchers lay on the floor. He stood them against the walls: twelve stretchers, twelve square holes; he was back where he always began, at square one. But this time he was not frightened. There was a lure. And the pull was so great that everything else within him was submerged. He wanted to go up to the surface. Where he could breathe. It did not fill him with pleasure, but with impatience, as if the pictures he had within him, the pictures he could see in his mind and which did not yet exist were so fragile that he would lose them, too, if he were not quick enough. And he thought, for a moment he thought: it was all worth it. Then he heard someone coming. He put the glasses back on. It was Helene. She stood outside the doors. He could see her shadow, restless. He went over and slid them open.

She said, 'I just want to help you.'

Peter let her in and shut the doors.

'You can help me stretch the canvasses.'

Helene shivered.

'It's colder in here than outside,' she whispered.

'You'll get used to it.'

Peter placed his smock over her shoulders.

She laughed. The breath issued forth from her mouth.

'Thanks.'

'If you're cold, you shouldn't stay here.'

She stared at him.

'Shall we start?'

They stretched the canvasses, twelve of them, one after the

other, fixed them first on to the cross in the middle and tightened them from the sides until there was not a single dimple; they had not done this together for a long time, worked together, and they worked well. It was an old habit they almost believed they had forgotten, and yet they remembered as soon as they started, as soon as they touched the materials again; their hands had a better memory than they did.

Peter was reminded of the rules prescribed by old masters. There should be as few hindrances between the hand and the canvas as possible; between the idea, the hand and the canvas. The first commandment of any artist was to clear the way.

'Shouldn't you ask Hall to have a look at you, too?' Helene said.

Peter wheeled round.

'Has he rung?'

'No.'

'Have you talked to him?'

'No, Peter. Not since we were there with Kaia.'

Helene turned on the tap and washed her hands.

Peter put the tubes on the table.

'Did you have a nice New Year's Eve?' he asked.

'You know I don't like fireworks.'

'What did you tell Ben?'

'I told it like it was, Peter.'

'Like it was? What did you say, Helene?'

'That you were in Estonia. Wasn't that what we agreed?'

'Did he ask any questions?'

Helene dried her hands on a dirty towel, slowly, with care; then she went over to Peter, quickly, as though she did not want to have any more time to think, and thrust him against the wall.

'What is it we're supposed to be hiding, Peter?'

Peter stayed there, against the wall, bent double; he had to draw breath, he had to collect himself and he did not know what to say.

Helene, impatient, waited. She repeated:

'What is it we're supposed to be hiding?'

Peter looked up.

'I visited some children,' he began.

'Yes?'

'In a disused transformer station. On New Year's Eve.'

Helene, baffled:

'Why did you do that?'

'We lit candles for them.'

Helene had a sudden change of heart. She raised her hands to her face and cut him off.

'I don't want to hear.'

'We lit candles for them, Helene.'

'I don't want to hear! Do you hear me?'

Peter tried to hold her, but she pulled away and threw his smock over the chair. Something fell out of the pocket. She picked it up and walked back to him. It was Thomas Hammer's business card. Peter ripped it into pieces and scattered them on to the floor.

Helene said, 'Have you got rid of him now?'

Peter looked at her:

'Do you know what I was thinking when you were standing on the doorstep today?'

She shook her head.

'I no longer know what you think.'

He tried to smile.

'You looked exactly as you did the time you found me.'

'I didn't find you.'

'Yes, you did, you found me, Helene.'

She leaned against his shoulder and whispered:

'And we don't want to lose you again, Peter.'

Peter could have cried. He did not.

22

Peter was working.

Kaia was sitting in his studio, silent, patient, her face averted, a semi-profile pose; she was staring at a point above the door, at the stopped clock. Peter worked fast. He was not taking his time. Now that he had time, he was not taking it. He did not begin with detail. He began from the other end, from the whole. No monochrome surface this time, no anatomical section, no lines, only colours that met, clashed and merged into a new light, for what else is the line if not the intimate contact of two colours? He painted with carefree abandon and yet determined fury. If the conception of pictures can take months, years, a succession of years and constitutes the invisible period, the birth is different. When the picture emerges, it is in motion. He was inside a bow, a taut bow, and not a triangle. See, don't think; don't think, see. He painted *alle prima;* he knew what he was going to paint and that was all he knew.

Every day Kaia sat with him, silent and patient, while Helene was at the theatre. It was not long to the premiere now.

One morning they heard a scream, a shriek. Peter went to the doors and peered between the curtains. Just below the gate Ben lay struggling on the ground. He was trying to get to his feet. He seemed to be trying to climb the gilt stick he had armed himself with again, but it must also have got a knock in the fall. It snapped and he slipped back down and fell badly, this time on to his back. Kaia also wanted to see. She went to Peter's side. They stood watching Ben, the helpless old man who had lost all his agility and elegance, all his style and dignity, in this simple fall on a patch of ice.

Peter did not move.

In the end Kaia tugged his coat and pointed, wanting to draw his attention to Ben, who at this point was on his back, beating the ground with half of the stick and shouting for help. Soon he did not even have the energy to do that.

'Do you remember our little secret, Kaia?'

She nodded.

Then Peter opened the doors and went out. Ben was furious

when he caught sight of him and his voice rose to a near scream.

'For fuck's sake, don't you put any sand down here?'

Peter looked down at him.

'We stay on our feet, old man.'

'I can sue you! I will sue you!'

'There doesn't seem to be anything the matter with you.'

Ben lay still for a moment, looking up at Peter.

'Why didn't you come and help me straight away?'

'I didn't see you, Ben.'

'You didn't see me?'

'I was working.'

'I saw you behind the curtains! Have you already gone blind?'

'You're disturbing me.'

Peter began to walk towards the studio again. He could make out Kaia, behind the curtains. She was standing there, motionless.

Ben shouted, his voice quivering.

'What the hell's up with you?'

Peter waited for a few more seconds before stopping and turning.

'Do you want some help or can you manage?'

Ben, meekly:

'Help me.'

Peter went back, grabbed him under the arms, lifted up the thin, stiff-limbed, cursing man and lugged him to the studio. Kaia had sat down on the chair, staring in the same direction, at the clock above the door. Ben softened and kissed her on the forehead.

'So this is where you are, little princess.'

Kaia gave an imperceptible nod.

Peter was about to close the doors. Ben put his hand in the gap.

'I must have dropped my keys when I fell. Could you find them for me, Kaia?'

Kaia jumped down off the chair and ran out.

Peter drew the curtains.

Ben stood looking around, for a long time, before commenting:

'Good to see you in uniform again, Peter.'

'I'm working. You're disturbing me.'

'Has Hall asked you to wear sunglasses?'

'They're comfortable, Ben.'

'But it's not very comfortable to talk to you when you're wearing them.'

'Then you'd better stop talking to me or go,' Peter said.

Ben did not go. He stood quietly observing the canvasses for a while, with his back to Peter. He said nothing about what he saw. He said:

'Journalists have started pestering, Peter.'

'Let them pester.'

'Especially after you gave him-whose-name-I-will-not-utter a well-deserved clout.'

Peter laughed.

'A clout? I knocked him to the ground, Ben. My knuckles are still sore.'

'Good. Especially since you punched him-whose-name-I-will-not-utter, the journalists have been pestering.'

'Do you mean Patrick?'

Ben, impatient, irritable:

'You haven't punched so many people that you're beginning to get confused, have you?'

'I don't talk to anyone before an exhibition.'

'You need publicity, Peter.'

'I need peace and quiet to work.'

Ben thrust his hands in his pockets and took a deep breath.

'I thought perhaps, and don't take this amiss, dear Peter, that we should let it be known, if you get my meaning, to a few, selected journalists that you are going blind.'

'What the hell do you mean?'

'I mean it will stimulate interest.'

Peter looked at him.

'Is it comfortable talking with your back to me?'

'You need it, Peter. And you know that.'

Peter moved a step closer and raised his hand. The brush between his fingers was at breaking point. In a low voice, he said:

'Don't come back here until I've finished and the pictures have to be taken to the gallery. Is that clear?'

'What happened in Estonia, Peter?'

'Have you been talking to Helene?'

'What do you mean?'

'Has she asked you to ask me?'

Ben swivelled round, his face pale, drawn, the skin over his cheekbones taut. He pointed his stick at Peter.

'You have to think of Helene, too. Not just about yourself.'

'I do think of her.'

'Don't forget that Helene is also under great pressure.'

'I haven't forgotten.'

'She has the premiere soon and on top of that she has you to take care of.'

'No one needs to take care of me.'

'Oh, yes, they do, Peter Wihl. You always need someone to take care of you. And you know that very well.'

Peter repeated:

'You're disturbing me.'

Ben moved a step closer.

'And now, on my own initiative, because I'm curious, impatient and concerned, and not least because I can no longer do the washing-up with you if I do not have your confidence, I'm asking you one more time to tell me what actually happened in Estonia?'

Peter glanced towards the glass doors, towards the curtains which billowed up in the chilly wind.

'I drank myself senseless,' he whispered.

Kaia appeared from between the curtains. She had not found any keys. Ben began to rummage through all his pockets and, with a deep sigh and a despairing shake of his head at himself and no one else, at length produced a bunch of keys. Kaia laughed. Then he limped to the doors which she had left open, dragging one leg as though he were in great pain or simply wanted to remind Peter of his fall. Ben came to a halt, threw the silver ferrule from the broken stick into the litter bin and straightened up.

'I think we all need some distraction,' he said.

Peter pointed the brush at him.

'It would be an excellent distraction if you left now.'

Ben ignored him and looked at Kaia instead.

'I have some cinema tickets for us for this evening, you know.'

Kaia clapped her hands and with quiet expectation turned to Peter.

'I'm not going to the cinema,' he said.

Ben asked, 'Can't or won't?'

'Perhaps I just don't feel like going,' Peter answered.

'Helene said you wanted to see it.'

'So you have been talking to her?'

'Helene rang to tell me you'd arrived back home. And I can assure you that she does need something to take her mind off this tragic theatre.'

'And which film did she say I wanted to see?'

'Girl with a Pearl Earring.'

Peter was reminded of the symmetry, the accursed symmetry, in everything, in everything surrounding him, which some confuse with fate, with meaning, but which is no more than an ungodly, empty pattern of chance, moments in time, impulses, a harmonious prison, it was nothing more than a *trompe l'oeil*, an optical illusion, as though a pedantic and mediocre artist had smeared existence together, this was the symmetry he had to break out of, he had to smash the reflection.

Kaia took his hand.

'Please,' she begged.

'It's not a film for you,' Peter said.

Ben laughed.

'If she can put up with *The Wild Duck*, she can also manage Vermeer.'

'Please,' Kaia repeated.

'No,' Peter said.

Ben sighed.

'Listen to what your wise daughter is saying, Peter. We need to be amused and entertained to steel ourselves for grumpy old Ibsen.'

And Peter thought: Perhaps it would be for the best after all, to do normal things in abnormal times, to go to the cinema wearing dark glasses.

'Of course we'll go to the cinema,' he said.

Ben gave Kaia two tickets and finally he left. Kaia, obedient, happy, sat on the chair staring at the clock above the door, in the same position as before. She clung to the tickets, hardly daring to breathe. Peter applied a few brushstrokes, but the bow was slack, the colours did not glow, they withered and sank. He was already distracted. For devilry he smeared a large yellow blob on all the canvasses, a dirty mark which upset everything he had done hitherto. Then he put the brushes down, hung his smock and scarf on the nail, took Kaia's hand and went down to the house, where he made them lunch. He heated up a few leftovers, and while they ate, or rather Kaia ate – happily she had her appetite back and Peter was still not hungry – he leaned over the table and whispered, as if to take care no one heard them, although apart from Kaia and Peter, no one else was there:

'We won't tell everyone yet that I'm well. Do you understand?'

Kaia looked at him, nodded, and said, also in a low voice:

'Not even Uncle Ben?'

'Not even Uncle Ben. Just you, Mummy and me.'

'Just you, Mummy and me,' Kaia repeated.

And Peter knew he was binding her to the lie, to the obligations of the lie, no, not the lie, but that which he did not want to know, the ignorance, the lie's wilful close relative, which he concealed with good news, with truths, with solace. He drew Kaia into this informed ignorance; it was a black dog that kept running up and he had no choice but to chase it away.

'It'll be a surprise,' Peter said.

Afterwards, he stood in the bathroom with the door locked; he stood with his back to the mirror and gingerly took off his dark glasses. The light blinded him, stung; he was on the point of screaming and had to hide his face in his hands. Then it passed. He did not scream. He lowered his arms and felt nothing. He took the eye drops, leaned back and pressed: four drops in each eye. He felt nothing. He could see and he felt nothing. He was healed. He could see and it was not painful. He ran water into the bath, as hot as possible, and undressed. He could barely get in the water, it scalded him, his toes, thighs, back, but soon he was used to it, or the water was already cooling down, it did not matter, he put a plastic cushion behind his head, sank deeper into the water and watched the steam drifting around the room and attaching itself to things, pulling them loose, this feeling of numbness, numbness and sudden childhood, he shut his eyes, floated and slept, slept and floated away, in semi-slumber, timeless, in the state where all times meet at a point smaller than a pinhead and culminate in being suspended in dreams, memories, visions, Peter's father scrubbing his back with a firm, rough hand, the coarse soap, *Sunlight*, and talking about new cars, horsepower, mahogany dashboards, gear levers between seats, radio aerials, there are at this moment only four of them in the country, there is a drink on the ledge beneath the mirror, Father's drink, it is Friday evening, music, voices, from the television in the living room where his mother is sitting ready with supper, three slices of bread, each cut into two on a small plate, a glass of juice, red juice since it is Friday evening, it is the Friday evening amnesty, a break from the sublime frugality, the superfluous frugality, which was not a virtue of necessity, but asceticism, purification, it is Peter Wihl who remembers, dreams or sees this before him, it does not matter which, it is just vestiges of the middle-class dream, faint steaming tableaux, and his father who asks, while scrubbing ever harder, why are you not dirty, boy, you should be dirty before I wash you, and he sees the glow of car headlamps move along the walls, fog lamps, but that is not possible, lights cannot go through walls, that much he does know, ridiculous, the light is shattered against the exterior walls into circles and hurled back through the darkness of the garden, between the apple trees and over the hedge, long after the cars have passed, it must be other lights shining, agitated flickering flames, a forest of lights, and Peter Wihl heard someone shout, not at him, but at his father, someone was shouting at his father, and he thought, idiots, don't you know Father is dead, the water cascaded off him, the steam dispersed and defined things in sharp contours, he sat in the bath, out of breath, nauseous, the smell of soap and candles, from which he could not escape, he could not stand it and vomited, he threw up in the water he was sitting in, Kaia was knocking at the door and shouting to him, and he shouted back to her, it seemed, without a voice:

'I'll be out in a minute.'

Peter dressed, swallowed a pill, put on his glasses and rang for a taxi.

The others were waiting for them outside the cinema in the town centre: Ben, Helene and the stage manager – he had also joined them. *The Wild Duck* must be going very badly if he had chosen to leave the building. This was a rare occurrence, it only happened on the occasion of funerals, public holidays and major natural catastrophes for preference, or perhaps everything was already set up for the premiere. Anyway, he was there, in his old coat buttoned right up to his Adam's apple, complete with galoshes and earmuffs. Kaia ran straight to Helene, who seemed both happy and worried. She gave Peter a fleeting kiss on both cheeks and whispered:

'You didn't have to come.'

'Do you want me to go home again?'

Helene sniggered.

'I thought you didn't have the energy.'

'I'm fine.'

'Sure? Will your eyes be all right?'

Peter kissed her.

'I'm fine,' he repeated.

They went into the cinema foyer, the film was due to start, Helene and Kaia bought chocolate, the stage manager had to go to the toilet first. Ben watched him leave with a pained grimace on his face, and pulled Peter closer.

'Please God, may I not have to sit next to that tedious stuffed shirt.'

'The stage manager?'

'Yes, who else? What seat have you got?'

'Don't speak so ill of the stage manager, Ben.'

'The man smells of vinegar.'

'He smells of theatre.'

Ben lost patience.

'Every time I see him I think about changing sexual orientation.'

Soon they were all assembled and stood in the queue. The usher hesitated when he saw Kaia, but Ben put his arm around her and said:

'She's sitting next to me and I promise she'll close her eyes if there's anything too nasty.'

They were let in and they found their seats. The cinema was full. Finally the lights went off and the chocolate came out, the rustling of paper, an orchestra of polite noises in the dark. The stage manager leaned over to Peter and said in a dry, matter-of-fact voice, without a hint of irony or surprise, merely forbearance, after a long life in the service of the theatre:

'I would just point out that you are still wearing your sunglasses.'

'I am supposed to,' Peter said.

The stage manager nodded and refocused on the screen.

'Of course.'

No more was said.

The film could start.

Girl with a Pearl Earring.

Even before the first scene was over Peter had had enough. Once again he was taken aback by the seductively fraudulent symmetry, this time in this fallacious story based on reality, as was claimed in the blurb, and no stories can be more fallacious than those based on so-called reality: the blind artisan who is forced to send his only daughter away, the beautiful daughter, who becomes a servant girl in Vermeer's house and in due course his model. It was too much for Peter. It was romantic and evil. It hit a raw nerve and upset him. He could not tolerate it. It was more than he could endure. He had to go. He had never left a film in the middle before. He had always stayed in his seat whether he was dying for a pee, thirsty, drunk, ill or desperate; no matter how trashy the film was, he had stayed in the cinema as if cast under a spell by politeness, fear, habit, good manners until it was over and the guilty parties were named in the credits. Now he had to get out. It was like a conspiracy, the conspiracy of symmetry and he was being encircled and crowded in. It was becoming ever more stifling. He could not breathe. Soon he would have a panic attack. He had to get out, the sooner the better. He had to get away from this extravagant delusion, this symmetrical hell. He found Kaia's hand.

'Let's go,' he said.

But Kaia did not want to go. And she did not let go of his hand, either. She held it tight and Peter was surprised, almost frightened, at the strength in the small fingers that squeezed his. In the end he had to pull his hand away. Helene had also become restless; this restlessness, annoyance, impatience spread to the seats around them, and she leaned forward.

'Not long to go.'

Someone shushed them.

Peter found it difficult to maintain his composure.

'I have to go for a pee,' he whispered.

And he began to edge his way along the row to the central aisle where he could make out luminous numbers on the steps leading down to the exits on either side, one was also an emergency exit with green lights. One by one, people in the row had to stand up for him, they were probably the same people who would come to his exhibition, it was his public, affluent, liberal and conservative to the core, the squinters who would stand in front of the pictures, take a step back, smile, maybe shake their heads, demonstrative yet discreet, appreciative, judgemental, all depending, as they balanced glasses and the price list in their right hand and gesticulated with the left, and in contrast to other art forms like novels, plays, even dreadful films which stretch out in time, time is the very premise of the experience, a painting can be experienced quite literally in the blink of an eye, in the time it takes to see, one blink and a judgement can be formed at that very moment, years of work submitted for judgement in the frail courtroom of the moment, and now Peter could not remember what the etiquette was, whether you should worm your way out showing your face or back, that is, your backside to those sitting, all he knew was that this varied from country to country, in some it was polite to turn your back, that is your backside, in others the custom was to turn your face, Peter chose the former, the back, he turned his back to the audience, in that way there was less chance of being recognised if indeed anyone still knew him, then he tripped over a foot and fell headlong, managed to catch hold of the back of a seat, or a shoulder, someone shouted, *Take off your sunglasses, you prat*, at long last he emerged into the central aisle and walked as fast as he dared down the broad, slightly sloping steps, the axis of the auditorium, facing the screen, with the audience on either side, like a reflection of each other, but when he got down to the emergency exit, he was unable to open the door, it was downright impossible, no matter how much he pulled or pushed the solid bar across the steel door, it refused to budge, he tried the other exit, the usual one, the same thing there, he yanked at the bar, he put all his weight against it and shoved as hard as he was able, that didn't help either, the doors were jammed, or he didn't know how to open them, it didn't much matter, he couldn't get out and no one came to help him, he was quite simply locked inside, locked in with his public, and Peter Wihl was gripped by a desperation, by a fury so profound and all-pervasive that he could only ever remember having experienced it in a dream, in the absurd dreams of childhood when the unbearable recurring scene, which was always unresolved, woke him with a scream, and he thought he could hear laughter, it might well have been in the film, or something in the film the audience was laughing at, and at this moment he had no more strength left, he gave up, he could have sat down where he was and stayed there, but he did not, instead he set out on an even more humiliating retreat, he went with bowed head up the central aisle, this time with his face to the audience, who once again had to stand up, in reverse order, and finally Peter Wihl found his seat next to Kaia, who was sitting with eyes closed and hands folded in her lap, not because of what was happening on the screen, but because she was ashamed of him, her father, and in deference he sat right through the film until Colin Firth, who played Vermeer in a becomingly helpless way, had finished painting his fallacious portrait of a girl with a pearl earring, and the film was over.

When they came out, it had begun to drizzle. Ben said:

'Now we could damn well do with a drink, couldn't we, Kaia.'

Kaia looked up at Helene, who shook her head, and turned to Peter.

'We're going home, aren't we?'

Peter smiled and put his arm around her shoulders.

'Of course we'll go and have a drink.'

'Sure?'

'Yes indeed. We'll go and you can have a drink. I need a pee.'

With that, they went to the nearest bar, right next to the cinema. Peter was not in the mood, of course. He was dying to get home as soon as possible; he was exhausted and upset. And by good fortune the place was packed – they might have to turn round and go home after all. Sadly, however, Helene saw some people she knew, a couple of actors from a different theatre and a hoarse prompter, there were waves and shouts, and they had to join their table. Ben ordered wine for those who wanted it, Peter asked for a soft drink for Kaia and water for himself, the actors – both better known for their pasts – glanced at him with indulgence, perhaps sympathy, even condescension, they probably assumed he had a hangover, wearing sunglasses and drinking water on a Friday evening. Peter cared little, they could believe they could read him like an open book, out loud if they wanted, and they could interpret him any way they liked, from the front or the back, as long as they were wrong. And the conversation flowed past him, he could not be bothered to follow, the words were background noise and he did not listen, he was not involved, he sat behind his glasses and drank water until the stage manager, as ill-at-ease and awkward as Peter – away from the theatre he did not have his frame of reference, he was out of his element, he was not in control of this dimension of the world – banged his glass on the table and said with all the indignation, contempt and revulsion he could bring to his dry voice:

'Changes! Changes and more changes! It's a living hell!'

There was a momentary silence. Everyone looked at the stage manager who, as if in shock, peered down at his fingers which were wet from the wine.

Ben smiled.

'Aren't changes a blessing?'

The stage manager gulped several times.

'Changes are a curse when they are never-ending.'

Ben was amused.

'But isn't that the nature of change? Changes also have to change?'

The stage manager came close to banging the table again, this time with his fist, but controlled himself.

'One day Ekdal has to stand at the edge of the stage. The next he has to stand in the wings. Yesterday, Hedvig's lines in the last act were struck out. Tomorrow, in all probability, they'll be put back. It can't go on like this. No, it can't go on like this.'

Now Ben laughed.

'Didn't Ibsen himself change the ending of *A Doll's House* when it premiered in Germany?'

The stage manager shook his head.

'I don't know anything about that.'

'Yes, he did in fact. He let Nora come back because, you see, the audience wanted it.'

'I don't know anything about that,' repeated the stage manager.

Ben would not let go.

'So I think you could change the ending of *The Wild Duck* as well. Hedvig doesn't shoot herself, instead she shoots Werle. That would have appeal.'

The stage manager had almost returned to his old self. In a dry, dispassionate voice, he said:

'Ibsen's plays should be performed as they were written. That's all there is to say.'

Ben, however, wanted the last word.

'Yes, right, then old Ekdal will have to light his pipe and break the smoking regulations.'

A waiter put another bottle of wine on the table. Peter looked around for a toilet door. He needed a pee. He didn't see any doors, just a green glass partition which reminded him of an aquarium. Someone came out of the partition, just shoved it to the side and came into view. Peter waited for the room to be filled with, or drained of, water. Everything seemed both thoroughly modern and old-fashioned. The architect must have thought that bad taste was still good taste, if you had sufficient good taste to know at all times what bad taste was. Some people at the other tables, recognising him now, nodded, this imperceptible knowing nod to show you belonged to the same circle, you were among those who nod, although they don't know each other, a nod so scant that it can also be perceived as a neutral movement, to avoid an embarrassing and degrading situation, should the nod be reciprocated with a corresponding nod, in other words: a risk-free nod. Someone placed a hand on his shoulder, it was Ben, he asked:

'You're the expert, Peter. What do you think?'

Peter spun round, his mouth dry. He had lost the thread of the conversation. Now everyone was looking at him, even Kaia was looking at him, waiting.

'About what?'

Ben sighed.

'About the film, of course. We've just been to the cinema, Peter.'

Peter took a mouthful of water. It did not help; his mouth was still dry. He mumbled:

'It doesn't happen like that.'

Ben's thin face loomed closer.

'What did you say?'

Peter repeated, 'It doesn't happen like that.'

Ben leaned back.

'Elaborate, Peter.'

They waited for him, for what he had to say, but he still did not know what to say. He could say something about Vermeer's severe interiors and how the Dutch master filled these ordinary rooms, ordinariness itself, our surroundings, what we live in, a kitchen, a living room, a studio, with a light the world had never seen the like of before. He could say something about the fragile balance between the gravity of the model and the lightness of the portrait, the impossible mathematics of imitation, so to speak, or that Vermeer, in the one self-portrait he ever painted, sat with his back to us, or he could just say that Colin Firth, who played Vermeer in this romantic cabal where everyone was out to deceive, was still holding the brush wrong. He said nothing of this; he said:

'In the painting known as *The Milkmaid* Vermeer painted a nail in the bare wall behind her. It casts a small shadow. That's all. It is perhaps the most beautiful thing ever painted. A nail on a bare wall. And if you run your hand gently across the picture you can feel the nail scrape against the surface of your hand. All art should have a nail like this.'

Helene looked at Peter and smiled, the smile for which he always yearned, perhaps that was even why he continued to paint, to be met by this smile, one of both acknowledgement and admiration. He felt an urge to rip off his glasses and confront her gaze; he raised his hand, paused.

Peter stood up, shoved the partition to the side, went into the green toilet, undid his fly and peed. Soon afterwards Ben also came in and stood in front of the second urinal with his back to him.

'Did you mean what you said?' he asked.

'What did I say?'

'You said you didn't want me to visit you in the studio any more?'

'Yes. I meant it.'

'I didn't like what I saw there, Peter. I didn't see a nail.'

'I don't give a shit.'

'No change in your mood then.'

Peter rinsed his hands under the tap.

'You'll have to trust me.'

Ben laughed.

'Trust you?'

Peter could not find a towel and pressed the hand dryer, which drowned them out with the electric stream of air and they said nothing until it switched itself off.

Then it was even quieter, a silence that resembled coldness, green coldness, their faces were pale, distorted, in this aquarium-light.

'Did you mean what you said?'

Ben was drying his hands on a serviette.

'I meant that I was quite unable to see where you were going with the pictures.'

'I meant when you were talking about a leak to the press.'

Ben folded the serviette, put it in his pocket and sighed.

'What do you want me to do, Peter?'

'I told you, Ben. I'm not talking to anyone before the exhibition.'

Peter made to leave, but Ben held him back.

'So you want me to trust you?'

'Yes.'

'Trust a man wearing ridiculous sunglasses?'

'Let it go, Ben.'

Ben did not.

'Seven days on the piss in Estonia? Do you think I believe that, Peter Wihl?'

Peter tore his arm away, re-joined the others and sat down.

Helene looked at Ben who came right behind him, hobbling a few steps before sitting down, far too heavily.

'Have you hurt yourself?' she asked.

'I fell. On the ice outside Peter Wihl's studio.'

Ben put a hand on Peter's shoulder.

'The great artist has enough to cope with and, naturally, had forgotten to put down any sand.'

Helene shook her head.

'Didn't you have your stick with you?'

'Yes, dear Helene. I had my stick, but not even that helped. It snapped!'

Helene laughed.

'By the way, have you heard where Ben got hold of that stick? He bought it at an auction after the scenographer at the National died.'

'We've heard it,' Peter said.

'*We* haven't,' said the hoarse prompter.

Helene hesitated for a second and turned to the prompter and actors.

'When he died, his beautiful home was sold piecemeal, everything, powder box, grand piano, bedlinen.'

'We've heard it,' Peter repeated.

Ben kicked his leg and said, loudly:

'And, of course, because I bought his silver stick Helene thinks I have necrophilic tendencies.'

Helene took a deep breath, looked at Peter for a moment, then looked past him as she continued:

'And this beautiful, warm, extravagant house, designed and composed down to the tiniest detail, was just turned into an ordinary flea market when it was dismantled.

Peter could not take any more. He interrupted her again.

'Why do you keep telling that bloody story? Can't you find something new to talk about?'

The table went quiet. Everyone in the entire room seemed to go quiet at the same time.

The stage manager studied his watch.

Helene got up, buttoned up Kaia's duffle coat, took her hand and walked to the door.

Ben leaned over to Peter.

'I would love to whack you with my stick right now, but regrettably, as you know, it's broken. The least you can do, however, is ring for a taxi.'

Peter, perplexed, reeling, said:

'I haven't got my mobile on me.'

Ben almost pushed him off his chair.

'Then go after them, you self-centred vandal.'

Peter caught up outside. It was raining. The wind was blowing umbrellas inside out. There was a taxi free in the next street. Helene and Kaia got into the back. Peter sat in the front and gave the address. Otherwise no one said a word throughout the journey. In the garden, rain was falling like snow. They went in. Peter waited in the kitchen while Helene put Kaia to bed. He drank two glasses of water. Finally, she came, pushed the door to and stood leaning against the closed door, her arms crossed, like a knot across her bosom.

'I know it is the sick person's privilege to behave like an asshole,' she said.

'I'm well now.'

'You mean you're just an asshole?'

'Sorry.'

'Don't interrupt me.'

Peter sat down.

Helene moved closer.

'But don't take your anger or whatever the hell it is out on me. And if it isn't too much to ask, at least do it when there's no one else present, and especially not Kaia. Especially not Kaia. Have you got that?'

Peter nodded.

'Have you got that?' she repeated. 'Talk to me, for Christ's sake!'

'It won't happen again.'

'And how can I know that?'

'I said I'm sorry. It won't happen again. What else do you want me to say?'

Helene sat at the table, opposite him, drank some water and breathed out.

'That film was a bloody awful idea,' she said.

'And it was an even worse idea to let Kaia see it. She is not going to see *The Wild Duck*.'

Helene ignored him.

'But that does not give you the right to insult and humiliate me.'

Peter looked up.

'How many times do I have to say sorry? Eight? Ten? Nineteen times? Or do you want me to whip myself as well?'

Helene shook her head.

'I don't recognise you, Peter.'

'I'm the same person.'

'No, you're not. You've changed. And I'm not sure I like what you've become.'

Peter stood up, knocking his chair over behind him, and shouted:

'I'm the same person! Do you hear me? I'm just the same!'

'You'll wake up Kaia, you idiot!'

Both of them looked at the door.

The house was silent. All they could hear was the wind.

'I'm the same,' Peter repeated in a low voice.

'As who, Peter?'

He leaned on the table.

'The same as before, Helene. I just haven't said it before.'

'Said what?'

'That I hate the story about the bloody scenographer and how his beautiful bloody home was taken apart and ended up as a pile of junk inside glass display cases in the middle-class art business.'

Helene smiled.

'Dare I ask why you hate it so much, apart from the fact that you have obviously heard it several times already?'

'Because it scares me, Helene. It scares the wits out of me, for God's sake. Don't you understand that?'

He took her hand in his.

She turned to the wall, to the hook, from which nothing was hanging.

'When will you have finished the portrait of Kaia?' she asked.

23

When Peter awoke Helene had gone. The space beside him was empty. When he put his hand there, he could feel the taut sheet; the duvet cover and the pillow were already cold. He must have slept late. The wind had woken him. Sometimes it made the walls tremble. He lay there waiting for it to hurt. It did not. Kaia stood at the foot of the bed. Peter sat up with a start, worried for a moment, raised a hand: he was wearing glasses, he had slept with his glasses on.

'What's the time?' he asked.

Kaia looked down at her arm. The thin, slanting veins in her temples were clearly outlined against her skin.

'Six minutes to ten,' she said at last.

Peter smiled and shook his head.

'My goodness. Soon I'll have to go back to bed.'

Kaia was as serious as before.

'There's a letter for you.'

'Have you got it with you?'

'In the kitchen. Shall I get it?'

Peter shook his head.

'Why don't you run on to the studio. I'll be right there.'

Kaia hesitated, preferring to stay.

'It's blowy,' she said, softly.

'That doesn't matter, does it?'

Kaia stood for a little longer, she seemed disappointed, and Peter was going to say something, that they could go together, but then she ran off anyway.

He heard the front door shut after her, and a current of air swept through the house.

He got out of bed, put drops in his eyes, washed, dressed and went into the kitchen. Kaia had set the table for him and she must have gone to extra trouble: a coffee cup, a glass, a small plate, a basket with three slices of bread, the newspaper, wet at the edges – she had even tried to dry it, but she had laid the cutlery incorrectly. The knife was on the left, and this tiny mistake filled him with enormous tenderness; this lapse was so beautiful, the way he saw it that morning, that he was on the verge of tears; he could have cried at the sight of this table and the knife and fork placed the wrong way round.

The letter had fallen on the floor. It was from the Institute for the Blind. Peter did not open the envelope. He tore it into strips and threw the pieces into the fire. He was not hungry. He left the breakfast untouched and went to the studio. The wind was blowing the snow away. The thin grass lay flat against the ground. He closed the doors. Kaia was sitting in the chair waiting for him. Impatient to start, he kissed her on the cheek and set to work with a will. Today, he was going to paint Kaia the way she had laid the table. He would paint with the same dedication. His hand was light, the brush had the effortless flow of the virtuoso: precise, fluid strokes, as if the twelve canvasses were one picture, bound together by the shadow each cast. But it did not work. The virtuosity went flat. He met no resistance. He was just repeating himself and painting in the air. He was unable to manoeuvre the nail into position. He lacked a nail. Something was bothering him. Something was different in the studio. At first he could not see what it was; he just sensed it. The canvasses were in the same order. The curtains were drawn. Nothing had been touched. Then he knew what it was. He turned to Kaia. She had moved the chair closer to Peter. She was sitting directly behind him, as if she wanted him to see her better. Peter put the brushes down on the workbench and stood silent for a moment.

'That's enough for today,' he concluded.

Kaia looked at him with an inquisitive expression, almost anxious.

'Have you finished, Daddy?'

'Daddy's finished for today, Kaia.'

'I can sit for a little longer. I'm not tired. Look.'

She raised her chin, swept her hair back from her forehead, focused her gaze on the clock above the door and stayed like that, in semi-profile, and all the light there was in the studio was concentrated on her face.

'It's Daddy who's tired,' Peter said.

Kaia got off her chair.

'We can go for a walk.'

'Do you want to? It's blowy.'

'That's OK.'

They wrapped up warmly and went out. The wind was warm, the clouds scudded across the sky, the trees behind the quiet, abandoned streets were bent over, shaking. Then they came to the park. Peter stopped and took Kaia's hand. The same avenue lay in front of them, bare trees on either side of the gravel path. Branches and twigs flapped between the trunks. Not a soul to be seen. No barking dogs.

'Shall we walk round the park?' Peter asked.

Kaia looked up at him.

'Where?'

Peter chuckled.

'Where we'll walk? It was you who wanted to go for a walk, wasn't it?'

Kaia went silent. Peter squeezed her hand with affection.

'I'll show you something. In the churchyard.'

'Then we'll have to go through the park, won't we?'

'We can walk round it, Kaia. If you want.'

Kaia shook her head.

'We'll go through the park.'

And Peter thought: she is braver than me.

They went on, hand in hand, up the avenue. They held each other tight. At one point they could lean into the wind without falling. Kaia laughed. Peter laughed, too. They laughed and leaned into the wind. A lightness came over Peter as the wind almost lifted them off their feet. For a short time it seemed like happiness. They tried to run, but the gale would not let them. A vast cloud drifted across the park. At the end of the avenue they turned into the path up the gentle slope and went into the churchyard. The pointed, almost black, poplars stood at an angle, swaying. The 'Dogs should be kept on a lead' sign was daubed with cryptic tags. Peter struggled to remember the last time he had been there. He had paid the church office to look after the grave indefinitely, but indefinite time also has a limit: fifty years. In twenty-five years the remains of his parents would be transferred to the corner of the cemetery, to make room for new bodies, by which time Kaia would be thirty-one and he would be seventy-five. Several of the headstones had been overturned, by the wind, hooligans, or just neglect; impossible to know. Cars filled the parking area behind the chapel, which from the outside looked like an old industrial building, no windows, just heavy grey walls. It reminded Peter of the transformer station in Tallinn, apart from the tall cross on the roof. He stopped and looked around, disorientated, confused, frightened he wouldn't find the grave. The lightness had gone, instead he felt a heaviness, it pushed him down, down, he had to force himself up. A wall of rain approached from the mountain ridges in the west, and then he knew where to go. It was the smell, a hint of a smell, which instantly reminded him of the way: past the pissoir, the moist green rotunda between the bushes, and his parents' grave was in the space to the left. Peter was pleased that the grave was tidy and well tended, that the headstone had not been knocked over and Peter was just as pleased that he was pleased.

They crouched down.

Kaia was silent and serious.

Peter scraped some ice and leaves off the names.

'My father sold cars. The finest cars in town. And every summer he would buy a new car. Sometimes he would let me sit on his lap and hold the steering wheel while he drove.'

Peter fell silent.

Kaia looked at him.

'And Grandma?'

Peter was touched that Kaia, who had never met her, said *Grandma.* She seemed to acquire greater definition; the word *Grandma* in Kaia's mouth brought her to life.

'My mother was the finest passenger in the world,' he said, quietly. They sat there, crouching, without speaking for a while. Lightning struck, somewhere between the fjord and the forests. The thunder rolled past. Peter forgot to count the seconds.

'Did they love you?' Kaia asked.

Peter was taken aback.

'Love me?'

Kaia looked away.

'Your mother and father?'

Peter pulled her close.

'Of course they loved me.'

Kaia still had the figures, the small painted figures, in her duffle coat pocket. Now she positioned them in a circle on the grave, one by one. And just then the rain hit them, rain and hail, as big as bullets. It was the storm that had caught up with him at long last, thought Peter. The weather forecast had been right. He took Kaia's hand and they ran, bent double, down to the car park. Then she tripped over a kerb. He was unable to catch her. She fell headlong, with her hands beneath her. He had to lift her up, she did not cry, at least he couldn't see her crying in the rain. The wind almost blew her over again. She didn't hear what he was saying. A litter bin was hurled through the air and landed on a car. They had to take shelter in the chapel. He half-carried her and barged open the heavy door with his shoulder. A verger met them, gave Peter a programme and said in a whisper:

'It has just started.'

They took seats at the very back, in the semi-darkness. No windows, just the blue stained-glass paintings in the background, and candles. Now, Peter realised they had stumbled into a funeral service. The same as the last time he had been there too, twenty-five years ago, his parents' funeral. The white coffin lay on the catafalque, wreaths and flowers in the aisle, silk ribbons bearing valedictory messages. The chapel was full. A boy with long hair stood by the pulpit, playing guitar and singing a popular melody. Some turned towards them, with smiles of curiosity and solace. Kaia was crying. Peter pulled out a handkerchief and dabbed at her face. She continued to cry.

'Did you hurt yourself?' he whispered.

She showed him her hand, impatient, almost angry.

But Peter could not see very well in the darkness of the chapel. He just saw the shadow of her hand.

The boy finished the song and sat down beside a woman in the first row, probably his mother, who put her arm around him. Those sitting behind them patted the boy on the shoulder. The priest greeted the next of kin, the woman and the boy, and stood in silence, facing the coffin and the baroque triptych, which with all its shiny ornaments and excess seemed so beautiful and out of place here in this spartan, golden chapel, and in the centre of the triptych was God's eye, enclosed in a triangular halo, this one eye, wide open, God's eye, the same eye as twenty-five years ago, the same eye as always, God's omniscience as a symbol, it was an image of a symbol, God's presence.

Kaia was the only person crying.

Peter took off his glasses and could see that one finger was bleeding, the middle finger of the right hand, which she had grazed in the fall. It was nothing serious, he was relieved, he wiped off the blood and blew on the graze, but Kaia pulled her hand away.

He looked at her.

'Did that hurt?'

She just stared at him, scared; her face was mute and pale, her mouth pinched. She was not crying any more.

Peter leaned closer.

'What is it, Kaia?'

She shook her head and turned away. Peter grabbed her arm, but she didn't want to look at him. She struggled. He tried to force her; he was frightened, too. It was no use.

'What is it?' he repeated.

The verger appeared behind Kaia and made a sign: Shh.

Peter let go.

Everyone in the chapel, except Kaia, was looking at him.

The priest knelt down by the altar.

At last, the organist began to play.

Then Kaia turned after all, looked at Peter, raised her hand – the ungrazed one – and pointed at his eyes.

24

Peter was in the way.

The flowers he was holding were in the way.

Wherever he stood, he was in the way.

Everyone was running around everyone else, actors, props people, technicians, wardrobe supervisors, prompters, they were talking to themselves, changing costumes, shouting messages, meditating, swearing, laughing in near-hysteria, weeping quietly, it was chaos and turmoil on a grand scale, chaos and turmoil which, in thirty minutes, when the bells rang for the third time, would be superseded by the very strictest discipline, it was the premiere of *The Wild Duck*.

Peter caught a glimpse of Helene on the stage. She was making her final preparations, moving a chair closer to the red wall, straightening a curtain, cleaning a glass. He had always loved to see her like this, in her own world, a self-preoccupation which was to the benefit of all; that was also how he had seen her for the first time. It was a different world from his, yet he knew it so well, his world was tangential to hers. He waved, but she didn't see him.

A door was opened, a smell of perfume and vinegar, Kaia sitting in the make-up room waiting. She had a new plaster on the graze and a little bandage and she showed her hand, as though proud of it. Peter's eyes met Helene's in the mirror under the bright lamp, green, but then her eyes strayed. She did not see him, or she did not want to.

Peter regretted having come. He was in the way. The flowers were in the way.

The bell rang in the foyer.

The stage manager passed by on his way to his office, or cage, stopped in mid-stride, and with the whole theatre at fever pitch he was the only person to retain his composure, he smiled and said:

'This is going to be bloody, Peter Wihl.'

He walked on before Peter managed to say anything, but then stopped again and turned.

'What's the matter with you?'

Peter took a step back.

'With me?'

'You look as if you're about to do a turn on the stage.'

'I'm just nervous on Helene's behalf.'

The stage manager laid a hand on Peter's shoulder, an act of shocking intimacy for him.

'She, of all people, has nothing to be nervous about. She's the best.'

Peter handed him the flowers and stepped back.

'You take them.'

Weary, the stage manager smiled.

'Are they for me?'

'Of course not.'

Peter went to the little washroom by the lift. Gregor Werle was there – or the poor wretch who had to try to play this pathetic, humourless character – throwing up in the basin. Peter could not stay. He about-faced in the doorway. The bells rang for the second time. Helene and Kaia, impatient, were waiting for him. They took their seats in the gallery. Ben was already there. He shook his head.

'Do you really have to torment Kaia with Ibsen before she's even school-age?'

He said it in such a loud voice that everyone around them turned; he had probably been drinking dry white wine to find the courage to be able to stomach both the play and a gunshot.

'You'll have to hold her hand,' Helene whispered

'I want to borrow Peter's sunglasses,' Ben shouted.

Ben went to take them off him.

Peter pushed Ben away.

'Why don't you have a sleep!'

It was like a show, some laughed, some shushed, it took Helene a few moments to calm them down and they took their seats. But now Kaia did not want to sit next to Peter. Instead she sat between Helene and Ben, neither of whom noticed this little change of plan, switch of positions, only Peter, who straightened his glasses, put on a smile, pretended nothing had happened, stared at his hands, ashamed, nervous, not on Helene's behalf, but for himself, this was no heroic nervousness which would be of benefit to others, it was him in his own world, immured, and it made him even more ashamed, and even more nervous, because he did not know whether he was in control of this world any more.

What had Kaia seen in his eyes?

Peter could not think the thought through to its conclusion.

The theatre was soon full, the same premiere public; the bells rang for the third time.

Helene leaned over to Peter.

'What do you think of the red wall?'

'It's too late to change anything now, isn't it?'

'Well, thank you very much indeed.'

Peter clasped her hand in his; it was warm, moist and he could sense the beating of her heart deep in her palm.

'The wall's fine,' he whispered. 'You're the best.'

A voice in the loudspeaker, it was the stage manager, art's purist, requesting the audience to switch off their mobile phones.

Then, Peter caught sight of Thomas Hammer in the auditorium below. He was sitting in the front row reading the programme; he put it in his pocket, where his hand stayed. Perhaps he was switching off his mobile as he looked around. Peter was gripped by a sudden queasiness, nausea. What if Dr Hall was there too? That would not be so improbable, and feverishly Peter thought, from now on he would stay at home, he would not leave the studio, he would no longer show his face out of doors, he would concentrate on finishing his work. Then the lights were dimmed, the colossal chandelier above them was extinguished, for a moment everything went black, applause and darkness, until the projectors lit up the stage and everything was flooded in red. The play could begin. It began. But Peter could not follow. It did not concern him, it did not mean anything to him, like the funeral, the coffin, the dead man he had not known, and so it did not move him, did not concern him, he was on the outside, it was both a relief and a curse, he was on the inside, he was in his own world, which he did not share with Helene, but with Thomas Hammer. He heard a few lines. He noticed old Ekdal's pipe, which the ageing actor made great play of, searching for matches as he sucked valiantly on the cold mouthpiece, and when he did find a box, he was unable to light the tobacco. He was rewarded for his efforts, reaping a steady ripple of chortles, now and then laughter. The interval came. Peter saw Thomas Hammer stand up and go to the toilets. Most people moved towards the bar in the foyer. Helene wanted to go backstage. She turned to him.

'Aren't you coming?'

'I need some fresh air,' Peter said.

'Sure? You're not leaving, are you?'

Peter smiled.

'I want to see the open solution.'

Helene, Kaia and Ben disappeared behind the stage. Peter went down to the gentlemen's toilet. Thomas, standing by the furthest urinal, had his back to him. There was a queue in front of the three cubicles, a monotonous buzz of voices, mumbling; premiere mumble. Peter picked up words such as *gripping, bombastic, classic, slow, wonderful, superficial.* He took his place in front of the second urinal, which had dark urine in the white bowl and there were hairs on the curved edge; he was unable to pee.

'This is the place where you hear the truth,' Thomas Hammer said.

'This is where you hear tittle-tattle,' Peter said.

Thomas Hammer laughed.

'Call it what you will. It stinks anyway.'

Behind them people were coming and going, the same public, the same mumbling. Peter took a paper towel from the machine on the wall, went back to Thomas Hammer.

'What happened in Estonia?' he asked.

'What happened? We hardly needed to give you an anaesthetic. How much had you drunk?'

'Answer me, Thomas.'

'You can see, can't you? Isn't that enough?'

'You're not answering my question, Thomas.'

'Shall we have a smoke?'

'What?'

Thomas Hammer held out a packet of cigarettes.

'Help yourself.'

Peter, tired, resigned:

'You're not allowed to smoke in here.'

'But that's half the fun, Peter.'

The bell rang in the foyer. They were alone. Thomas Hammer lit a cigarette, took a few quick drags and flicked the butt in a urinal.

'What happened in Estonia?' Peter repeated.

Thomas Hammer turned on the tap, pressed liquid soap out of the dispenser and washed his hands.

'You didn't tell me the truth that time,' he said.

Peter, bewildered:

'When? When didn't I tell you the truth?'

'You said you would rather be a mediocre artist and survive, than a dead master.'

'I don't remember saying that.'

'But I remember it well, Peter. And I knew you were lying. I knew you would do everything in your power to survive and be a master. You want it all, you do. Cost what it may. That's why I almost like you.'

'Don't kid yourself that you know anything about me at all.'

Thomas Hammer turned to face Peter.

'You went along, didn't you?'

Peter looked away, at the door, the mirror, the urinals, no longer believing his own words.

'I had no choice,' he said.

'No one forced you to do anything, my dear Peter.'

'I didn't know what I was getting myself into.'

Thomas Hammer raised his hand and interrupted him.

'Shh.'

They listened. All the sounds, footsteps, voices drifted away from them. They heard the doors being opened in the auditorium, and at last everything was still.

Thomas Hammer sniggered.

'We'll be late for the lesson,' he whispered.

Peter felt like punching him. He clenched his fists in his pocket, took a step forward and whispered in a hoarse voice:

'You said the sum total of suffering would decrease. In the hotel room. Do you remember? Do you remember saying that?'

Thomas Hammer took off Peter's glasses, bent closer, pressed his thumb lightly against both eyes and smiled.

'I'm so bloody good, even if I have to say so myself. And now it's up to you, Peter Wihl.'

'Up to me?'

'To paint your next masterpiece. By the way, you don't need to wear dark glasses any more.'

Peter snatched back his glasses.

In desperation he asked for the third time. It was like his unbearable recurring dreams, marking time, not moving.

'What happened to me in Estonia, Thomas? What did you do?'

'You said you didn't want to know.'

'No, you said I didn't want to know. Now I want to know.'

Thomas Hammer leaned against the wall. He also seemed fatigued, as though bored, when he said:

'The sum total of suffering is definitely no greater. The morality account is in credit. Not in the red.'

Peter looked at him, at his puffed up, bloated face in which his features were beginning to disappear: the fat earlobes and the thin, near-invisible lips.

'What do you mean?'

Thomas Hammer glanced at his watch.

'I would prefer not to miss the climax of the play.'

Thomas Hammer made a move to go. Peter shoved him against the wall.

'What the fuck do you mean by a morality account?'

Thomas Hammer smiled.

'Do you think anyone will miss an orphaned, abandoned kid no one knew anything about?'

'Shut up, Thomas!'

'You said you wanted to hear, Peter. Now make up your mind.'

Peter turned away.

'Yes. Tell me. Tell me.'

Thomas Hammer put his hand on his shoulder.

'This abandoned child no one knew anything about and therefore doesn't exist, Peter, was given the opportunity to do the world a small service, that is, to give you new eyesight. I am sure she will go to heaven.'

Peter swivelled and struck. Thomas Hammer sank to his knees, groaned, held his hands over his face, his mouth. Peter stood over him. Thomas Hammer crawled around on the floor, confused, cursing, then he got up, staggered, took some paper and wiped his nose.

'Why did you take me to the transformer station?' whispered Peter.

Thomas Hammer was not listening, or could not talk, drank water from the tap, coughed, got his voice back.

'By the way, I've been trying to reach you on your mobile. Have you changed your number?'

'I threw it away.'

Thomas Hammer spun round.

'Threw it away? Where?'

'In Estonia.'

'In Estonia? You threw your phone away in Estonia? Where in Estonia, if I might ask?'

'At the hotel. On the way to the airport. I don't remember.'

'Right. Did you delete the message from me?'

'I don't remember. I just threw away the phone.'

Thomas Hammer stood speechless for a few seconds, breathing heavily, his face white now, drawn, as if for a moment, and not until now, he had lost his composure. He stared at Peter in disbelief and pointed, his whole hand shaking.

'Idiot. You bloody idiot.'

Thomas Hammer went to the door. He turned, calmer, but just as pale.

'This time it's my turn to say it.'

'What?'

'That I never want to see you again, Peter Wihl.'

Then Thomas Hammer was gone. The door fell to after him, soundless. Peter stayed where he was, in the silence, amid the stench of liquid soap. He looked in the mirror, went closer, hesitant, he looked at himself in the mirror, closed his eyes, bent over the sink and heaved.

Afterwards Peter put on his glasses and went upstairs to the gallery. The kind usherette showed him the way without delay or fuss, and he found his seat, beside Helene, who just shook her head. Kaia was holding her hand. Ben was asleep. The play continued with Peter in a world of his own. He saw that Thomas Hammer's seat, in the front row downstairs, was unoccupied. Peter thought: It's too late. I will have to live with this. It is too late. Would he be able to live with it? This was the sordid inspiration. Peter thought: See, don't think. Don't think, see. This was all he could think. He clung to all the things he didn't know. It was a comfort. It was a mitigating circumstance. He could just as well have said: There is no comfort. And there are no mitigating circumstances. All he did not know was more than he would ever be able to know. He drew a sharp breath. Helene whispered, without taking her eyes off the stage:

'What's up?'

'Nothing.'

'Is something the matter?'

'Nothing's the matter.'

'At least try and follow.'

Not a sound was to be heard in the theatre, Peter noticed. The audience was waiting, in a kind of multiplied silence, a concentrated coma, for the end, which of course they already knew, but which they had never seen: the red wall slides open and the child, Hedvig, sitting at the back of the stage in the loft, facing the audience, presses the pistol, the muzzle, to the waist of her bodice, hesitates, and with a smile, a beautiful triumphant smile, she pulls the trigger.

Then there was the inquest and the final insight, when sentimentality merges with cynicism in the dialogue between Dr Relling and Gregers Werle, and from the mouth of the retching actor Peter heard the absurd line: *Hedvig did not die in vain.*

Peter leaned back in his seat, relieved for a brief instant, relieved, it was appropriate to feel relief, to feel that everything was relinquishing its hold on him.

Afterwards, clapping and stamping of feet, a standing ovation.

The cast was called back three times.

Peter did not go to the premiere party. He left Helene in Ben's care, or vice versa, he left Ben in Helene's care, and took a taxi home with Kaia. She went straight to the bathroom and got herself ready for bed. Peter stood outside the door, listening. And when she was in bed, under the duvet, Peter sat with her, holding the hand which she had hurt. The little bandage around her middle finger was moist.

'Is it painful?' he asked.

Kaia did not answer. But she let him hold her. He waited. Then he said:

'Daddy's eyes are a bit sore. That's why I have to wear dark glasses all the time. In fact, I am not allowed to take them off. Do you understand?'

Kaia turned her head away from Peter.

He continued to hold her hand.

'This is our little secret, isn't it? Isn't it, Kaia?'

Kaia lay quiet for a while. Then she turned to face him. Her thin face was a shadow on the soft pillow.

'It still hurts,' she whispered.

Peter leaned closer.

'It'll pass, sweetheart. It'll pass.'

Kaia looked up at him.

'Are you sure?'

Peter shut his eyes behind the glasses and kissed her on the cheek.

'Positive.'

Peter rose and went to the door.

Kaia said, 'Switch off the light.'

Peter turned in surprise.

'What did you say?'

'Switch off the light, Daddy.'

'Sure?'

She nodded, several times.

Peter switched off the light and stood waiting in the dark until he could hear Kaia was still; just her light breathing was visible. Then he crept out, pulled the door to, took one of the living-room lamps to the studio, plugged it in, changed clothes and started to work in the light, doing the only thing he knew: painting. And he remembered a time when he had hidden in an apple tree, in the spring. He was sitting on the highest branches, hidden by the leaves and the white blossoms, and as his father stalked to and fro in the garden shouting for him he had thought he could stay there at least until autumn. It was a Sunday and they were going to eat soon and his father could not find him; his mother came out on the terrace too, in her blue gingham apron, and called him, shouted his name. Then he was found after all. A bird, it might have been a magpie, had circled him, screaming. Perhaps he had been sitting near a nest, he had not intended to, and his father saw him and stood under the tree with the long-handled net which they used to take down apples from the top of the tree. This is what Peter Wihl was dreaming after he had gone for a rest on the mezzanine floor over the studio in the early morning light, and he fell asleep in an instant.

25

Peter woke to a distant sound. It was Helene. She closed the glass doors behind her, and it was this sound, the sharp bang – in other words she had used a great deal of force – which woke him. She had not knocked. She had not waited until he woke of his own accord. She had just forced her way in. Those were the first words he thought, forced her way in. He ran his hand across his face, straightened his glasses. He had fallen asleep with the lights on. Helene was wearing the same dress as yesterday. Her hair was untidy. Perhaps she had come straight from the party. In her hand she was holding the morning newspaper. Peter got up.

'How are the reviews?'

'They start with the scenography.'

'Congratulations.'

'That means the play has got terrible reviews.'

'Let me see.'

Helene threw the paper over to him. There was a reference to the play on the front page, a photograph of Hedvig with the gun. He flicked through to the culture section. Helene remained standing by the doors. There was something wrong. She looked around her. She had forced her way into the studio.

'What's this lamp doing here?' she asked.

Peter walked towards her.

'You've got a brilliant review, for Christ's sake. Limp production in wonderful scenery. Aren't you happy?'

'Everything is interconnected, isn't it? Perhaps the play was worse because I chose the wrong scenery.'

'Rubbish. Do you really think old Ekdal would have performed better with blue walls?'

'What's this lamp doing here?' she repeated.

Peter put down the newspaper.

'I needed light.'

'What the hell is going on with you, Peter?'

Peter stopped.

'What's going on with me? I needed light.'

Helene moved closer.

'You leave Kaia alone in the house all night. With the door shut. In the dark. What the hell's got into you?'

'She asked me to.'

Helene stared at him.

'Asked you to?'

'Yes. She asked me to switch off the light, so I switched off the light.'

'I tried to ring you. On the mobile. Why didn't you answer?'

Peter looked down.

'I switched it off.'

'Switched it off? I got through, but you didn't answer.'

'I might have pressed the wrong button.'

Peter passed the newspaper to Helene. She didn't want it.

'You frightened Kaia, Peter.'

Peter, despondent:

'I didn't mean to. You know that.'

'You frightened her. That's as much as I know.'

She sat down on the chair, ran her fingers through her hair, breathing heavily.

Peter put his hand on her shoulder. She shook it off.

'Let's go and see Kaia now,' he whispered.

Helene sat in the chair, silent now, resting her head in her hands.

She looked up.

'What happened when you two went for a walk yesterday?' she asked.

Peter stood with his back to her, by the glass doors. One of the shutters on the kitchen window had worked itself loose and was hanging at a slant, thin twigs from the apple tree lay scattered around the garden, the bench was on its side.

'Kaia fell.'

'I know.'

'I was showing her the grave. Of Mum and Dad. She laid the figures there. On the grave. It made me – how shall I put it? – happy.'

'And then?'

'It began to hail. We ran for it. And Kaia tripped. I couldn't do anything to prevent it.'

'Good grief, that's not what I'm trying to suggest.'

'I tried to grab her.'

Helene interrupted him.

'She said you were at a funeral.'

'We had to take shelter in the chapel. Could that have frightened her?'

'Kaia said something. She said you took off your glasses.'

Peter turned to Helene. She was still sitting on the chair, without looking at him. He whispered:

'I am the same.'

But Helene was not listening. She jumped to her feet, as if she had not noticed the pictures until now; she approached one of them, stood contemplating it for a long time, without saying a word, then went on to the other canvasses. Peter waited, had never waited so long, could have thrown her out, he switched off the lamp. Then, pointing at the pictures, she turned.

'Who is this?'

'What do you mean?'

'Who is this girl? It's not Kaia.'

'Why do you ask?'

Helene laughed. A short, disconcerted laugh.

'I thought you were painting Kaia.'

'I just paint,' Peter said.

'Kaia has been sitting for you every day.'

'I just paint,' Peter repeated.

Helene went closer.

'Who is she?'

'Who?'

'Who is she, Peter? The girl in the pictures.'

Peter avoided her. He said:

'Anyone.'

Helene followed him.

'Anyone?'

'Yes, anyone. All right?'

'Are you painting twelve pictures of anyone? Are you? Who the hell is she?'

Peter pointed at her. He could hardly speak.

'You are not supposed to be here.'

Helene stopped.

'I beg your pardon.'

'You are not supposed to be here, Helene. You have forced your way in.'

Helene just whispered, 'Take off the glasses.'

Peter shook his head.

Helene switched the light back on.

'Please, Peter. Take off the glasses.'

Peter raised his hands in defence.

'I am the same,' he repeated.

Helene lunged towards him and knocked off his glasses; he was not quick enough to stop her. She stared at him, at his eyes, stumbled back a few steps, and now she was the one holding her hands in front of her face.

'What have you done, Peter?'

Peter tried to put his arms around her, but she resisted, she recoiled even further away from him.

'What have you done?' she repeated.

Peter stood still, frightened, and yet almost relieved. The glasses were on the floor. He had nothing else to hide. She had seen him.

'Not in the red,' he said at last.

'What?'

'The morality account is not in the red.'

'The morality account? How much did you pay?'

'That's neither here nor there.'

Helene dropped her hands. A sound emanated from her; it was like a sob.

'You're sick, Peter.'

Peter took a step closer. She shook her head.

'What do you want me to say, Helene?'

'The truth.'

Peter laughed.

'The truth? I didn't know what was going to happen. In fact, I don't know what did happen.'

'You didn't want to know, Peter. That's the difference.'

'I can see. Isn't that enough?'

Helene stamped on the glasses. They were crushed beneath her shoes. He let her do it; she had already seen him. And she asked, in a low voice:

'Is she one of the children you saw in the transformer station?'

Peter said, 'No. She wasn't there.'

Helene turned to the picture once more and looked back at

Peter in such a slow, horror-filled way, as though she had confronted a sudden realisation she had not been prepared for.

'That's her, isn't it?'

'What do you mean?'

Helene rubbed the back of her hand across her forehead, her cheeks. She searched for words, as she inched closer to the doors and said:

'She's the one who saved you. She's the one who saved your sight, isn't she?'

Peter followed her.

'I did it for Kaia's sake.'

'Don't play pathetic and put the blame on Kaia as well. You did it for your own sake.'

Peter shouted, 'I did it for our sake! For yours! For Kaia's! For mine! Do you hear me? For our sake! Don't you understand that?'

Helene stopped.

'What happened to the girl?'

'I don't know, Helene. I don't know.'

Helene raised her palms.

'Don't touch me.'

'Helene, please.'

She averted her face and repeated:

'Don't touch me.'

Peter wanted to bring this to an end. He said:

'Let's go down and see Kaia.'

Helene shook her head.

'You've frightened her, Peter,'

'I want to talk to her.'

Helene opened the door and stood barring his way.

'You stay here.'

Peter felt his mouth go dry – there was no more saliva, no moisture – and instead it was filled with a raw, heavy taste, which caused him to talk in a slow, laborious manner to be sure that he could be heard.

'We'll have to live with it, Helene.'

She gave him another look, different now; there was a kind of calm coldness in her eyes, a determined sorrow.

'You will have to live with it, Peter.'

Peter stood by the glass doors watching her walk down to the house. After some time, maybe half an hour, Helene came back out, with Kaia. Helene was carrying a bag, with a strap over her shoulder. She opened the boot of the car and put it in. Kaia paused and looked up towards the studio, unhappy or scared, it was impossible to see from this distance, she was probably both, unhappy and scared, and for a moment she seemed to be on the point of running up to him, but Helene called her. Kaia hesitated for a little longer and raised her hand, a forlorn greeting, before clambering on to the front seat. Peter let the curtains fall back into place. Soon afterwards he heard the car driving away.

Peter went back to the workbench where his brushes lay ready. There may be as many kinds of brush as there are artists, for artists make brushes their own whether they are made of hair from oxen's ears, ermine, sable or silk, or whether the bristles are oval, pointed or diagonal. Nevertheless, there are in point of fact only two kinds: one lasts a few hours, maybe no more than minutes, then it has to be changed, discarded; the other lasts for several years, or the rest of your life, for as long as you paint. It is like two worlds. But no one can say one is better than the other, that the slow brush paints greater art or the quick brush paints pictures that can be forgotten just as quickly. It all depends. It depends on the hand holding the brush.

Peter could not choose.

He swept up the remains of the dark glasses and threw them in the bin.

Helene and Kaia still had not returned.

So he put on his outdoor clothes and began to walk to town. The sun was high in the sky, shining through the low-level mist which wound in orange billows around the rooftops and church spires. The light stung his eyes and made them water. His face became wet and stiff. He had to stop, avert his eyes, shade them. Gradually he got used to it, the light, and could go on. No taxis passed and he walked all the way to the casualty department, on the other side of the river, and asked at the reception desk for Thomas Hammer, the eye specialist. Thomas Hammer had stopped working there. Could anyone else help him? Peter made his way back across the river, to the streets in the town centre and the building where Thomas Hammer had his private practice; he took the lift to the third floor. As he pushed the grille door to the side and emerged into the narrow corridor, he could hear the same piece of music as the previous time: Bach's *Sicilienne.* The doors to the waiting room and surgery were open. No one was there. No one was waiting for an appointment. The surgery was abandoned, cleared away for ever, it seemed. All that was left was his picture hanging on the wall in the waiting room. Peter was overcome by a deep terror, which felt like it was devouring him, and he had to lean against the door frame for support. He was alone. It was Helene's words, the purport of her words, which stood out in his mind: *You'll have to live with it.* He was alone. Then he noticed the music had stopped. He was alone and someone was standing directly behind him. He turned. A young man with long hair, a crooked feminine face, his lips stretched tight over his teeth, transforming the smile into a sullen grin, dark lines in the grey skin beneath his eyes, white shirt over black, baggy trousers. He was bare-legged and held a violin in one hand, the bow in the other.

'Can I help you?' he asked.

Peter breathed in.

'I'm looking for Thomas Hammer. The ophthalmic surgeon.'

'He's left.'

'Left?'

'Yes, he left. Packed and upped sticks. As you can see.'

The young man, or old boy, gave a brief chortle.

Peter leaned back against the door frame.

'Did he say where?'

'Not a word.'

The violinist made to go.

Peter said, 'If you could choose, what would you rather be: blind or deaf?'

'Blind, of course.'

The violinist plucked the strings and walked off towards his music room further down the corridor. Peter lifted the picture *Hand II* off the wall and followed him.

'Do you want this?'

'No, thank you.'

'No, thank you? You can have it.'

'I don't want it.'

'You could sell it for a tidy sum.'

The violinist came to a halt.

'Something wrong with your hearing? I don't want the confounded picture!'

He slammed the door after him and locked it.

Peter stood in the narrow, green corridor: the tired, scuff-marked linoleum sloped down towards the fire door at one end and up towards the lift at the other. The violinist resumed his practising, at a faster tempo now, with several notes coming out wrong, but he just kept going. Peter tore the painting out of the frame, rolled it up, threw it down the rubbish chute and listened to the picture falling from floor to floor, landing at the bottom of the building in the heap which was removed once a week.

He left the frame where it was, took the lift down, went out into the dark and searched for a taxi.

On arriving back home, he saw a light in the kitchen. He ran down the path, impatient, almost happy, and let himself in. It was Ben. He was sitting at the kitchen table. Two suitcases stood on the floor. Ben was holding the house keys in his hand.

'What's going on?' Ben asked.

Peter stopped short:

'Shouldn't I be asking that?'

Ben interrupted:

'I hope I haven't overstepped the mark, Peter. At least I haven't been in the studio.'

'What's going on, Ben?'

'Helene asked me to pick up a few things.'

'Are they staying with you?'

Now Ben seemed both embarrassed and furious at the same time.

'Have you been looking for them?'

Peter didn't answer. He asked:

'What did Helene say?'

Ben gave him a brief stare, more in surprise than fury, as if for a moment he had been seized by doubt.

'By the way, you're looking unconscionably well. I thought you were on the booze again.'

'What did Helene say?' Peter repeated.

'She said she couldn't live with it. Take a seat.'

Peter took a seat.

'What did Kaia say?'

Ben ran his hand across his scalp.

'She thinks my hair's beginning to grow back well. And Helene said she could no longer stand being in this house. And I don't know if I want to know what the problem is. But I do know you're turning fifty and about to open a fair-sized exhibition in my gallery in less than a month. Will you do it?'

Peter nodded.

'Perhaps that's for the best,' he said.

Ben was taken aback.

'What?'

'If they stay with you for a bit.'

Ben pushed the keys across the table.

'Is this the illness beginning to make inroads? Is this what Helene can't live with?'

Peter struggled out of his coat and hung it on the back of his chair.

'I'm well, Ben.'

Ben was impatient, annoyed:

'Yes, as I said, you look unconscionably well for, in essence, a dried out alcoholic who has just been left by his wife and daughter and is about to go blind. Have you changed your hairstyle? New shirt? Have you been to the solarium? Tell me your secret, Peter.'

And staring at Ben, who leaned closer, Peter repeated what he had said:

'I'm well.'

Ben's smile died as he fell back against his chair and sat, silent, temporarily lost for words, before leaning forwards again.

'Now I see what it is,' he whispered.

'What do you see?'

'Your eyes.'

Peter folded his hands and contemplated them.

'I was operated on in Tallinn. They exchanged a few parts. I won't go blind.'

Ben continued to whisper.

'Kristoffer said it was incurable, didn't he?'

'He was mistaken.'

'But couldn't Kristoffer have operated on you? Why did you have to go to Tallinn?'

'Because he doesn't do that kind of thing.'

'What kind of thing?'

'New parts had to be procured.'

Ben was silent again.

Peter waited. Ben still said nothing. Peter could not stand it any longer.

'Aren't you happy? I can see now. Say something for fuck's sake.'

'How are new parts procured?' Ben asked, at length.

Peter got to his feet and walked over to the window. He saw his face in the dark, as if someone, or he himself, were standing somewhere in the garden and looking in at them.

'You can tell Kristoffer Hall that I am no longer his patient.'

'I would prefer not to be drawn into any of your lies.'

'A secret is not the same as a lie.'

'So far you have told me more lies than secrets.'

Peter stood with his back to Ben, and when he leaned closer to the window and touched the cold glass, the other face, which resembled his, did not move, but stayed firmly in the garden between the apple tree and the moon.

'There was a disused transformer station. A hall. It was full of children. Abandoned children in desperate straits. I suppose their mothers are whores in the West, or dead, or both. I lit bloody candles for them. And a boy showed me a photograph. A tattered photograph. Of his sister and mother. At one time they had been happy too, Ben.'

Peter banged his head on the window.

Ben raised his voice.

'I would rather you sat here while you told me this.'

Peter sat down again.

'If I could tell you, I wouldn't need to paint it.'

Ben's eyes lingered on him, not in an accusatory way, more disappointed, and, Ben's disappointment was worse, it was also redolent of loathing, he loathed everything that disappointed him, everything that stood in his path, he was the swimmer who had to keep moving, otherwise he would sink.

Peter looked down at the keys in front of him. Ben moved his hands.

'Perhaps I won't do the washing-up with you,' he said.

'What do you mean?'

Ben stood up and rang for a taxi.

'What do you mean?' Peter repeated.

Ben spun round.

'Perhaps I don't want the things you paint in my gallery, Peter. What do you say to that?'

'I did it for our sakes, Ben.'

Ben laughed.

'For our sakes. What's that supposed to mean?'

'Do you remember what we were talking about on Christmas Eve? When you got the straw hat?'

'I'm trying to look to the future, Peter.'

Peter stood up, too. He said:

'I just went for my sordid inspiration.'

Ben laid a hand on Peter's shoulder. The contact seemed hasty, reluctant. He whispered:

'I hope it was worth it.'

Then he picked up the two suitcases and carried them to the taxi.

Peter thought: But I'll have to live with it.

The dim light from the headlamps passed over the walls and stopped in the corner.

Ben was back at the doorstep, anxious, peering in at Peter.

'Since it has fallen to my lot to be the messenger this evening, the anticipation of which does not fill me with any pleasure, tell me what I should say to Helene and Kaia. And I would prefer to be spared having to say that this is for the best, as, strictly speaking, you are not the one setting the terms and conditions now.'

'Just say I will have to live with it.'

'That you will have to live with it? Actually, I would rather not say that, either. You almost make it sound heroic.'

'That wasn't what I said.'

'No, because you are not the hero here, Peter. You are not the one to feel sorry for. You're well.'

'Tell them I love them.'

'They know that already. Is that the best you can come up with?'

Peter hesitated. He was frozen, from the draught, the cold floor.

'Say that at least they have to come to the opening.'

Ben shook his head in sorrow, or disappointment.

'You mean to your fiftieth birthday?'

'No, just say that.'

'What, Peter? The messenger is confused.'

'That I love them.'

Ben was about to leave, but changed his mind. He asked:

'By the way, what were you thinking of calling the exhibition? If it has a name at all, that is.'

Peter said, '*Écorché*. It will be called *Écorché*.'

Ben stood there.

'*Écorché*. Long, long time since I heard that word.'

'Yes. No one says *écorché* any more.'

'Only you, Peter.'

Ben closed the door.

The light jerked away from the corner, ran along the ceiling and disappeared once more.

Afterwards Peter went to the studio. He put on his smock, scarf and sandals. It was quiet now. He examined his brushes with circumspection, felt the bristles, blew on them, but was unable to make up his mind now, either. It was a long time since he had heard such silence. The sounds of the world had been switched off. He thought: This is what it is like to be alone. Then he made up his mind. He put the brushes aside and instead squeezed paint out on to his hand: cobalt, magan, ultramarine, azure, shades of blue. It is not the eyes that are blue, it is the gaze. He mixed everything in his hands and ran a finger across the canvasses, gentle at first, then firmer and firmer.

26

We had been trying for a long time to contact Peter Wihl, to no avail. He did not answer the telephone or letters. It is not unusual for people in such a situation as his to isolate themselves and refuse to accept help or support, for the simple reason that it frightens them. They find it humiliating, or they shut their eyes to their own fate, to use a rather inappropriate expression in this context, and that is why the aid we can offer is seen as a confirmation of all they refuse to accept. Aid becomes a punishment. They react with anger, which is taken out on the family in particular. During such times many homes disintegrate, and sometimes the fury is taken out on us, too. We can handle that. And that is why we broach these matters with circumspection and caution. We give them time. We cannot force anyone. But when Peter Wihl broke off contact with his doctor, Kristoffer Hall, I decided I would call by and get him talking, and I readily confess that I also had ulterior motives. As well as being a therapist, you see, I am the editor of our little magazine in which we write for the most part about new medicines, cataracts and the Paralympics, and I thought that an interview, if he was at all keen to be interviewed, which of course deepest down I doubted, might be a scoop, as they say in the media. I have heard of deaf, to varying degrees, composers, but never about a blind artist, and so in this way he would be able to articulate and share his unique experience with others, which ultimately would also be of use to himself, I am quite convinced. By the way, I was born without eyes.

On the last Friday of February I took a taxi to the place where he lived and worked. It was morning, overcast, zero degrees, yet spring was in the air. I was very nervous, the first time for many years, not an unwelcome feeling. I thought it sharpened my wits and gave me an edge.

When I said we could help, I don't mean that we can save someone's sight, we can't, but we can help people to live with it, with the darkness.

All I knew about Peter Wihl was that he would be fifty in just under a month and in this context was about to open an exhibition. He was married to Helene Sander, a scenographer, with whom he had a six-year-old daughter, Kaia, and he made his debut as an artist with the exhibition entitled *Amputations* in 1977. Most of the museums and collections around here had one of his works, and he was reckoned to be one of the most significant artists of his generation, but critics had begun to accuse him of repeating himself. His motifs were not strong enough to bear this repetition and he diluted his painting until it was transparent and in poor taste, they wrote. He had been very quiet in recent years, no hits, apart from the juicy incident when he punched a younger colleague, not so long ago, which gave him a whiff of fame again, media focus at least, before that too was forgotten. It was the same old story, which repeats itself ad nauseam. He had been passed over and left in the shade by new generations who regarded him as reactionary and old-fashioned (what a wonderful, old-fashioned word!), he was behind the times, as they say, or perhaps he had lost his way in time, the man who called painting the last *acoustic art*, and for his part despised all art that required electricity to function. I have often thought that modernity, or the experience of modernity, is so closely connected to sight. Eyes force speed upon us, a furious superficiality which makes us impatient and dissatisfied, and that is why there is nothing which goes out of fashion as fast as modernity, the modernity that always wants more. But naturally, as one might appreciate, in this regard I am somewhat prejudiced. And I knew that Peter Wihl would be blind within a very short time, perhaps a matter of weeks.

The driver was a friendly, considerate man. He opened the gate and wanted to escort me right to the door, an offer which I refused. Instead, I asked him to describe the way to the house for me. A gentle downward slope, about thirty metres, and at the bottom there were two broad steps up to a doorstep. He was a good guide, concise and accurate with a good eye for detail, but in his kindness he thought I also had hearing problems. It was not unusual; people often assume for some reason that the blind also having hearing difficulties, as if a single handicap spreads all over your body. You become your handicap, so to speak, and therefore they come close to your face and shout. It is exceptionally unnerving. The thing is, of course, that we hear much better than most because sounds are the light we can extract from the world. I usually say, 'Sorry, could you speak a little louder, I can't see, you know,' but this time I refrained. As I said, I had other things on my mind.

The taxi drove away. And at that moment I had a feeling that Peter Wihl was standing somewhere and observing me, behind a window or door, I suppose, because I hadn't heard him yet. I kept on walking, down to the house. Luckily the path had been sanded. Then I heard someone come out, not ahead of me, but to the left. The steps were light, a shuffle, nevertheless a man's, the heaviness, the rhythm of a man. I presumed it was Peter Wihl. I stopped and turned in his direction. He stopped too, I could hear, a fair distance away.

'Are you looking for someone?'

'Peter Wihl?'

'Who are you?'

His voice was strained, not quite unfriendly, more grudging, I would say, as someone who was being disturbed, tormented in some way, might react, but there was something else. He didn't look at me when he was talking, his voice trailed off and floated away, that is, he kept turning his head away, and this evasive posture, which at best might be put down to shyness, was reinforced by the distance he kept.

I told him my name and ventured a step closer. Off the path it was slippery. He stood still.

'Do I know you?'

I showed him my identity card, which I keep on a string around my neck.

'I come from the Institute for the Blind.'

I soon sensed his hostility, a heavy, almost desperate expulsion of air. He said, 'Are you selling lottery tickets?'

This had begun very badly. I was furious with myself. I had to try to get the conversation back on an even keel and decided to approach the issue head on.

'I would like to speak to you about your illness.'

His voice was tenacious, as if his jaw were clenched when he spoke:

'But I don't want to speak to you about anything. Clear off.'

Peter Wihl started to stride towards the building he had emerged from, his studio, I guessed. I walked after him. Then I slipped and came a cropper. As I said, it was slippery. There were icy patches away from the path. I was unhurt, and as luck would have it, my dark glasses didn't fall off, but I lay there like an idiot flailing my arms, even more furious with myself now for not being careful enough, or having more foresight, as we like to say, during all these manoeuvres. The nervousness had not sharpened my wits after all; it had just made me single-minded. I could hear that Peter Wihl had stopped and was standing still while I dragged myself to my feet, and for a moment I lost my sense of direction. My compass was temporarily defunct. It is an unpleasant experience, like feeling darkness on the inside. Then, to my surprise, he came back and I turned round to face him, breathless and embarrassed. This time he came closer.

'Are you also blind?' he asked.

His voice was different now, gentler, not so suspicious and aggressive any more, and he spoke directly to me, I noticed.

I took out the white stick, without which I had been foolhardy or vain enough to suppose I could manage today, extended it with a snap and laughed.

'Yes, I'm also blind.'

Peter Wihl said, 'I'm sorry.'

'You don't need to be. It's me who should be sorry. For disturbing you, I mean.'

'Did you hurt yourself?'

'I'm fine.'

He came even closer.

'Who sent you?'

'No one sent me.'

'You mentioned the illness. How do you know about that?'

'Dr Hall informed us early on in the process.'

Peter Wihl was silent for a few moments, anxious, I could hear, as if his feet were shifting weight.

'Isn't that a breach of professional secrecy?'

'We also take an oath to help.'

'I am no longer Dr Hall's patient.'

'You can't do this on your own, Peter Wihl.'

I knew straight away that I should not have said this; it was accusatory, moralistic, patronising and threatening. In other words, it was all I had taught myself not to say. I waited for him to run me off his property with every justification.

Instead he said, 'My feet are cold.'

This was so unexpected that, in my stupidity, I said, 'Poor you.'

Now he laughed.

'I'm afraid I'm not wearing any socks. Shall we go in?'

Peter Wihl took my arm, something which as a rule I dislike. It is the sort of helpfulness that deprives me of control, and I must have control, otherwise I lose my ability to reason. My fragile world falls apart if I lean on others, but this time I let it pass. I had used up my quota of blunders, so to speak, and dutifully followed him to what must have been his studio. The heavy odour of pigment, turpentine and oil was evident anyway. It reminded me of the smell of wilting flowers and the water they stand in.

He pushed some doors to and drew the curtains, a light swish, a hissing sound.

I stopped, with my back to the door, and said, mostly for the sake of speaking:

'Is this where you paint?'

Peter Wihl did not answer at once. Perhaps he had forgotten himself and nodded. He hurried past me, turned on a tap and rinsed his hands, I presumed, and now we were indoors it was easier to form an image of him. A room delimits people and enables you to cut out silhouettes of sound, smell and touch. He was quite short, at least no taller than me. I noticed that when his shoulder brushed against me as he walked past and I could hear it in his breathing. I guessed he was robust as well, not fat, but a strong build, athletic. The way he had held my arm suggested that, and particularly his heavy footsteps, which I could still feel from where I was standing. The floor vibrated, even though he was not wearing socks. He turned off the tap and said:

'Yes, the whole of my new exhibition is hanging here. In fact, you're the first to see it.'

At first I didn't know whether he was being ironic or funny, or if he was just thoughtless. Anyway, the sighted have bad memories, they take seeing for granted, even if they are on the point of losing it, and it would be a long time before Peter Wihl, and not least his family, got used to this darkness, and it would be very painful. Of course, I didn't say that, though.

'Tell me about the pictures,' I said.

He was on his guard once again and stepped closer.

'I don't need your help or anyone else's. Have I made myself clear?'

'Nor indeed have I come to help you,' I said.

Peter Wihl paused and threw something down, a towel, a cloth, something like that.

'So you are selling lottery tickets after all? What can I win? A dog?'

I waited a little before answering, unsure for a moment about the tenor of the conversation, about the sincerity or seriousness of his sarcasm. Then I heard him laughing, and I realised he was teasing me, and that is a whole lot better than being looked down on, that is, being made to seem pitiful. I have met a lot of well-bred louts who say that I am clever and brave, and ask in a whisper how I imagine the world, whether I can imagine anything at all, as though I had also been born without a brain, an amusing monster, so you can't respond, you are not on a level playing field. However, teasing is something else, teasing is playing on equal terms, teasing is dialogue. I did not have time to play.

'I would like to interview you for our magazine,' I said.

He went quiet for a few moments.

'What about?'

'About your art. Your situation.'

I was about to go on, about the magazine and its readers, but he interrupted me with resolve.

'You're a cynical young lady, you are.'

I decided to join in the game and laughed.

'Oh, I'm not so young any more.'

'Take off your glasses,' he said.

'What?'

'Take off your glasses.'

I hesitated, not because I had any kind of scruples about showing these prostheses of mine, but because he ordered me. There was something unwholesome about the situation, the tone, as if he wanted to test my limits and in so doing find out if I was worthy of trust. This was no game.

I took off my glasses.

Peter Wihl stood staring at me. I could sense that from his

breathing, the calm flow coming towards me. He seemed tired, on the verge of exhaustion.

'Glass eyes,' was all he said.

'We call them prostheses.'

'Accident?'

'I was born blind.'

'Tell me about it.'

Peter Wihl pushed something across the floor, a chair. I didn't sit down. And it struck me that the roles had been reversed. He was asking, I was answering, and if that was what was required to make him talk, fine by me. I chose the abridged version.

'My mother took the wrong medicine during pregnancy.'

'Medicine?'

'Dope. Pills. Call it what you will.'

'So it's your mother's fault?'

'I don't like the word *fault*.'

'Why not?'

'It doesn't serve any useful purpose.'

Peter Wihl went quiet. He was moving about, it was confusing and a little eerie, because he was walking around me, could I say 'restlessly'?

'Do you hate her?' he blurted.

I was astonished by the use of the word *hate* and above all by the force or the fury with which he said it; he almost spat at me. It was a long time since I had used the word myself. It was painful. Perhaps that was what surprised me most, that it still hurt me.

'I blamed her for a long time,' I said.

'Blamed?'

'I may also have hated her when I was younger.'

'But you don't hate her any more?'

'She didn't know she was doing anything wrong. She didn't even know she was pregnant when she was taking those drugs.'

'That doesn't help you.'

'Yes, it does. It helps me that I don't have to hate.'

'But that doesn't make her situation any better, does it? She must hate herself.'

I shook my head, something which I do very seldom. It is not a very becoming gesture or movement for us.

'I've forgiven her.'

And something happened to Peter Wihl when I said this. He released his breath as though he had been holding it while talking. That was how it sounded at any rate, like a groan, a whimper. He was standing right next to me and I turned to face him. It was time to revert to our original roles.

'Now, it's your turn,' I said.

He whispered, 'If I could tell you about the pictures, I wouldn't need to paint them.'

'Try anyway.'

Instead, Peter Wihl took my hand and placed it against one of the canvasses. The surface was rough, jagged, the paint seemed to have been applied in slapdash, thick, indeed ferocious brushstrokes, I could imagine, and there was no longer a smell of wilting flowers. My hand transmitted other signals to me. The colours were warm, as if he had just finished. He took his hand away and I let my fingers glide over the picture, carefully, and it struck me that I had never felt a painting before, and I had touched most things. This was the first time, and at once I was filled with a certain sorrow, something I had thought I was well over, because at this very moment I was reminded of all the things I would never be allowed to see, such as colours.

'Can you feel the nail?'

His voice was very close. I didn't understand what he meant. I didn't answer. I moved my hand and placed it on his cheek. He let me do that. His skin was dry, perhaps pale too, his face lean, no deep wrinkles or furrows, taut eyelids, he seemed to be without features, just a scar on his forehead provided any resistance, like a twisted thread beneath my fingers. I stroked his cheek again and, to my surprise, noticed that it was moist. Peter Wihl was crying. Not a sound issued from him, but he was crying and turned away.

Afterwards, he followed me out. He held my arm as we struggled to stay upright between the patches of ice on the lawn from the studio to the house, which was quiet. It was obvious his family was not at home. He seemed thoughtful, in a rather exaggerated way. Perhaps it was sheer embarrassment.

'A souvenir from the sea,' he said.

'What?'

'The scar. Fitter beat me up. Four stitches. Never been so proud.'

'The fitter?'

'Ship's engineer. A bloody Arab from Haugesund.'

He chuckled as he opened the gate.

'You started at art college when you came back from sea, didn't you?'

He stood there, still holding my arm, but the ground wasn't slippery now. No cause for alarm.

'You'll get your chance to interview me,' he said finally.

'When?'

'When the exhibition is under way. Then I'll tell you everything.'

Once again I was taken aback, by the choice of words. He would tell me everything.

'Everything?'

'Isn't that enough?'

Now it was my turn to laugh.

'I may be able to make it to the opening,' I said.

Peter Wihl released my arm. I could almost hear him smiling.

'That would be nice. But you've already seen the pictures.'

I smiled back.

'Thank you.'

I began to walk alongside the fence, on the sanded pavement, my flat shoes crunching beneath me. He called after me.

'Shall I get you a taxi?'

I spun around.

'Not necessary.'

'You can find your way?'

'Yes.'

Epilogue

There was a queue outside The New Gallery. The poster was displayed in an illuminated case: *Peter Wihl: Écorché. Paintings.* It was the same public. Peter recognised them. They were just twenty-five years older. He sat by the window table in the restaurant directly opposite, as he had done twenty-five years before. He did not want to be the first to arrive. He wanted to be the last to arrive and the first to go. This was his night. Patrick stood in the doorway next to Ben, receiving the invited guests. Peter had not seen Helene or Kaia yet.

The waiter topped up his coffee.

'The first time it was champagne,' he said.

Peter looked up.

'Sorry?'

'When you made your debut. Champagne by the bucket. Your coat was hanging in the cloakroom for three weeks.'

Peter smiled.

'Yes, those were the days.'

The waiter bent closer and lit the candle in the holder.

'What about some cake on the house?'

'No, thank you.'

The waiter withdrew without a sound. Peter peered out again and could see them through the windows, in the gallery, the invited guests, in evening dress, holding glasses, canapés, gliding round in a slow circle, along the walls where the pictures hung. He couldn't see either Helene or Kaia. He sat waiting. The street outside was deserted now. The cobblestones were wet and shone beneath the arched street lamps. He could not recall it having rained. The town seemed to be distant or fading. His thoughts and nerves were not connected. They were running on different circuits. He stroked the white tablecloth and stared at the flame and the thick drops of wax running down on to the copper candle holder. He saw, but did not feel. He felt the tablecloth under his hand, but not the table. Then Ben appeared on the doorstep, impatiently casting his eyes in both directions and at length spotting Peter, who stood up, collected his coat and crossed the street to join him, to get it all over and done with.

Ben put his arm around his shoulders.

'Putting off the evil moment, as always?'

'Old habit, you know.'

'You're the king, Peter. Now let's go in and crown you.'

Peter held him back.

'What the hell's Patrick doing here?'

Ben lowered his voice.

'Let's call tonight the evening of reconciliation, shall we?'

Peter dropped his hand.

'Are Helene and Kaia coming too?'

Ben was standing on the step above him.

'I think you should all go on a long holiday, Peter. Go away. Until Kaia starts school. You can afford to do that now.'

'Are Helene and Kaia coming?' Peter repeated.

'They're coming.'

Then they went in.

Peter was received with applause, devotion, or was it a kind of pity because Helene and Kaia were not there? Peter did not know. He noticed the red tickets by several of the pictures. The catalogue prices: 90,000 kroner. Number eight had been bought by the Riksmuseum. A gift table in the corner was covered with bottles, cards and flowers. It was too hot. It was too stuffy. The air was stagnant. He could hardly breathe. Soon someone would have to open the door. He greeted everyone and looked no one in the eye. In the end Ben came to his aid. They withdrew to the side and the guests continued to glide leisurely along the walls. The geometry of the private viewing: the circle and the square.

'The critics were here earlier today,' Ben said.

'Was it worth the bother?'

Ben had to mull that over for a moment, then was reminded of his words and gave Peter a hasty kiss on the cheek before tapping his glass to attract attention. The guests came to a halt, like a merry-go-round losing power. Peter took a step backwards, feeling it was too early, it was too early to give a speech. Helene and Kaia had not come yet. From his pocket Ben pulled a sheet of paper, a closely typed printout.

'As I imagine you don't want to listen for hours to an old bugger eulogising about Peter, who despite his fifty years seems to get younger and younger, I will instead read a review which will appear in tomorrow morning's newspaper!'

Ben waited for the laughter to subside. Then he began to read:

'Peter Wihl exhibits his latest paintings at The New Gallery. There are no words to describe how good they are. A colouristic pièce de résistance.'

Ben paused and looked around.

'That was just the title and preamble,' he said.

'*The twelve paintings revolve around the same motif, a girl, a child, in a setting which is both realistic and mythical, in which we can make out a big Ferris wheel, mechanical horses, lanterns, a kind of lost paradise. And let's be clear from the outset, when Peter Wihl is at his best, and he is never far shy of it, he is unsurpassed and he has no peers. The pictures give the impression that they have been painted at a furious tempo and every single brushstroke reeks of an obvious unwillingness to compromise, something which most artists would give their right arm for. Peter Wihl has a sense of history and yet is so cutting-edge that he makes most contemporary art seem the stuff of museums.*'

Ben serenely folded the sheet, put it in his pocket and turned to Peter.

'Say something to us,' he said.

The applause broke out again, even louder than before. The rhythmic clapping brought Peter to the front, admiration brought with it an onus, applause an obligation. Then he saw the woman from the Institute for the Blind. She was his rescuing angel, dressed in dark clothes, a bag over her shoulder, her hair bound in a tight knot this time, her face almost enveloped by the same large glasses, the white stick, the raincoat with two reflectors on either side, which still shone. Patrick stopped her at the door. She had not been invited; she did not have an invitation. Peter went over to them, and it occurred to him, once again, as guests allowed him to pass and he walked the few steps to the open door, that to her, to the blind woman, he could say everything, it was an opportunity, and he put his hand on her shoulder. She turned sharply, smiled, she had recognised him anyway before he had said a single word; she had recognised his hand. And bending closer, he said:

'Let's go now.'

'What?'

'Let's go and do the interview.'

And so Peter Wihl left his exhibition, his private viewing and the astonished guests in triumph and in the cold, as though his senses were suffering from a delayed reaction, and he followed the blind woman across the street, into the restaurant and sat at the same window table from which he could see whether anyone was arriving.

She seemed troubled.

'I didn't mean to bother you.'

'You did me a favour.'

'A favour.'

'Where shall we begin?'

She took off her raincoat.

'Wherever you like.'

'Would you like some champagne?'

She smiled again.

'Then I'll have to take a taxi home.'

Peter laughed and waved to the waiter, who came over post-haste.

'A glass of champagne and some cake on the house.'

The waiter bowed and went to the bar to fetch the order.

Peter turned towards the window. Some people were already beginning to leave. Ben ushered them out of the gallery. Ben cleared the dishes. Ben did the washing-up on his own.

'Is it all right if I use a tape recorder?'

Peter forgot himself and just nodded.

She waited. Peter waited.

Then he remembered she was blind.

'Of course,' he said.

She opened her bag and put a small, shiny recorder on the tablecloth between them.

'Do you always carry a tape recorder around with you?'

'I might have an idea and then it's very handy.'

The waiter returned with champagne and the cake. She raised her glass and took discrete sips. A drop ran down her chin, as if her lips were not used to this drink. She blushed. Peter passed her a serviette.

'Is it on?' he asked.

'Not yet.'

She pressed a button and a red light glowed on the top. Now Peter did not know where to begin. He put the fork in the cake, through the hard crust, which was almost completely covered with icing sugar, and into the soft, dark centre: hot liquid chocolate.

'Help me,' he said at length.

'Why do you paint?'

'Because I can see.'

There was a little pause. Peter regretted saying what he had, and was about to add something, but she asked first:

'What can you see?'

'The surface.'

She pressed another button and rewound the tape.

'Just checking it's working.'

Straight afterwards Peter heard his voice again. It could easily have been someone else talking: *The surface.*

He went on:

'Sometimes I think it was the devil that liberated the colours from objects.'

She was listening with her head cocked, but she seemed impatient at the same time. She was expecting something else.

Peter looked through the window.

Crowds of people were heading down the street.

Ben was standing alone on the step, beside the poster in the display case, looking across at the restaurant.

In the background he could make out Patrick going round and clearing up the glasses, serviettes and leftovers.

'Where did you get your inspiration from?' she asked.

Peter put down the fork, scattering crumbs over the tablecloth, and spoke in a hurry.

'The world is like a dictionary, right? But the dictionary is not a work of art in itself. Those who don't possess imagination paint only the dictionary. But those with imagination put the words together in their own way. That fundamentally is what I try to do. To articulate what I can see. In my own way.'

She interrupted him.

'Were you ever frightened you wouldn't finish?'

'Finish?'

She waited a little, then said:

'Finish the exhibition paintings while you could still see.'

Peter moved the dessert plate, leaned closer to her and then said in as composed a manner as he could:

'You don't finish a picture. You forsake it.'

At that moment Helene and Kaia arrived. Peter saw them. They were walking hand in hand along the pavement on the other side of the street. Kaia was carrying a big parcel, in yellow paper, with red ribbon around it. Peter smiled. Of course Helene would come at the end, when all the others had gone. It was the evening of reconciliation. Ben was standing on the step waiting for them. Peter said as he got up:

'Excuse me for a moment. My wife and daughter are here.'

He went out on to the pavement.

The town came closer again, traffic, wheels, he heard a car, tyres on the cobblestones, coming nearer and nearer, at a speed he could not comprehend. Kaia saw him, let go of Helene's hand and ran across the street with the present, straight in front of the car, he screamed and ran towards her, he just caught a glimpse of the driver in the confusion and chaos, and there was something familiar about the face, but that was the last he thought and the last he saw, and Peter Wihl's punishment was that he would never know whether he managed to save Kaia.